WHAT IS TIME TO A PIG?

Books by John Straley

WHAT IS TIME TO A PIG?

JOHN STRALEY

Published by Soho Press
Soho Press, Inc.
227 W 17th Street
New York, NY 10011

Library of Congress Cataloging-in-Publication Data

Straley, John.
What is time to a pig? / John Straley.
Series: The Cold Storage novels; 3

ISBN 978-1-64129-084-5
eISBN 978-1-64129-085-2

1. Prisoners—Fiction. 2. Men—Fiction.
3. Suspense fiction.
LCC PS3569.T687 W48 2020 | DDC 813/.54—dc23

Printed in the United States

10 9 8 7 6 5 4 3 2 1

This book is dedicated to Simon Ortiz

Disorder increases with time because we measure time in the direction in which disorder increases.

—STEPHEN W. HAWKING

PROLOGUE

It was late fall on the road to the dump just outside of Cold Storage, Alaska, when the mouse that would save the world scampered across the snow and first smelled a hint of rotten food. What puzzled her most was that the smell emanated not from the landfill but from beneath her four pink and taloned feet. It was the first snowfall of the year, and just a few inches covered the ground. The smell came up from a vent in the snow, up from the damp mineral soil. Her whiskers flicked the surface and her pink nose pushed away the crust of ice, then she began to dig, following the air that carried the smell of something sour and edible.

Down she went, through the veins of frozen roots and heart-sized stones; she followed the scent as it became stronger, her shrunken stomach rumbling. In a few feet she came to a hard iron wall that resisted her digging, and she crawled along its edge until she encountered a long crack where the wall had buried itself into the rocks of a roadbed. There near the edge was a tiny gap where something had pulled against the hard wall and bent it back just enough for a thin mouse to squeeze through. After her skull was through, her stomach was nothing, and her pelvis, the other large bone in the mouse's body, could wiggle through.

Once in she smelled a world of decay and fecundity. Her stomach cinched down, she could make a nest here as long as there were no dangers. She had seen no evidence of big animals having come this way, but still she would be careful, blend in, not rush toward the food, for that could be foolish. She would be invisible for as long as she could stand it. The mouse that would save the world was not rash . . . nor ignorant.

She worked her way around the enclosure. She heard nothing. She smelled no breath of mammal. No breath of meat eater. No footfall of hunter. She stood still for long series of heartbeats . . . then moved again, then stood still again. She climbed up boxes and found rotten meat. She ate a bit and nothing moved; no traps snapped. She ate again. She found something incredibly sweet but covered in green mold. She ate a bite but then decided to save it. There were good materials to make nests. She began to relax. She peed on the box with the food to mark it as hers. She climbed another crate.

She froze. Barely breathing, she stared. In the corner behind a tangle of wires was an animal with one eye, something that breathed in a way she had never heard before. As she stood stalk still, the mouse that would save the world could not take a breath. The monster lay purring as it slowly . . . slowly . . . opened and closed its one eye.

Chapter One

It might be easier to understand this story from the point of view of the mouse, for her motivations are simple: fear, hunger, procreation, and survival: living in the now as a Buddhist might understand it. But for us, the Western Homo sapiens who have grown past the mysteries of peek-a-boo magic tricks and object impermanence, the flow of time becomes a complicating factor. Besides, the mouse died few days from when we left her, tragically for her, but not for the human beings in this story, most of whom experienced life as a kind of hallucination, unstuck from traditional time as a result of being kept in cages where nothing happened according to their own will.

IT WAS SEVEN years after the US president's war with North Korea, and the whole world had gone a little crazy. It was as if all the bottled-up frustration of the administration, the repressed class hatred and racism, the fear of the Other, and the unquenched greed had started to spray from sprinkler systems in every office, every classroom, every store, and every network in the country: icy water raining down through high-pressure rubber tubes onto

everything and everyone. All bets were off, and the future
was chaos. At least that's how it seemed.

THE FIZZLED NORTH Korean missile was nothing more
than a bundle of sparklers that sprinkled warheads over a
small section of southeastern Alaska. The warheads had
apparently been meant for Valdez, Prudhoe Bay, and
down into Wyoming and Colorado. The North Koreans
had thought to contaminate most of America's oil supplies
to frighten US leaders to the negotiating table, but what
really happened was a mad rush by military and terrorist groups from around the globe to gather the missing
nukes, while the rest of the world watched the US Army
and subcontractors liberate the hungry North Koreans.
First came fire and destruction, then a river of American
food: MREs and then fatty grain-fed beef, along with tele-
visions playing dubbed American films over steam tables
laden with limp yellowy pork chops, grease-limp cheeseburgers, and boiled cabbage with brisket—all under the
watchful eye of white men with black guns and sunglasses.

But none of that mattered to the men serving time out
on the island where the Ted Stevens High-Security Federal
Penitentiary had been built. "Olympus," as it was known
to its full-time inhabitants, or T.S.H.S.F.P. on their paperwork. The employees, who rotated on- and off-site, called
it "Tough Shit." Whatever you decided to call it, it was a
concrete facility built on a rocky outcropping off the coast
of Yakobi Island. The nearest civilian town was Cold Storage, Alaska. Now it was 17:30, October 31, 2027, almost
five years after the final peace accord with China/North
Korea and the end of hostilities. The world was still in a
frenzy of nervous breast beating and anxiety about dodging the bullet of nuclear annihilation. The United States

had somehow balanced its trade deficit with Asia, there was no more Republican Party but a new Democratic Business Party and the Constitutionalist Party of the American Nation. The evening meal had been served in the Red and Blue Units, and the White Unit was just finishing up its Sobriety, Substance, and Spirituality class in the cooldown space, which had thick windows overlooking the North Pacific and was plumbed with pipes to flood the room with either salt water from the surrounding ocean or imported military gas.

Gloomy Knob was the speaker on this day. Gloomy, of course, wasn't his real name, but the name given to him as a boy by the community. Gloomy Knob had grown up in Cold Storage and had graduated from the local high school. He had earned money working in the woods cutting trees and working on machinery in Alaska, Washington, and Idaho. He had been living at home and building a cabin when he was arrested; he had been building a new life—or so he thought.

He was one of only two inmates who were locals. He and Ishmael Muhammad were the only two prisoners from Cold Storage held on Olympus. Gloomy had been given his nickname—and, really, the only name he used— for a cliff face in Glacier Bay he had liked to visit as a boy. Gloomy Knob was a bluff where to this day mountain goats loved to climb up and down from tidewater all the way to the alpine willows. It was a place where Tlingit elders went to gather goat hair that had sloughed onto the willow branches. Gloomy's father, Clive, had taken him there, and his mother had shown him how the old people would make yarn and small panels of rough cloth that they eventually stitched together into a blanket. Clive had run a bar that also served as a small nondenominational and eclectic church in the tiny village of Cold Storage, which was how Gloomy Knob had become the unofficial nondenominational "pastor" of the clearly non-Christian and non-Islamic Sobriety, Substance, and Spirituality discussion group at Ted Stevens High-Security Federal Penitentiary, even though he abhorred most public speaking. Yes, Gloomy had become a preacher in jail.

"Gentlemen," Gloomy began, "I will start today as I often do, with a story."

The men groaned. They sat on shiny steep pillars that had emerged from the floor and were immovable. Tables and a lectern could also rise through the steel-plated concrete floor by hydraulic force when needed, but nothing could be moved or thrown. Twenty-eight men in lime-green jumpsuits sat on pillars. Some wore tight-fitting skullcaps, some had shaved heads. Some had vivid tattoos, while some conspicuously did not.

"So," Gloomy continued despite protests, "a farmer was in his orchard with his pig, as a city slicker was driving by in his sports car, clearly in a hurry."

"I got this already. The pig is a filthy beast. It represents the fallen sinner. The farmer is your false prophet, Jesus," a man with a beard called out as others nodded.

"Gentlemen, please . . ." Gloomy raised his hands, palms up. "In some stories, a man is just a farmer and a pig is just a pig. Please . . ." And the grunting subsided.

"So, as the city slicker is driving by, the farmer lifts up the pig to the apple tree and lets the pig feed on an apple. The pig chews away on the nice big apple, and the farmer sets him back down. Then as the car gets closer, the farmer does it again, and the city slicker sees that this is a big fat pig, and the farmer is straining a lot to lift the animal up. The city slicker slams on the brakes and grinds to a stop, then jumps out of the sports car and walks over to the farmer."

"What did he say?" a black inmate said unself-consciously.

"I will tell you, sir." And Gloomy walks toward the inmates, a row of cameras in the ceiling following his every move.

"The city slicker says, 'I was watching you, mister, and I think it would be much easier if you tried something else, Mr. Farmer.'"

"I'm sure he did!"

Now the black inmates were laughing.

"Thank you for the encouragement," said Gloomy Knob, pausing to look each and every one of them gathered there in that antiseptic holding facility in the eye. "Then the farmer lifts that pig up again, straining every muscle. The pig eats another sweet and delicious apple, then the farmer sets the pig back down. The city slicker says, 'I think if you were to climb up in the tree and shake all the limbs and knock the apples down on the ground, the pig could just eat the apples off the ground. It would be a lot easier for you and the pig, and it would save a lot of time.'"

"What he *say*, Gloomy? What the farmer *say*?"

And Gloomy Knob held up both his hands again and said, "That farmer walked over to that city slicker as his fine sports car was idling like a purring cat by the side of the road, and said, 'Well, yes, sir, I suppose you are right, but what is *time* to a pig?'" And here the gathering resorted to a respectful and knowing laugh, and they rocked back and forth on their uncomfortable perches.

After Gloomy's father's generation, everyone in Cold Storage went by nicknames. Gloomy Knob took his name into prison. Gloomy Knob was convicted of murdering his sister and kidnapping his mother. His sister was called NoNo. His mother was called Nix. His cousin had taken the name Ishmael Muhammad, but he was known as "Itchy" to his family. They had both been convicted for involvement in the kidnapping of Gloomy's mother, who had long ago been a bass player in a cruise-ship band and had married into the bar, but neither of them felt guilty for the kidnapping. Someone else had taken Nix and buried her in a box in a tideflat with a breathing tube to motivate both the boys. They never counted that as a charge against them, even though the government had added it onto their sentence. Gloomy didn't talk about the past much due to his grief and guilt over NoNo's death, and Ishmael never spoke up, apparently for ideological reasons. At the time, Ishmael had deep religious beliefs to explain his actions. In prison, each prisoner had to discover his own particular way of doing time.

In the last few months, Gloomy hadn't seen his cousin in the prison, and his memory had become a stuttering and chaotic dream that interrupted his waking life. Gloomy could look at a clock and then look again and have lost hours while visiting some other time in his life, which gave him great anxiety as to how time was *actually passing*. Hence the pig joke. What interested him most was why many of the other inmates found the odd joke funny.

NIX KEPT REPLAYING the events in her mind. She didn't see the men who took her. She had been walking down the gravel lane and it was suddenly dark. She twisted inside a scratchy bag for several moments and then everything was gone; there was no struggle, no scratchiness, and no sounds of boots running down the gravel lane.

Sometime later, she awoke in darkness so pure that

she couldn't be certain her eyes were even open. Her arms were pinned to her side, and as she twisted her torso, she could feel the rough surface of the wooden box she had been buried in. She kicked her feet and heard dirt shifting down around her head. Her breath came back against her face as she struggled. The smell of peanut butter from her sandwich at lunch mingled with the yeasty scent of the wet rocky sand that had been heaped on top of her.

She banged her head against the surface of the box, and her forehead butted against the end of a pipe. Cool air came down the pipe, and she could hear the shooshing sound of waves breaking on a beach. Somewhere in the dark was the barking call of a raven. A drop of water dripped down the pipe and landed on her lips.

"Our Father, who art in heaven—" she began.

Then a voice interrupted her. She didn't recognize the voice. It was a distant hiss that seemed to be riding down the air through the pipe.

"Hush," the voice said.

"Help me. Please help me out of here," Nix said.

"Hush . . ." the voice wheezed again. "I will . . ."

"Why am I in here? When will you let me out? I'm sorry. I'm sorry." She felt her tears track down her cheek and get cradled in the folds of her ears.

"Don't ask questions," the voice said soothingly. "There is only one answer worth knowing."

"What?" she said, stammering. Her heart was beating inside her chest as if it were kicking to get out. "What is it? Please, what is it?"

"Close your eyes." The voice came all around her body. She could still hear waves breaking. She kicked against the box, shaking dirt down the sides.

"In a few moments you will know the answer," the voice said.

The darkness sat on her, and the smell of the earth filled her nose and mouth. A fat drop of water landed on her open eye.

AS GLOOMY AND the other prisoners filed back to their cells to read their religious materials, a technician spun on his chair in a bunker buried three levels down beneath the housing floor of the prison. This was a secure area with just two entrances, its own communications trunk, and a dedicated dock and helipad on the far side of the facility. This security team had one office at the prison and one temporary communications center and interview room in the town of Cold Storage. The technician handed his boss a file.

"It took the Iranians fucking years to give the specs to the Koreans, and then it took their people forever to work through their lawyers before we could get it to our technicians and sort out all the noise and what looked like chatter and background stuff—"

"Enough with the caveats, Pete. Just tell me."

"There is a faint but intermittent transmission of a power source being fed to one detonator."

"Where is it?"

"Here. Alaska."

"Alaska? Really?"

"They didn't have satellites; they didn't have GPS; they didn't expect they would be hard to find."

"How far along are we to detonation?"

"Unknown."

"Unknown? A thermonuclear device. Unknown?"

"Jasper . . ." The technician cupped his head in his

hands and took a long breath. "You want me to quit and go home?"

"I want you to wander around in the fucking woods until you find it or it goes off . . . that is what I want." Jasper, the supervisor, wore a short-sleeved shirt with brown stains down the front. After he read the memo one last time he clipped the document to his board and drank a long swallow, one of many, of cold, bitter coffee. Both Jasper and Pete were discovering a new and irritable way of experiencing time, a way that felt like a jittering caffeine nightmare, as if they were both drowning in the surf and trying to drag themselves back to shore without touching bottom.

NOW WHILE GLOOMY was telling the joke about the pig and the farmer in prison and Jasper was feeling his stomach ache about the bomb, Nix was in Cold Storage, Alaska, wiping the cedar bar top with a dry towel. She had set her sketchpad down a moment before, and one of her drawings had been smeared with beer. She came to the bar sometimes when she couldn't stand the atmosphere of the house where her husband lay dying. Lilly, the nurse who usually slept above the old cold storage, had agreed to stay the night. She had been making bread and was reading a book from Clive's library. In the last few weeks, when it seemed that he was going to die at any moment, Lilly had virtually moved in. Lilly was strong and patient with him. Patience was what Nix had wished for, patience while lifting him onto the commode or changing his diaper in the middle of the night.

"If we're lucky," Lilly had said to Nix just that night, "if we're lucky this is how we end up, I suppose"—she paused—"at home with people who care about you."

Nix had been putting on her slicker to go out to the bar as Lilly stood in the kitchen kneading bread dough. "Yes . . ." Nix said.

Lilly was looking down at the floor. "I don't mind it," Lilly said softly. "He's got the long trip ahead. I don't mind helping him get ready now."

Lilly was a blessing to Nix. She gave her time to get out of the house. Time to sit and work on her drawings. Blessed time away from the dying in the upstairs bedroom.

Nix hated it. She hated the smell of the house, the disinfectant in the bucket for dirty linens, the sour smell that made even the warm kitchen with baking bread smell boggy.

NORMA THE BARMAID on duty brought Nix a martini. Nix held her mechanical pencil above the paper. Every time she was about to begin a new drawing she would remember the words her art teacher had made her write in ink all around the top of her computer monitor at school. She had looked at those words every day whether she consciously read them or not: *When beginning any depiction, the artist must consider the angle and the source of the light.*

She held her pencil steady and took a drink. She didn't really like martinis, but she wanted something that would change her mood. Yet, when she sipped the cocktail, all she tasted was the disinfectant in Clive's room. She set the long-stemmed glass down gently and took a deep breath.

This moment of beginning a new drawing always created tension within Nix. It was a delicious tension, like the moment just before kissing a stranger. She placed the tip of her pencil down and drew the first curve of a raven's beak. Like with the kiss, she could tell how propitious the next move and the one after that would be. There was the curve of the head in profile; there was the raucous call and the weird intelligence. There was the source of light slanting in at a long angle from the southwest, where Raven stood on the ridge of a roof, tipping forward and ready to fall into the gliding first curve of flight.

This first feeling having been revealed to her, Nix hurried on to capture the moment. She sketched from the top down. She even put in a faint background. The world itself became visible as the new light fell upon the bird.

Norma walked down her side of the bar, turning and twisting her back to loosen her tight muscles. "You wanna trade for your tab?" Norma joked.

"Can't afford to." Nix smiled as her forearm moved across the page. "I might, if I drank more. But I've got to zap these down to the editors and the book designers in three weeks or I don't get the second half of the advance."

Norma craned her head and watched Nix draw. Raven on a roofline, the islands in the background. Raven leaning forward as if he were going to spill out the rest of the drawing. Norma was some twenty years younger than Nix. She was thin, weathered, with short brown hair and a bright scar on the left side of her throat. Nix never asked about the scar—not because she wasn't curious but because she already knew part of the story and didn't care to know any more. She knew because she had shared in the events that had left the mark on her old friend's throat.

"How's it going at home?" Norma said, and her voice softened, hesitant to ask.

"It's going . . ." Nix said absently, then stopped and looked up at the barmaid. "It's going slowly," Nix said finally, staring into her friend's eyes. "I had to get out of there."

Norma reached over and covered Nix's hand with her

own, and she let it sit there a moment without saying a word. "Well, tonight will be some distraction"—Norma's voice brightened—"Halloween. My God, there will be some loonies in here for sure."

Nix swiveled around in her chair, looking out the windows of the bar as if to remind herself what time it was, and what month. "Halloween?" she said. "I must have forgotten."

It was early evening and already very dark. The wires above the boardwalk along the beach swung crazily in the gusts of wind. Rain sheeted down the smudged window-panes, the windows fogged where they reached the level of the booths. Outside, one light flickered as if it couldn't decide whether it was going to burn out. The rain fell through the light as if it were a ripped curtain flapping there. Two electric carts hummed by and a rusted-out gas cart sputtered down the boardwalk like a rockslide. Dance music wheezed out of a radio and then faded into the clatter of the bar. A guy by the pool table was bobbing his head in time to the sound effects of the game he was playing on his goggles. His vision obscured, he slowly pulled his beer glass toward his mouth by instinct and feel alone.

Nix thought of the man dying in her house. He had been a jailbird and a drug dealer long ago. But he and his brother were good men and had built a community in Cold Storage that she had grown to love. She loved him. She loved his crazy preaching on Sundays. She had sat with him for days during his sickness, she had cried, and now she was ready for him to die.

She looked down and pictured his shrunken body as his bony chest slowly rose and fell.

"I'm not worried," Clive said as if he could read her

thoughts. Then he said in his reed-thin voice, "Not near as worried as you are, girl."

Nix tried to smile. "That's good," she stammered. "I don't think there's anything to worry about." But as she said the words she felt icy gravel gather in her chest.

"There's nothing to worry about," she said again, this time with a little more force. Clive had been so much fun, so irreverent and funny, but now he was pale and his eyes were still. He blinked once in slow, reptilian consideration. She felt her hands shake, and he gripped them firmly, as if to apologize for the awkwardness of dying.

"Here we go," Norma said, and took a deep breath.

At the door some kids were running back and forth, daring each other to knock. They were all wearing sheets over their heads.

"Come on," Norma said. She elbowed Nix as she reached under the bar for two big handfuls of wrapped toffee. "Let's give the ghouls something . . ." she said as she moved around the end of the bar.

A couple of fishermen in wool coats with the sleeves cut off pushed their dirty linen caps back off their faces and sat up straight in the booth by the window. They made faces at the specters running back and forth on the sidewalk. They looked through the records that the bar kept near the old stereo system, and one looked at Nix to make sure he had her approval. Nix smiled at him because she recognized him and liked his taste. The fisherman put on Louis Armstrong and Ella Fitzgerald. Knowing there was a scratch on side one, he put on the second side and sat down with his partner, who spilled his beer. The other started swearing as he squeezed back into the booth, never taking either of his hands off his beer. Nix threw them a bar rag because Norma's hands were full of candy.

Both women arrived at the door at the same time and just as the smallest of the four ghosts was about to knock, Norma jerked the door open.

"Boo!" she shouted, and she sent the ghosts shrieking and jumping back. They laughed and then eased forward, holding out plastic bags with their dark mouths open.

"Trick or treat!" the four of them sang out in unison.

Nix stood behind Norma's right shoulder. She looked at the children and for some reason felt short of breath. It was a familiar feeling, that of struggling for air. She did not move but stared at the tiny ghosts with half dollar–sized holes in the white sheets. Their eyes were far back from their ill-defined skulls. The smallest wore a plastic garland of flowers that had been used in last year's fifth-grade play.

As Norma was doling out the candy, a rumble came from the south as a plastic garbage can rolled in the middle of the boardwalk, for there were no roads in this little boardwalk town in the Alaskan wilderness. The wires running to the back of the hotel started howling and a great gust of wind hit the side of the building.

The kids shrieked and the wind pushed the door wide open against the wall. The napkins on the bars scattered like leaves, and the kids howled all the louder, wind billowing up underneath their costumes and lifting the sheets up off their heads faster than they could grab them while still holding on to their bags of candy.

Norma stepped back, turning away from the blast of wind, but Nix watched with a kind of fixed panic as the ghosts' costumes rose up into the air, twisting and spinning like single sheets of newspaper blown down the canyon of the street. They rose straight up above the roofline, toward the waterfront, until all four sheets became entangled in the power lines running down to the harbor.

The rain came suddenly, pelting down out of the blackness of the squall. The little-girl ghosts ran into the bar shivering and laughing, holding on to their candy bags with both hands.

Norma got a dry towel and the fishermen ordered another round of beers. The embarrassed little girls covered their mouths as they spoke and sucked down their giggles as they asked if they could call their mothers. Nix walked over to the windows and watched the wind push the twisted sheets against the power lines. When the wet tip of one of the sheets slapped against another, sparks showered down on the street and the bar went black.

"There's no saving them now," Nix said aloud, although she hadn't meant to.

The girls who had once been ghosts laughed and shivered in their thin, wet clothes, as Ella Fitzgerald's voice skittered up into the darkness.

Chapter Two

Like all inmates on Olympus, Gloomy Knob had tags around his neck. On these metal tags were stamped his real name and his identification number. These tags could either be swiped through a reader or placed into a machine, and, given the proper access codes, the corresponding inmate's entire file would be pulled up, including his medical, legal, military, NSA, OGA, and CIA files—and even nuclear regulatory and security information. Almost any bonehead at the prison could read that Gloomy's real name was Christopher McCahon. What they might not have known was his father was Clive McCahon, and that Gloomy had grown up in a bar in Cold Storage, Alaska, called Mouse Miller's Love Nest—the very same bar Nix was sitting in at this moment. Clive ran the bar as a genuine community center, and on Sundays it was a spiritual meeting place. Clive once told his brother, Miles, who had been a medical practitioner for the village, that he "loved Jesus like Elvis loved his momma." Clive loved Jesus the way he loved Duke Ellington or the great Satchmo, or the early music of Joni Mitchell or Bonnie Raitt. He loved Jesus the way he loved the opening paragraph of *One Hundred Years of Solitude* or all the novels of

P. G. Wodehouse. This is not to say that Clive McCahon was a pious man—remember his house of worship served mixed drinks—but Clive McCahon was a man who had been moved by the Spirit.

Gloomy Knob grew up both in the bar and in his grandma's house, where his father and mother lived. His mother had been a bass player in the first house band at the Love Nest. The band had been called Blind Donkey, his mother was named Maya, but everyone called her Nix. Gloomy had a sister who had been baptized (in the bar) as Nancy Vishnu McCahon, but everyone called her NoNo. Gloomy was serving a life sentence for the death of NoNo. Gloomy had never given a statement as to the circumstances surrounding her death and had insisted upon pleading guilty to the crime. He refused to testify against his codefendant in his implicated crimes.

Gloomy Knob, his sister, and Ishmael grew up together in Cold Storage, Alaska. There are no roads either in or around Cold Storage. The only road is a short lane up to the dump used by the city truck, which serves as a police van and also pulls the garbage trailer up. The only ways into the village are by boat or float plane. The nearest large towns are Juneau to the east and Sitka to the south. Pelican, Alaska, lies up the coast a bit, and Gustavus is across Icy Strait toward Glacier Bay. Cold Storage has a hot springs, a small ice plant, and a fish-buying station for the small boat fleet. It also now houses a few prison employees along the coast, though not many, since most of the employees choose to take their two weeks a month off in a more lively setting. All told, Cold Storage has about two hundred year-round residents, and in the summer there are a few more charter fishermen and operators along with some lodge operators.

Gloomy's great-aunt was an anarchist named Ellie Hobbes. She was the one who built the bar in the first place after she came to Cold Storage in the thirties with the man who would be her husband, Slippery Wilson. He had been a rancher, but they were on the lam when they arrived in Alaska. Gloomy never knew her and he never knew his grandmother Annabelle, who had also made the trip up in the dory with Ellie and Slippery, but he had heard the stories told endlessly in the bar at night. His father would toast to them at closing time. Somehow, there was a strong link with both anarchism and Christianity in Clive McCahon's faith, which had begun to irritate Gloomy in his early teenage years. When Gloomy started hanging out in Glacier Bay and sitting up on the actual Gloomy Knob in the national park, he would take only the scriptures and read them under a tarp. And there he would pray out toward the water and try to imagine the arid Holy Lands as the rain sluiced down the sheer face of the black rocks, where the mountain goats gamboled and would sometimes stop stalk-still and stare at him.

Nicknames for their generation had become almost required. There had become a naming ceremony that took place on thirteenth birthdays, like a bar or bat mitzvah, which happened at the Love Nest. The young initiate had to give a spiritual reading, and their mentor also gave a talk as to their spiritual progress. Gloomy gave a reading from *Moby-Dick*, and, as a poke in the eye to his father, he asked the pastor from the other church in town to talk about Gloomy's faith in Jesus. Nix played a favorite family song called "Love Is the Answer, but What Is the Question?" and Clive played an old vinyl recording of the Barrett Sisters singing "I Don't Feel No Ways Tired," followed by scratchy gospel records all night long.

Gloomy didn't like that his father had been a drug dealer. He didn't like that he sold alcohol six days a week and only quoted scripture about God's love and never about our duty to be obedient: our absolute duty . . . what Gloomy saw as the first commandment. "No truth. No justice"? Wasn't that what all the people chanted out in front of the buildings? He had seen them in the news. He could not imagine his father crusading for anything. He was a good-times Christian. He was only in it for the love, the art, and the beauty. But none of that mattered now. Gloomy was being put through his own trial. He had killed his own sister. There were no more good times to be had. There was only his prison job tending a bonfire at the construction site for the new women's prison. That was the best life he could hope for, or want.

Gloomy loved this job. It got him outside. It made him feel at home. Others didn't want it, thinking it cold and awful, but he could think of nothing he wanted more than to stand on the beach and burn construction trash with a guard holding a gun on him.

A short piece of pipe insulation floated out into the inlet. It was curled like a piece of macaroni, moving toward a rock in the middle of the channel. The moon was pulling all the water of the world to one side of the planet and pulling this bit of pipe insulation along with it. The rock looked like an elephant garlanded in slippery kelp banners. An eagle launched from an overhanging spruce and swept down for a look. Gloomy blew his warm breath on his hands and watched the whole scene. The eagle flew close to the pipe insulation and lowered its talons toward the gray-green water but at the last moment pulled up and flew around the point of the island and out of sight.

A fat guard came out of the construction shack, carrying

a propane torch. He had been at this work site a long time with Gloomy and over time he had let the convict refer to him by his first name: Tommy. As long as no other prison personnel were around, Tommy didn't mind. It seemed to make the time go faster. Tommy lumbered clumsily over the slick rocks and, in his full uniform and heavy utility belt, bent over the firepit and flicked the lighter in front of the torch. The blue flame jumped toward a corner of a cardboard box filled with two-by-four scraps. Smoke rose and curled out into the gray sky. Ravens hopped near the firepit, where Tommy always threw the remains of his pastries from the day before. The ravens had come to expect it and arrived as soon as the shore boat pulled up to the construction float, which was ten yards from the firepit. Tommy threw a vanilla almond croissant to a big black bird and then jacked a shell into the chamber of his rifle. He set the safety and slung the gun with the laser sight around his shoulder using the clip sling, which would let him pull the gun into a firing position with one motion. Tommy kicked more boxes over to Gloomy and motioned with his chin that it was all right for Gloomy to pick up his fire tool.

The tool was a pitchfork with four blunted tines and a bright red four-foot handle. Gloomy pitched a roll of electrical wire into the fire, and black smoke sizzled out of the flames. Tommy nodded at the wire. "Geez. They still getting rid of that order?"

Gloomy nodded and said nothing, just as he was supposed to. He had been burning a roll of this wire every day for more than a month. Apparently the wrong shipment had come in and because of problems in purchasing it was better to burn the first order. Gloomy poked the roll of expensive wire into the flames and watched the insulation burn black, exposing the glass and silver core.

"Did you hear about the penguin who rented a car in Arizona?" Tommy asked, and Gloomy shook his head. Tommy went on, but Gloomy didn't listen, just as he hadn't listened for the last 654 days that Tommy had been working. Rain began to fall and Gloomy pushed dry wood from some broken pallets around the burning spool of fiber optic wire. The raven had lumbered away with the croissant. Three small crows were harassing the larger bird. Two other ravens pulled a cruller apart and then hopped in and out of the smoke while they tried to fly away with their booty. Sparks rose up in the smoke and blinked out.

"I mean, it's a real penguin . . . from the north pole or wherever. Not a nun." Tommy kept telling the joke and Gloomy nodded as if listening while he stood on his tiptoes, watching the pipe insulation disappear.

The tide kept running. The rock was up on its haunches now because the tide was going out, garlands sagging down to the sand sculpted around its base. A helicopter circled like an injured bug far above the fire.

Gloomy's side hurt. This was only his third day back on the job, following an attack. He had had to fill out a wellness form, lie to the doctor, and write something in his official journal, which he hated to do, but not as much as he hated being on Ward 11 with the meat pumps. The clinics were full, and Gloomy would rather be out in the rain with his broken ribs and infection anyway because he so loved being a fire tender.

The attack had been over before he was aware of being hurt. He was in a crowd outside the pharmacy. He didn't need any meds, but as he pushed his way around an inmate, he felt pain run up his side: sharp, then dull.

Gloomy remembered men walking quickly away, the sound of their footsteps receding as he stared up at himself in the smoky glass ceiling. Soon there was an alarm and the sound of closing doors. Blood spread across his white shirt and down his tan pants slowly, like a time-lapse image of a flower blooming on TV.

Gloomy didn't know who had shanked him, and he wasn't that concerned as long as it meant he could have a single unit. He was back in population, which was not the usual drill, but Gloomy didn't file a grievance because being in protective segregation was worse than being in the hole.

Protective seg was twenty-four-hour lockdown with three hours a day in a private yard so you could throw a ball at a bare hoop. You never saw the other convicts, but you could hear them. Protective seg was full of rapists and snitches. They were the worst kinds of talkers. These were men who gained advantage by insinuating themselves into whatever nonviolent nature you had left. They attached themselves to you like sea anemones to a tarred piling. Once they had you in a conversation through the bars there was never a moment's peace. You would hear their dreams, anxieties, and fantasies. They were always niggling for a confession from you. Always looking for a bond. Gloomy had once spent a stretch in protective seg with a towel wrapped tightly around his ears. He was glad to be back in population now even if it meant he might be killed.

Gloomy turned a burning two-by-four over and flipped it into the flames. The guard kicked another box of scrap wood over toward the fire. They were supposed to go through all the materials to make sure there wasn't any contraband or dangerous materials. Gloomy was serving a life sentence, so he had a high-security rating: SR-100. The SR rating should have made it illegal for Gloomy to have his hands on any sharp tools or materials that could be fashioned into tools. But the truth was that Gloomy was a thirty-four-year-old lifer who would do anything the guards asked rather than risk losing this job, which got him off the main campus.

The construction site was to be the new women's facility. There was a stream of federal dollars for prison construction after the Soledad and Pelican Bay riots and the corrections strike of 2021.

The California riots and corrections strike had been uglier than the Arizona riots in the seventies and had changed the prison industry forever. In the summer of 2021, prisoners started killing and dismembering guards, spraying the walls red with arterial blood. After the first four days, they naturally turned to the snitches and trustees. After the first seven days, all structure in the convicts' community was lost, and the killing became a random and chaotic ballet of suffering. Prisoners eventually became hungry and fatigued by the weight of so much death. Some tried to escape and were shot by snipers on the perimeter. The prisoner representatives asked for nothing more than humanitarian relief akin to a peacekeeping force to be sent back into the prisons. But by then the corrections officers had called for a strike. They were not going back in to face the survivors of the worst prison riots in American history. Not without a new contract, at least.

So the new federal program came into being. The Republican president maintained that it was a new era and communities had to take a proactive stance toward prison reform. This was to be the new Public-Private Partnership where business, government, and community would usher in a new era of public corrections. Public correctional facilities would become as important and as ubiquitous as public education. Prisons were good for communities—particularly the small rural communities of the west and the north.

The revitalized American economy, in conjunction with the telecommunications and computer industries, began building a whole new style of prison. Gloomy was now serving time in Stevens, a three-year-old high-security work facility built on Yakobi Island off the coast of southeastern Alaska. Named for a powerful Alaskan senator (who had been convicted, then pardoned for accepting expensive gifts from powerful lobbyists), Stevens may have been a model prison at the time, but the new women's facility being constructed would be an even finer example of confinement, control, and protection. Olympus had originally been intended as one of the few maximum-security prisons for the upper echelons of criminals, but after the nuclear exchange it became a holding station for suspects and terrorist debriefing in what had been one of the biggest embarrassments in nuclear whack-a-mole that the spy world and security agencies had ever known. There was a mass murderer who had been featured in a popular movie and one drug lord from Mexico, but truth be told there weren't enough prestigious criminals in America, so Olympus filled up with terrorist wannabes; uncharged suspects from Korea, Saudi Arabia, the Gaza Strip, North Dakota; and a surprising number of people from Harlan, Montana, along with some run-of-the-mill criminals from old-fashioned prisons, or "gladiator schools," in Texas and around the country.

Gloomy was ostensibly serving a life sentence. But at first they moved him around. No one knew where he was and they kept him moving, so if he had confederates out in the world they would not know where to find him. Only Gloomy's lawyer could find him, but that didn't matter because Gloomy never wanted to speak with her. Probably because everything about his arrest and conviction was hurried and covered in the smoke and mirrors of "national security," his sentence was to be carried out in a media black hole where no one could see or photograph him. The government was not done with Christopher McCahon.

Gloomy tried to do his time as peacefully as possible, but he could not settle in anywhere. If that meant getting outside to look at the birds and watch the fish jump, that was what he aspired to do. He didn't think about the past. He didn't care to remember how young he felt when he first came inside, or how old he felt after his first month. The first nights after being transported from a pretrial facility to the hard rock where his life was going to end are lost to Gloomy now. No memories remain of his early incarceration. But there are lessons, and those lessons have a backdrop. He's not sure if it happened to him, but he knows that every new client who comes in cries until they fall asleep. All night in every lockdown, the new fish cry. Some call out names. Some stifle coughs and choking sounds, as if the grief in their lives was trying to jump up out of their chests.

On a transport bus once—Gloomy couldn't recall which one, and the state had been boarding out its prisoners at the time—there was a white kid with a new haircut and pimples staring out the grating welded over the bus windows. The kid watched the passing buildings warily, as if each one were a wild animal clawing its way toward him. "Is that it?" he'd ask breathlessly as they passed some institutional white buildings with metal fencing. "Is that it?" Some old convict from the back yelled forward, "Just look at the wire on top of the fence. What direction is it leaning?"

The boy looked and said almost as if to himself, "It's tilted toward the outside of the fence. So what?"

"So, you ever hear of anybody ever wanting to stop people from climbing *into* a prison?"

Then the bus was past the place, and the kid leaned back in his seat and started to cry. He was cuffed to an older con and this older man turned away in a perfect gesture of indifference and contempt.

After the California riots, American prisons became cleaner, more like high-tech cattle pens, just as the new public schools are today. Olympus looked more like a fortified junior college than it did an old-style stir. The warehouses and communication center resembled gymnasiums. The largest building was the four-acre clinic unit. From the outside, the prison's tannish gray walls matched the island's rock bluffs, and the blue metal roofing recalled the sky on a late fall day when the first snowstorm was breaking.

All the housing units were two stories. The first floor was called "Earth," and the one above it was "Heaven." Earth was where the prisoners lived and worked. Heaven was where the guards looked down on them from catwalks. Men lived in units or "cubes." Six cubes were joined into "suites" that had a common room and work stations. There were monitors built into the desks at the work stations, and each workstation had both styles of input pads. There were plug-ins for headsets. The walls were white with pale blue outlines of mountain peaks painted at eye level. Each suite could be locked down from the main control; the whole facility could be separated off into no larger than hundred-foot areas.

The ceilings to Heaven could be opened anywhere to allow armed teams to enter an isolated cube. The prisoners could be gassed to the floor, cuffed, and extracted from the cube without an extraction team ever having to actually enter a large hostile territory. In Heaven, the rooms and corridors of Earth could be controlled like a mechanical maze, and because of this convicts were not allowed on the catwalks of Heaven. The entryways on and off the secure catwalks were the most secure areas of the prison. No prisoner was ever allowed up, and if you were caught there, you were "tagged"—meaning killed.

There were still high jinks among the convicts: blanket parties and beatdowns, rapes and sexual predation. There were dealers and bankers but nothing that wasn't in some way or another allowed by the prison administration.

As far as Gloomy knew most of the boys at Olympus were there for "the rest of the day," meaning they were serving life sentences. This made it somewhat more mellow because there were older convicts from other facilities and not many crack babies or maniacs trying to crawl their way out. Most guys were trying to do easy time. There were fewer snitches at Olympus than at McNeil. There were fewer guys looking to make a deal, mostly because if you were on the bench for the rest of the day, there were fewer deals to be had. It was a work facility meant to pay its way. The lifers were given meaningful work to do in exchange for a relatively safe place to live. If you wanted to stay political or be a bloodletter, you were usually sent down to one of the killing farms in Texas or to the exchange prisons in Mexico.

The younger prisoners frightened almost all the older prisoners in the American penal system. The old men were relatively weak and physically vulnerable, while the young ones—the gladiators and guerrilla boys—were crazy. They really didn't seem concerned about survival. In some police precincts you might see an officer lose patience and stick a gun in a man's mouth to get him to confess, but the young ones were more likely to get an erection than they were to confess. Violent death was familiar to them. A head shot would be the last big rush. There were few ways to accommodate men like this. The new prison design reflected what it took to contain the violence on the streets of America. They were the containment boxes, the machines that separated good Americans from their wayward children.

Gloomy had done a fairly decent job at staying healthy. He got to move and breathe uncirculated air on the construction site, and he knew there would be no end of work as long as they kept building prisons. The prison industry had become the perfect vehicle for the redistribution of federal money; technically all the new jobs created had to be put out for the best bid, but nobody could compete with existing industry. In fact, industry was complicit in the creation of this cheap labor. The expanded use of convict labor had caused some squawking from some union heads, but there were always trade-offs. Higher-paying administrative jobs were created for the "free" population and the lower-skilled positions—keyboarding and "channeling" the complex switchboard systems—were perfectly suited to prison workers. And these jobs were counted as American jobs, which were always a win for politicians. Any job not going to an illegal immigrant was so much the better at election time. There were illegals in jail, of course, and though they claimed there had been no illegals building the prison, according to the locals working out there, there were plenty non–green card Mexican skilled laborers on the subcontractors' crews who signed on for the specialty painting, rocking, and pouring jobs—the hard stuff that union guys didn't want.

So, too, there was money to be skimmed off the top and into campaign coffers, as has always been the case in American politics. Prison work was flush with money—enough for everyone: legal, illegal, bosses, and gangsters—just as long as you could make prisoners work for nothing and the government kept printing the cash.

The new women's prison was being built with the best of laser and fiber trunk management. Prison workers would be taking credit card orders from the Philippines and reserving rental cars and hotel nights in Bangkok, all in a completely closed and secure "Island 3000" communications system. Inmates would scan NSA files for keywords or try to find patterns in coded bank transfers, never knowing what kinds of cases they were working on or what countries they were dealing with. And from there, they worked their way up to more preferred work as their diligence and reliability improved.

All the packing boxes at the construction site were marked with Chinese logos. Gloomy had seen so many of these logos over the years that he just ignored them now. He was burning another spool of excess wire when a tine of his fire tool clicked against a hard object in the thick ashes beneath the fire. He flipped it to the side and looked carefully at a sparkling gem-like object. It was melted glass from yesterday's fire. The wire had spun glass inside, and if the fire got hot enough the glass melted and pooled in the ash. He had seen many of these, but he didn't dare pick one up even if it had cooled off. An object like that would have been valuable contraband. A cooled glass chunk could slip fairly easily into a body cavity and would not be picked up on a metal detector. A good-sized chunk could be fashioned into several remarkably deadly weapons.

"Then the penguin says, 'I swear it was ice cream,'"

Tommy said to one of the construction grunts eating a doughnut next to him, and they both laughed and turned away from each other. Tommy patted his gun, and the construction grunt looked half embarrassed and tried to finish his snack so he could get back to work.

Gloomy was absorbed in looking at the glass. *Isn't that just the way*, he thought to himself. "Isn't that the way." The glass was beautiful. Gray to black but clear in some places. It was maybe a pound of curve and flow. As Gloomy stared at it he thought perhaps he could see the face of a saint. He didn't know the names, but he could see a woman in this abstract bubbled figure.

"How lucky," Gloomy said, and Tommy looked at him quizzically, then sipped his coffee. With the shattering of militant Christianity, the free Bible groups had been outlawed in American prisons. There were the April 19 groups and the New Left Christians. It had gotten so bad that the book of Revelation could not be preached at all and the New Christian services had to stick to prosocial, nonviolent themes. "McBible," the convicts called this new institutional Christianity, or "Scripture Lite." April 19 groups hailed back to the days when neo-Nazis began to merge with the David Koresh gun-loving Christians, and they all took common cause with the poor children killed by the FBI when the good reverend called the cops' bluff in Waco on April 19, 1993. Later McVeigh had blown up the Oklahoma federal building on the anniversary, and the American far right made a holiday out of April 19 and it stuck.

Gloomy vaguely remembered being a Christian. He still read his Bible, and sometimes pieces of scripture or an image of some biblical figure would come into his mind unbidden. Lately Gloomy was trying to remember his old beliefs and his childhood, but his mind was all jumbled up.

Gloomy was burning a wooden box with the strange construction logo on it, but he preferred to look at the molten glass. He thought maybe a miracle was something different from what everyone thought. He had once believed in miracles. He remembered that. Some voice (was it a woman's? It seemed high, almost like the hiss of the wind) spoke directly into his brain. "Look at a snowflake," this voice said explicitly into his ears, "and then look at a whole city covered in snow. That is a miracle of planning and design."

He had heard the voice periodically for the last month. It didn't frighten him, but he wondered what it might be doing in his head. This voice covered his brain during sleep like warm syrup and he was grateful for that.

"What if miracles are different than anyone supposes?" Gloomy said out loud. Tommy shook his head and made a "cuckoo" gesture, swirling his index finger around his temple before turning away, but Gloomy kept talking to himself in a low whisper. "What if someone threw some sand in the air and it came down in a heap." Gloomy turned a burning board over with his fire tool. "What if he did it again and it came down a little different? What if this person kept throwing sand up in the air for a whole year?" A raven circled the beach, landed, and waddled toward the fire. "Nothing but throwing sand up in the air and looking at the pattern. What if he did that for ten years? Or a hundred years or a hundred million years? And what if he threw the sand up in the air and it came down in the perfect likeness of a man? Wouldn't that be the miracle?" Gloomy kept thinking as he looked down at the molten glass figurine. "Wouldn't that be the miracle?" he said out loud in a conversational tone. He bent down to pick up the cooled molten glass. He heard Tommy pull his weapon off the shoulder clip.

"What are you thinking, Gloomy?" Tommy asked kindly, genuinely concerned as he gestured with the muzzle of the short rifle. "Just kick that over to the side. Then you throw it away in the barrel . . . like always." Tommy pointed with the gun to the row of seven galvanized barrels that were used for the unburnable waste. He looked for a time at Gloomy and then repeated, "What were you thinking? You ain't some new fish."

Tommy had been edgy with his gun lately. All the guards and employees seemed more on edge in the last few weeks. It could have been spring, the beginning of April and all the anniversaries coming up, or it could have been the natural ebb and flow of fear and disgust that seemed to run through the culture of prison life.

Gloomy flicked the molten glass to the side. It had been careless to try to reach for it, but he doubted that Tommy would write him up. It concerned Gloomy though. Lately he was getting more and more careless. It was as if he was dreaming more, while he was awake. He didn't want to think about it, but he had begun to hear the voices when he was awake. He knew they were in his head. He knew they were part of his imagination: a kind of shorthand for thinking. He had been getting kind of dopey, particularly since Lester had been killed.

After Lester was gone, and Gloomy got to be alone in his cube, he had begun to have more sex dreams. He often dreamed of a fair-skinned woman with dark hair, brown eyes, and thick eyebrows. She had a lot of body hair. He remembered she wore flannel nightgowns to bed. The dreams were all similar. He would put his hands underneath her nightgown, and she would roll into him, her mouth against his neck. He would run his hand up to her breasts and circle her nipples with his thumb and index finger. She would slightly arch her back while keeping her face hidden in the cleft of his throat. But he could never remember her name as soon as he had finished saying it. As if the words were gibberish. She would hold his wrist tightly, keeping it in place. Then, as if he were having a stroke, bright lights would flash through his brain. Intense pain would sear behind his eyes, and his head would ache. All images would be blotted out. All sensual and erotic feelings would be replaced with pain and an aching feeling in his chest.

This is where all his sex dreams ended. He wouldn't come during her visits, and in the morning he would have a painful dry piss erection, but he would be too sad to masturbate.

He had been in jail long enough to become old. First in Walla Walla and then at McNeil and only the last three years on Olympus. His underlying offenses had taken place in his hometown of Cold Storage, Alaska. Part of the new Public-Private corrections policy was that offenders were to be housed near the site of their offense whenever possible in order to promote community healing and personal accountability.

The smoke swirled around Gloomy's head and he squinted into it. The fire popped and he fed some broken lumber from the concrete forms into the fire. Gloomy could hear the waves breaking on an outside reef from the other side of the island. Workers were pounding concrete forms together inside the new prison building and Tommy was arguing with the birds. A fat raven was hopping down the beach with a croissant. Others hopped and chattered nearby. Tommy drew his weapon.

"Motherfucking crows." Tommy was in a bad mood now, and Gloomy did not know why. Tommy kept the hammer back on the nine-millimeter handgun, but Gloomy knew he wasn't going to fire. If he discharged his weapon, there would be a ton of report writing and forms to fill out at the computer terminal. Tommy hated keyboarding. Guards were not allowed to file their reports in the voice-recognition system because there were bugs in the VRS that compromised security. If Tommy could, he'd get a prisoner to make all his entries.

"Did you see that shit?" Tommy looked up at Gloomy, and the ravens tore the pastry apart, shaking their heads and beaks as if they were beading water from their backs. They walked like fat professors away from the fire.

"By God, Tommy, now, you know it's unlucky to mess with them," Gloomy said as Tommy took aim and made soft "cachoo, cachoo" sounds as he pretended to shoot.

The birds scattered, circling the fire and the remaining pastries. Tommy kept aiming straight up, making the little-boy shooting noises with his mouth. One large bird rattled and squawked, then, with a slight pause in the wing beat, tensed its body and let go. A whitewash of shit streaked down the side of the gun and splashed the side of Tommy's arm.

"Now, that's just too much," said Tommy, and he corked off a couple of rounds.

The cracking sound spiraled away quicker than the smoke, returning faintly as an echo. The ravens laughed up out of sight and behind the shelter of tall spruce trees. A couple of guys in hard hats poked their heads out of the building, wondering what was going on. They looked at Gloomy, half expecting him to be bleeding, but he stood with his prison-issue fire tool leaning against the crook of his arm as he stared up, trying to see where the ravens had gone.

"Now I'm in for it," Tommy said with a hangdog expression. He slowly got up from his seat and bent over to pick up the two spent shell casings. "I guess I'll just wait to see if anybody says anything. I'll just write up a report . . . I don't know . . . about how the ravens were messing with the perimeter alarm systems or something." Then he settled his bulk back into his chair and took a bite from another pastry.

Lester had been Gloomy's cube partner for two years. Lester was a Crow Indian from Montana. He went by the name Lester Face. That's what was on all his files and pleadings, but his full name was Lester Plays with His Face. The name was also the name of a legendary Crow warrior. Lester grew up with the name on the reservation, but he had shortened it for most situations out in the world.

Lester had worn long braids and the hair on top of his head stood up in a kind of pompadour, which had been traditional among the Crow. But Lester hadn't been traditional or very political. He was a gambler. Lester had carried a picture of himself in a perfect gray suit, red shirt, and silver hair ties. One of his gray cowboy boots with red toe caps was up on the tire of a white '65 Mustang, and he was smiling like it was the first sunny day of spring.

"Look at that suit!" Lester would say abruptly during a silence and point at the snapshot. "Just look at that suit. That car. I wasn't some poor-assed wagon burner. I was a pit boss in a real carpet place. Not some sawdust bingo hall on the rez. Fuck, no. I'd have a hundred-thousand-dollar drop at my tables in a single night. I *couldn't* pay for a steak in that place, but that's all I ate. You know what I'm saying?"

Gloomy never really knew. Lester had kept a box of pleadings under his bunk and was always working on legal stuff. Gloomy thought Lester was on Olympus for the rest of the day, the same as he was. It was a killing, Gloomy thought.

"Dumb, dumb, dumb," was all Lester had said about it. "I picked the wrong set of friends, man," he had told Gloomy once as he shook his head and stared down at his yellow legal pad. "The wrong set of friends with the wrong set of problems."

Before he died, Lester covered the spread and ran some games on Olympus. Lester did not like to lose big. But one time he had . . . the last time.

Gloomy hadn't actually seen the severed head in the shower room. He had heard yelling, and when he came around the corner the guards were there holding men back. There was a hazy puddle of bloody water creeping out onto the floor.

It wasn't the violence that shaped prison experience, though, Gloomy told himself, it was boredom. Prison life was violent, sure, but no more violent really than the lives most of these men left on the outside. But there was nothing on the outside to prepare any man for the long expanse of empty time. Men had carved names of women into their skin and dabbed the cuts with ink, or trained themselves to do five hundred push-ups without stopping, or simply stripped the paint off every inch of their metal bunk, all for the want of something to do. A white guerrilla boy named Ghost had killed Lester. It was supposed to be about money, but really Gloomy thought they had sawed Lester's head off with a cord of braided aluminum scraps out of sheer boredom . . . boredom and for the story they could tell about it the rest of their caged lives.

There was nothing to be done about it now, so Gloomy chose not to think of his cubemate's murder as some kind of mystery. It was a fact. It was a waste of time to imagine justice or rectitude in a place like Olympus. Ghost lived a protected life under the wing of some powerful angel in Heaven. There was nothing to do but try to stay out of the way of the bad luck the gods could bring. *Just do the time,* Gloomy thought, as each instant opened into the next.

Gloomy stepped around the smoke again. There was the weird yawping call of a blue heron lifting from the cove across the inlet. Tommy sighted his gun along the bird's flight and Gloomy turned away.

Gloomy thought about Lester's head. He imagined the eyes open on the gray pebbled concrete of the shower floor. The head sat for maybe an hour before anyone picked it up. The eyes staring, sucking up only darkness, the ears plugged with cottony silence. Gloomy flipped another piece of broken pallet onto the flames. Lester's head could have sat there for years, never moving, never blinking, never having another thought in its brain. Gloomy grinned a bit and wondered if they would let the head out if its parole date ever came up, for even if you were sentenced to three hundred years, which was Lester's rumored sentence, the head would still have a parole date. What was time to Lester's head?

Gloomy heard something and turned back toward his keeper. Tommy's phone buzzed against his belt and he flicked the switch and started speaking into the collar mic. He listened through the earpiece and spoke softly so Gloomy couldn't hear—not that Gloomy wanted to. But something was up. Tommy was listening intently and only speaking in short bursts, and he didn't look happy.

"God damn it now, Gloomy." Tommy snapped off his

phone. "You should have reminded me you had an admin appointment this afternoon. Now I got to schedule a pickup and go back inside."

"I don't have an admin appointment," Gloomy offered, looking back down at the burning pallet. The flames curled like the chrysalis of burning hair around a skull.

"The heck you don't," Tommy spat out. "You're meeting with your CO at one. That means we'll be on the skiff during lunch and that means I've got to type entries or walk walls until end of shift. Why didn't you tell me?"

"I don't know a thing about it." Gloomy repositioned his tool into the crook of his arm and held his hands palms up in the smoke. The fire flared on a collapsed cardboard box and just above them the heron broke over the trees like some awkward marionette.

Tommy threw the leg irons and manacles next to a drift log a few feet from the firepit. "Just put these on." He stuffed a doughnut into his mouth and kept it there while he tucked his uniform shirt into his pants.

Some prisoners who were working on release plans, men who had to complete certain jobs and courses before they were released, had probation and parole officers. Men who were going to be inside "all day" were assigned control officers or COs.

Once Gloomy was inside the second perimeter lockdown entrance, Tommy turned him loose. They had walked from the workboat up the dock and through the first of three outside gates and the first of the sliding metal doors on the outer wall itself. Tommy waved goodbye dismissively and went toward the break room. Tommy walked slowly; nothing but paperwork awaited him there. Heading the construction crew was considered "good duty" by the guards. There were never more than four guys, and

on many days, like today, there was just Gloomy. Most of
the other inmates preferred to stay in and pound on a keyboard to hack into some forbidden computer file so they
could access the film section. Men would watch anything
within the prison database that was off-limits to them—
educational training films, recreation films, emergency
medicine or basic anatomy films—anything to try to find
an image that recalled a woman's body. Men would stare
up at the wall-mounted monitors in their workstations
and sniff the air as they pointed, clicked, and typed. They
sniffed, hoping to catch any scent of the fertile world over
the walls.

But Gloomy didn't need it. He wasn't interested in
acquiring any new job skills. He had taken the unit on
work ethic just to get off Olympus's main campus. The fire
tender's job was used as punishment or motivation to work
harder at the typing classes. Gloomy kept going back to
the fire. The young ones didn't understand. To them the
computer felt like freedom, but to Gloomy, all it meant was
staying in the walls of the prison.

The doors buzzed open and Gloomy walked down the
sand-colored hall. There was only one door at the end
and as he walked the forty or so feet across the tile floor,
Gloomy could hear cameras in the dark mirrored ceiling
swiveling in their gimbaled braces. The designers could
have made them silent but opted not to, so the inmates
would constantly be aware they were being watched.
Gloomy tucked his shirt in and straightened out the front
of his pants, then knocked on the door. It buzzed and
jogged open slightly, and he slid it to the side into the wall
and walked into the CO's office.

There were dozens of cubicles and a front desk. A yellow line was painted on the floor about three feet from

the receptionist's desk. In this part of Olympus, convicts were called "clients." Clients were not allowed to step over a yellow line without permission from someone wearing a yellow badge or better. Yellow, red, blue was the order of access. A blue badge could countermand any other badge. A blue badge could go anywhere and it was said there were only a dozen or so of them on staff throughout all three of the shifts.

The receptionist was a tired-looking Filipino man wearing a blue sports coat and a yellow ID badge. Gloomy stood with his toes on the yellow line in front of the desk. The man scanned his paperwork, never looking up at Gloomy. The client stood there for some thirty seconds as men and women walked between the cubicles, carrying coffee cups. Gloomy could hear the sound of laughter coming from around the corner, mingled with the gurgle of a coffee maker spitting the last drops of water down into the filter.

"Yes?" the Filipino man said, as if Gloomy were interrupting something shockingly personal.

"Yes?" he said again.

"I was told I had an appointment with my CO."

"You were told, huh?" the man said sarcastically as he opened a three-ring binder. "And I don't suppose you have a pink slip for the appointment?"

"No," Gloomy said, and shook his head, looking down at his feet. Prison life was full of changing rules and policies. Some days you needed a pink slip and others you didn't. You were always supposed to follow the drill, but the drill always changed. The confusion was so constant that Gloomy had long ago formed the belief that it had been designed into the system to keep the clients off balance, and half-apologetic at all times.

"No," the yellow-badged clerk said loudly. For the first

time he looked up, then squinted across the three feet at the number stitched on Gloomy's shirt. "No. I didn't think so," he said as he mumbled and tried to enter the number with his keyboard. He scowled and then gestured with a backhanded wave, indicating Gloomy could approach the desk. "Give me your tag."

Gloomy reached under his shirt and lifted the tag around his neck over his head. The clerk ran it through the scanner and pulled up Gloomy's jacket—all his files.

"There it is," the clerk said down into the computer. "You are late, my friend. You've been bumped out, so just cool it on the bench there and maybe I'll get you in." The clerk pointed to a bench near the door. Gloomy held his open hand out and the clerk looked at him as if he were threatening to set himself on fire. "What?" the clerk said with an edge of panic to his voice, his hand sliding down under the desk.

"My tag," Gloomy said, and the clerk threw it to him, embarrassed.

"Yeah," the clerk said.

Gloomy sat. He slept, his mind wandered, and he lost track of time. There was nothing to read. He was not allowed to ask questions. There were no windows. Gloomy was expected to sit quietly and keep his hands visible to the clerk at all times. Gloomy thought of Lester's head again, the curve of the scalp and eye sockets. When he thought of it there was not blood and no body. There was just the head. He heard no screaming or crying. He looked down into the black eyes, into the black mouth that was parted slightly, the once pink tongue that had turned gray, the ears sucking silence and the mouth singing it back out over the air. Gloomy followed that silence out over the rocks, past the waves breaking in a jumbled foam; he followed it over the foothills of swells breaking in from the west, and, as he did so, he thought of nothing so much as distance, the gray horizon flattening out to the marbled sea. He floated there on the bench, waiting for his appointment.

GLOOMY'S GRANDFATHER—OR GREAT-UNCLE, technically—was named Slippery, and before he had gone into logging, he had been a fair hand on horseback. He had chased cows in the Palouse country of Washington state and had even followed the little country rodeos for a year or two. He rode the saddle bronc events and had done some calf roping. Sometimes on weekends after working the woods, he would put on a pearl-snap shirt and his riding boots and take his saddle horse in the back of the pickup to the old arena to team rope with some of his buddies.

There was a time Gloomy's grandpa would try to take him out on an Alaskan lake after work. The lake had no one on it in the evening, and they would pull the old wooden rowboat down through the weeds to the water-front. The only fish in the lake back then were little rainbow trout. Gloomy would sit in the stern, and Slippery would pull gingerly on the oars, not wanting to rip the rotting locks out of the boat.

He remembered Slippery wearing an oil-soaked hickory shirt and frayed pants with suspenders. He had a skinny chest that more often than not was burnt mahogany red around the opening of his shirt. But peeking out under the hard hat, his forehead was fish-belly white, and his hands were scarred with smooth pink slashes across the wrists and knuckles. Slippery's gym shoes were always getting soaked through with

water, and Gloomy worried about his feet. But Slippery
never seemed to notice or at least give anything away.
He would go to the west end of the lake just ten yards
from the shallow ledge and let the boat drift, then he'd
rig the spinning poles with salmon eggs, one miniature
marshmallow, and a bobber about six feet up. Then Slippery would open a beer, make his first cast, lean back,
and say the same words he said every day: "Hey, boys,
chow!" The hook would plop like a nickel in the murky
water, and the silver bobber would settle on the surface of the lake like a planet in the universe. They never
spoke unless it was to congratulate each other on their
technique. If they were lucky fishing, Gloomy and his
grandfather might bring home three fish.

The air in those remembered summer days seemed
clear as gin even to Gloomy, who had never let gin pass
his lips. Ravens disappearing into the red alder trees and
the lazy hush of a shallow summer river breathed dreams
through Gloomy all of his life. Memories were swirling
around Gloomy now, crisscrossing swiftly over his head,
and he reached up and pulled one down to relive.

Gloomy was sitting in the skiff at the dock in front of
Slippery's cabin. He rolled down the window and hung his
arm out the side of the boat, then looked at his forearm
vibrating in the sideview mirror and wondered if his arms
were almost as broad as Slippery's. He flexed and stole
glimpses of his arm as his grandpa smoked a cigarette and
sang a Marty Robbins song.

Once home Slippery gathered his gear up to clean and
lay out in his shop. He lugged the old yellow McCullah
chain saw with the thirty-four-inch bar against his leg.
He slung his chaps, gas jugs, and wedges over his shoulder. The McCullah was a wonder to Gloomy, especially

as he had grown older, because the old yellow saw was so huge, it was like carrying around a motorcycle engine with handles. Gloomy wondered why in the world his grandpa hadn't just cached it up in the woods somewhere rather than carry it all the way back down the cut to the skiff for the long ride into town.

"That there's my partner," Slippery had told him once, sitting on the tailgate and looking at the sleeping saw. "I take care of that old saw like my best buddy 'cause I count on it to earn my living. No sense being disrespectful to your tools, now, Gloom. It's bad luck." Gloomy remembered that and the smell of beer on his breath mixing with the oil on his clothes, the cool evening wind off the unnamed lake, and the evergreen smell of sap on the old man's hands. At that time Slippery Wilson was everything the boy wanted to be.

Once the tools were put up, Gloomy made sure the skiff was squared away and the gear was covered before he went into the cabin. Inside Ellie was propped up on the couch with her oxygen bottle by her elbow. There was a stack of pop cans on the coffee table and a large glass tumbler with the last smoothed cubes of melted-down ice. She could barely breathe. The skin on her face was a strange translucent white, made more strange by the lipstick, which was badly applied. She smiled at him and opened her arms for a hug. If she had been drinking the vodka she kept hidden under the sink, she would say expansive and sentimental things on the most ordinary of days. "Oh, my baby boy, my big strong baby boy, I'm so happy, happy, you're back and not all busted to splinters." Then she would start coughing so hard Gloomy would have to turn away. She would spit in a tissue and hide it under the crocheted blanket. If she had drunk enough she would try to smoke a cigarette and this would be all right as long as she remembered to turn off the oxygen, which it seemed she always did.

Slippery came in the house and said the same thing he always said as he walked in: "Hello, the house!" and he kicked off his wet gym shoes and walked over to the couch and leaned over to give his wife a kiss on the cheek. "By God, Ellie, I think you're looking a little better today."

He always said it in the same tone, and Gloomy's grandma would always nod and close her eyes for a moment before replying, "Yes, just a little better each day," and she'd make an attempt to clean up: rattling the cans and knocking the tumbler off the table.

Slippery came over to her and said, "Now leave that for tonight. We'll eat camp food until you're better." And he went to the shower. Gloomy went out to the back where they had built a washhouse and got clean clothes for him and his grandpa. They both had work clothes and house clothes. Slippery would have a clean set of house clothes with him in the bathroom and Gloomy would bring in a clean set of clothes for the woods and fold them by the door, so Slippery could pick them up the next day and dress out in the shop at four in the morning without waking anyone else.

After his shower Slippery made dinner. Per usual, there was some beef that he'd gotten from the locker downtown and some canned vegetables. Slippery fried slices of boiled spuds in the pan right next to the round steak. He served up the plates for Ellie and himself, and Gloomy got his own. Slippery cut the meat into tiny bits for his wife. After supper, Gloomy did the dishes and Slippery helped Ellie to bed, then Gloomy turned on the little TV that got terrible reception—not that it ever bothered Ellie. Then Slippery came out and drank another beer in the big chair near the heater and read *National Horseman* until he fell asleep around eight o'clock. Gloomy did his homework at the kitchen table and listened to the sound from the little TV as it mixed with his grandmother's labored breathing and ragged coughs.

He looked out the window. Some nights the stars above the inlet were so intense that if he stared at them long enough he'd become dizzy and feel himself lift away from the earth, the valley, that breathing cabin. He stood up and looked in the bedroom and watched his grandmother sleep, her chest moving slowly up and down. Her skin looked like it was bathed by the stars and the moon. He was unbelievably happy, then Ellie sat up straight in her bed as if she had been pulled by wires, pointed her knobby finger at him, and asked in her cracking voice:

"Tell me, boy, what did you rascals do with that other bomb?"

MEN AND WOMEN in the office began to move around more quickly. A woman put on her sweater and changed her shoes. A man stood with a companion, both talking and laughing in their overcoats. William Thompson walked past the bench and was startled to see Gloomy sitting there.

"Whoa, you're here then?" William took off his glasses and stared at Gloomy as if expecting a response.

Gloomy brought himself back from the edge of the earth and looked up. "I was told to see you."

William grabbed a quick look at his watch, then back to Gloomy. He let out a long sigh and watched the tired Filipino clerk walk out the door with his lunch cooler.

"That's right. I wasn't aware you had been brought in. How long have you been sitting here?"

Gloomy raised his hands palms up to the sky. "I'm not sure."

William walked straight back to his cube, motioning for Gloomy to follow.

The cube was a silver-sand color. The trim around the window was dark maroon, as was the desktop and the casing of the monitor. William Thompson had a photo of his wife and child on his desk. They were standing on the stern of a runabout, the boy holding a silver salmon nearly as tall as he was. The woman was laughing, her mouth full of sunlight. Gloomy sat down.

"I'm sorry you were out there, McCahon. They brought you in from work. I'm sorry."

William was fumbling to turn on the monitor and he squinted over his keypad. The monitor was cocked at an angle, so Gloomy could not see the screen. William mumbled as the images flickered, and he worked his way through several menus, tapping his finger on a pad near the keyboard.

"The reason I wanted to talk to you today, Mr. McCahon, is I got a yellow tickler in your file. That means we're coming up on an important date, and I wanted to give you a heads-up." He paused, squinting at the screen. "Hold on. Let me just make sure this is right." He stared at a calendar and did some mental calculations. "Yes, we are . . . ten weeks out from your first opportunity for petition."

"Petition?" Gloomy felt something in his chest tighten. A chill maybe.

"Yes, that's right. You have an opportunity to go before the parole board."

Gloomy shook his head. "No. That's not right. I'm not qualified. My sentence did not fall under the criterion. I mean, I'm not qualified for release. I'm . . ." There was something wrong both in his chest and his head. It felt as if his mind were a wet rag that someone was wringing out. He felt as if his eyes were crossing. "No," he finally managed. "No. It's my understanding that I am not qualified for parole."

William stared at him, then back at the screen. He lifted his finger, pointed at the screen and was about to speak, then stopped himself. His fellow COs were buzzing through the door at the end of the hallway. Gloomy and William could hear their voices leaving like rocks clattering down a spillway.

"You were injured recently." William looked at the screen with concern. "They got you on any new meds?"

"No," Gloomy asserted. "No . . . somebody poked me is all, and they don't have me on anything anymore. But Mr. Thompson, you must be wrong. I can't be eligible for parole." The door at the end of the hall slammed shut and the silence eased back around them.

William cleared his throat and slowly continued, "Well, I won't try to convince you, Gloomy, but it's true. Just think about it, anyway. You have to write some things for the board. You have to forward your journal entries, your autobiographical material, of course, and the narrative of the underlying offense."

Now there was a ringing in Gloomy's ears, and for a moment he felt so dizzy he thought his eyes just might actually be crossing. "The underlying offense," he mumbled.

"Yes," William said patiently. He almost looked at his watch but stopped himself. "Yes. The underlying offense. You have to communicate to the board what happened back in the summer of . . . You have to tell them the details about the deaths of Ali Sheik Muhammad and . . . of course your sister." William paused and looked at Gloomy, self-consciously calm. "And the criminal enterprise that led to these events," William finally added.

Gloomy gripped the edge of the desk and leaned forward.

"Whoa, you look pale. You okay?" William tried to back away from him but his chair banged into the file cabinet. He pushed his wastebasket in front of the convict.

Gloomy's stomach churned, and for some reason he smelled gas. It felt as if he had just taken a great swallow of gasoline. He gulped for breath and swallowed hard, but it was no use.

Gloomy leaned forward and vomited into the wastebasket. William Thompson patted him lightly on the back.

Gloomy covered his face with his hands and kept holding his head down. "I don't know what happened," he finally said, his voice echoing in the plastic can.

"That's all right. It's a big step, this parole hearing. You're having a stress reaction. Don't worry about it. It will be easy to clean up."

Gloomy stared at William. Gloomy thought he could smell smoke and that smoke circled in on itself like the springtime song of the gulls gathering for herring along the coast. Gloomy wanted to travel up out of his body with that smoke, up off this island because he felt the leaden weight of bad luck about to fall out of the sky. He rubbed his fingers through his scalp and wondered why his hair was wet.

"But I haven't had any debriefing sessions scheduled, I mean, at any time," Christopher McCahon said.

IN THE SECURITY bunker under the stone foundation of the prison, Jasper thought he had stomach cancer, when in fact he was just drinking far too much black coffee.

There were too many things to adjust in his new swivel chair; any lever he hit seemed to drop some part of his body toward the floor. He spun around toward the new federal prosecutor, who had been sent to help him. Jasper burped and scowled at the new printouts that all had red borders, indicating that the information contained on the pages was sensitive, secret, and high-priority, which pretty much described Jasper's stomach at the time.

"They say the Iranian security forces have people in the prison. They say the Iranians have people in town. Contractors. They don't say who they are." He spun around and looked at the woman, who wore some kind of pencil skirt and rubber boots. "I hate these fucking spies. What good are they? They tell you enough to make everything your fault when things go to shit but not enough to stop it from happening. Fuck them, the chicken-shit bastards. Jesus."

The prosecutor looked at him and arched a perfect eyebrow over her dark eyelid. "You kiss your mother with that mouth, Jasper?"

"Goddamn right I do, and she is grateful for it."

"What do these chicken-shit spies say?" she said, stretching up toward her reading light like a Siamese cat.

"I told you: the Iranians want to kill or kidnap our only two assets in the can."

"Well, which is it?"

"I suppose they want to kill the one that won't help them and kidnap the one that will," he said. "What do you think we should do?"

"I don't suppose there are any actual Iranian security forces on the ground in Alaska, are there?"

"Fuck no, the chicken-shit bastards."

"Then I say, let them do what they want."

Jasper took a long drink of coffee and winced as if his bowels were splitting. "Jesus, Billie, you are hard on those boys."

"The clock is ticking, Jasper, and you won't be kissing anybody if we mess this up. Can't hurt to have two teams working on this."

Chapter Three

After the war with the North Koreans, the US intelligence service's black prison sites started filling up with not only Shia terrorists who had tried to get ahold of the Alaskan warheads—and possibly, depending on what websites you read, had actually gotten ahold of one—but also, increasingly, members of the new, more radical segment of the Second Ghost Dance Movement, which had started taking hold throughout the American West and in the North. Most of the details have been covered in the media but very little of it is truthful. It all came back to the first Ghost Dance—or Medicine Shirt—Movement.

On January 1, 1889, in Mason Valley, Nevada, as the sun disappeared during a solar eclipse, the son of a failed Paiute prophet journeyed up to heaven and met with God. This man was named Wovoka; the white ranchers he lived with were named Wilson, and he was also called Jack Wilson. Some whites and some Paiutes suspected that his father was actually the white rancher Wilson, but Wovoka did not bring up the matter of his actual paternity with God.

As Wovoka looked around heaven he saw all of the game, the buffalo, the antelope, the thousands of geese and birds. The elk and deer that the white hunters had decimated off the land were also there. They were alive again in heaven along with all the Indians who had died of white man's disease and guns. God told Wovoka that Jesus was coming back to earth soon, possibly by 1892, and that the Indians should be ready. They should love one another. They should stop the harmful practices of their old ways, they should stop mutilating themselves, they should not drink the white man's whiskey, they should not lie to one another, and they should treat each other as they would want to be treated. If they did that, then Jesus would come back and all the animals would return, the Indians would return, and the earth would swallow up all the white men. Then the authentic human beings could live in peace, and there would be plenty of food to eat. The only thing they had to do was dance in a circle for four days straight, and on the end of the fourth afternoon, they should bathe in the river. God also told Wovoka that he, Jack Wilson, would be the new administrator over all the Indians of the American West when Jesus returned, and William Henry Harrison would remain the administer of all the white people in the east.

News of this spread quickly. Wovoka never left Nevada; people from all tribes came to hear his teaching. Navajo apparently rejected his vision, but the Lakota in Montana took to the prophecy, adding their own militancy to it. Wovoka preached to keep the Circle Dance Movement and the coming of Jesus a secret from the whites, but the Lakota openly flaunted the magic of the ceremony, claiming to their administrators that the Ghost Shirt or the Medicine Shirt worn in the circle dance became bulletproof against white men's bullets. Word of this spread throughout the west, making both soldiers and settlers anxious.

With all the talk of bulletproof clothing, the coming messiah, and the disappearance of the whites, some stories had lost the message of universal love and had Wovoka himself at the forefront of the rebellion.

In the end, Jesus did not return with all the buffalo, but the last great massacre of Native Americans at the hands of the Seventh Cavalry occurred at the end of December 1890. Men, women, and children had their bodies dumped into a frozen ditch outside the impoverished camp of Wounded Knee, South Dakota. Some say 130 women and children had been killed, but others estimated the number of dead to be upwards of three hundred. Wovoka was not among them but lived on to become an actor in silent movies, playing the same stoic, silent Indian in the same big black hat over and over. He died in 1932.

The Second Ghost Dance Movement had its beginnings in 1990 with Arnold Wild Horses, who was raised in Harlan, Montana. Arnold was a smart, severe young man with glasses who came from a violent alcoholic family, though he never took to alcohol himself. He rode out the turbulent times in his government house in the closet with a headlamp and a series of library books. He went to Princeton and Harvard and got degrees in literature, comparative religion, and philosophy. He became a follower of Islam in Boston and went on a hijrah in 2018. His first book was called *Crazy Horse, the Tash-shay River, and the Prophets of God*, in which he puts forth the argument that the Native Americans in North America lost the Indian wars ending with Wounded Knee because they couldn't maintain the unity they showed at Little Big Horn. The reason for this, he believes, was because they never fully embraced monotheism, and monotheism, he argued, was the anvil upon which the modern concept of universal

justice and fairness is forged. Wild Horses called monotheism the "balance beyond the horizon." The prophet
Wovoka understood this when he incorporated Christianity into the Ghost Dance Movement. Wild Horses went
on to make the argument that the prophet Muhammad
had been tasked by the angel Gabriel to unify all of the
polytheists under the word of God, in order to bring them
what Wild Horses started referring to as the "blessings
of balance beyond the horizon." He did not want Native
Americans to turn away from their traditional cultural lifeways. He found their belief in the sacredness of the land to
be foundational and fulfilling, citing Martin Heidegger's
principles of existential phenomenology. At the same
time, Wild Horses felt that Heidegger's work in *Being and
Time* was incomplete due to Heidegger's "refusal to con-
struct prescriptive analogisms," which prevented his work
from being incorporated into social constructions during the professor's lifetime and allowed Heidegger to be
subsumed by the National Socialist administration of his
university. In his speeches, Wild Horses told eager young
students that even though the Native warriors gained their
wisdom and strength through their relationship with the
land, the land alone was not capable of nurturing them
in their struggle once it had been stolen from them. Wild
Horses argued, "Without the land and the people's feet
on their own ground, engaging in their sovereign cultural
practices, the authentic human beings have no anvil upon
which to forge their tools of war."

Muhammad knew the same indivisible sacredness that
Sitting Bull had known. Muhammad and Gabriel exempli-
fied a unified sacred world imbued with and inseparable
from God's love and God's justice. God's followers were
the authentic human beings. The Plains Indians needed

the abstraction of monotheism to become modern warriors. Arnold Wild Horses' first book was reviewed in the *New York Times* and sold well. He was offered teaching positions at three Ivy League schools but ended up teaching in Missoula, Montana.

Eventually, small mosques started showing up in Montana and Wyoming. Native Americans began calling themselves "Indians" again, and they were seen praying three times a day in the Shia practice. They incorporated their traditional clothing and chants into their prayers. They prayed to the east, "where the sun rose," and where the "truth came from."

Arnold Wild Horses changed his name to Ali Wild Horses, and he was thought of as a holy man akin to an ayatollah. He published mostly pamphlets that were handed out in mosques to friends. Some of these pamphlets were found at crime scenes: liquor store heists and break-ins on the reservations. And later federal authorities found Qurans and New Ghost Dance literature, along with automatic weapons when they executed search warrants involving large bank robberies in Denver and Salt Lake City. There were entire sections of the dark web where people communicated in a new kind of pidgin language of English, Arabic, and Lakota Sioux.

From the very beginning, Wild Horses envisioned the Second Ghost Movement as a revolutionary movement. He thought of it in the tradition of the first movement. He wanted a separate state, he wanted land for his people to walk on and to practice their faith. He wanted the Great Plains and the lands of the buffalo, and, to the north, he wanted the caribou to once again belong to the native people of North America. Assuming America was not going to simply give the land back, he was encouraging an underground group of warriors to begin the fight to take it.

Deep in the concrete cells of Olympus, there were dozens of Second Ghost Dance followers who prayed three times a day. They were forbidden to know the direction of true east, but sequestered around the darkest parts of the lockdown were arrows scratched into the paint, or embossed somehow into the concrete: arrows with primitive points and what looked to be feather flights near the notches, and somehow these arrows all pointed due east. One of these inmates was Gloomy Knob's cousin Ishmael Muhammad, who had been part of the criminal conspiracy resulting in the death of NoNo and the near-detonation of a thermonuclear device, the first of its kind in North America. Gloomy and Itchy had never spoken to each other, though they had been yards apart for more than seven years inside the reinforced-concrete island cage. The prison authorities told Gloomy it was considered a security risk. Yet it seemed odd to Gloomy that he had never caught sight of his adopted cousin even once, not through the window of his cell or in a chow line, not walking across an exercise yard, or standing in a hall or a line. It was as if Ishmael "Itchy" Muhammad did not exist inside Ted Stevens Penitentiary.

Yet there was a cage with Itchy's name and number on it. The best-kept secret in the federal system was that in the cage next to Itchy's was the leader of the Second Ghost Dance Movement, lifted out of his shoes on the beach in Cold Storage, Alaska: Ali Wild Horses himself, who spent his time braiding his hair, praying to the east—a direction he knew in his heart. Wild Horses prayed three times a day in the tradition of the Shia followers of Islam. He taught such to all of his followers. Yet in prison he was not allowed a Quran. The one book he asked for and was permitted was *The Brothers Karamazov*. Ali Wild Horses kept his own council and was only allowed out of his cell for forty-five minutes a day to walk in a circle in the morning, and fifteen minutes a day to shower outside under a cold spigot rigged under a basketball hoop, where he could hear the ocean breakers working their chain-mailed fists against the rocky coast of the island. It was here he prayed his longest and deepest prayers.

NIX LIVED WITH the panic in her heart. She couldn't be sure, but now she thought the sound of the crashing waves was coming closer. She could see some daylight up through the end of the pipe. She had yelled herself hoarse, crying and pleading. She had said the Lord's Prayer countless times, and now she lay still, murmuring, "Please, God. Please, God. Please, God."

The box she was buried in was made of plywood, a simple box just big enough for her body, though it was not coffin shaped. She could sense it was not well made, for the plywood bowed in against her chest as the earth settled in the hole. She had no idea how deep in the ground she was. The circle of dim light in the end of the pipe could have been the sphere of Venus seen through a telescope. It could have been a baseball just inches from her face, but it didn't matter. She could not reach it.

She had wiggled her hands up the side of her torso, scraping her knuckles until they bled. She pushed against the top of the box, and as the nails gave way, clumps of damp sand fell through the seams like roaches scuttling inside the box. Water dribbled in. Mud formed in her hair, in her mouth. "Oh, God, please. Oh, God, please."

Now she lay and listened to the waves breaking. She

could even feel their rhythmic thudding through the soil in the ground. Had they buried her below tide line? Would the tide eventually rise up above the air hole? Would the water rush down the pipe, and if she held her hand over the opening, how long could she breathe?

"Oh, God, please, don't leave me down here," she pleaded, thinking that was a more modest request than salvation. She whimpered and started taking deep breaths as her chest pushed up against the thin wood buried in the ground.

FEW PEOPLE KNEW, and none in law enforcement, that the man who dug the hole had been the skipper of the luxury yacht the *Moondancer.* He was a Jamaican skipper who had been paid a half million dollars for the job. He received his orders over a satellite phone that he kept in his coat pocket. The voice that gave him his orders belonged to a woman and had a clipped British accent. His mission was only referred to as a job. He believed in his heart that it was industrial sabotage, stealing documents, or a machine or a prototype: rich-people problems . . . he didn't know or care, he just wanted to be paid. He had spent years developing an image as a self-styled pirate, but once the North Koreans sent their badly made missile into the air, he knew he was dealing with serious people. The nice lady mentioned that there were others in place to "finish the job" if he failed her, and he was starting to get paranoid. He began seeing other civilian men who appeared to have weapons secreted away in their coats walking the docks. Men who should not be walking a dock in Alaska.

The Jamaican skipper was told to motivate Ishmael and Gloomy, the men with the warheads, to work quickly, and he thought of the idea of burying Nix in the box at low tide, then he carried it out. He took a video of her with the bag over her head, crying out. Then he took the bag off so her face was visible. Threw her in her grave. The video was chaotic: he threw the camera on the ground as he nailed the box lid down, then picked it back up. For one jittery moment, one of his hands flew across the frame as he dropped wet sand on top of the coffin, then the video ended. According to the reports, the video was found on the dock, and a witness told police that a black man with a "reggae accent" had been seen talking and showing something to Ishmael Muhammad before the fire on the yacht, which led prosecutors to believe the Jamaican had given the local boys the instructions for the kidnapping.

WHEN NIX WAS done with her shift tending bar at Mouse Miller's Love Nest, she walked through the door of the communal house, where most of the Love Nesters lived. Lilly, the Tongan nurse caretaker, was sitting in the living room. The large kitchen monitor displayed Clive's vitals. Lilly smiled up at Nix as she took off her damp coat.

"We didn't get any kids. I think they're scared. You know, your man may be closer to a ghost than any of them want to think."

Nix took a towel off a hook by the door and dried her hair.

"You have a good time, though?" Lilly asked.

"I did," Nix said as she let out a long and tired sigh. "How about you, anything happen?"

"No," Lilly said, putting her book aside. "I'm about to go change him." She squinted at the monitor over by the stovetop. "He's got some moisture there. He'd be all right for a bit, but I'll change him before I go so you don't have to."

"You are the best, Lil. What about L.P.? Is he in bed?"

"That old Indian is up in his room playing the guitar. I think he's crazier all the time. I think he's crazier than even he thinks he is." Lilly laughed. L.P. was a guest from times past and from times ahead, she supposed. He was a man with secrets and with deep connections to the Love Nesters.

Nix looked up at the plank ceiling of the kitchen and listened to L.P. plucking on his guitar. The notes slid downstairs and seemed to fly out the window above the sink. She thought of L.P. sitting in his musty room crowded with magazines, playing his road-worn acoustic guitar. She sighed and turned to follow Lilly as she walked into Clive's room.

"I'll help you with it," Nix said.

The sick man lay still with his mouth open. His eyes stared up at the ceiling and he had a strange, wild expression on his face. Lilly leaned over and smiled. "We're going to get you cleaned up," she said in a voice that was not too loud or too saccharine. He snapped his mouth shut and looked around as if he were waking up in a strange place.

"That would be nice," he said, answering the voice above his head that seemed to come from somewhere.

Lilly threw back the sheet, exposing the old man's torso and legs to the light from the bedside lamp. His skin was so white, Nix thought the light would sear him. His body resembled a mollusk that had been ripped from its shell. His skin showed ravages of scar tissue up his torso from a fire he had been trapped in years ago. His legs were pearly sticks with more scar tissue scoring the length of one narrow thigh. He had once been a criminal and a cowboy, had once walked thirty miles in a day, and had run away from Cold Storage, buying a car in Skagway before he knew how to drive and taking off north on the great American Road. He had walked up the sides of steep wooded mountains, but those legs of his would never again carry him outside of that small room.

They lifted him and cleaned him, toweling and swabbing his shrunken sex and the tender red flesh around his bottom. Lilly put powder on his soft skin and the powder made him seem like a porcelain doll. They moved quickly and gently, neither of them saying anything, but the sick man grimaced up toward the ceiling, his mind reeling, trying to will himself away from this situation, where two women held him in their hands.

"I know, baby," Nix said. "Don't act shy now. I know you aren't shy."

"True that," murmured Lilly.

Clive heard them. He smiled. Or he thought he was smiling, but truth be told, he could not really tell if he was in the bed or taking a spin around the room. The revulsion for his physical self was lodged in his being, like a chunk of meat in his throat. He had no words for it and he was too weak to do anything but choke down his disgust. When he settled back into the collapsed tent of his own body, in his temporary home, he just lay there, both resisting and leaning into every tender touch.

In the last few weeks he had felt sleep coming on him with a heavier and darker hand than it ever had before. He noticed that he no longer remembered the moments before sleep, and he didn't know how or where he was waking up. He was just suddenly returned to that leaden body, staring up through a face that could have been some child's mask. It was as if now, in sleep, he was becoming acclimated to death.

None of this frightened him. He was tired and ready to have his bones release their grasp. He just didn't know when or how it would happen, and he didn't want to leave Nix standing there as the darkness came. He couldn't bear to think of it, for to do that made him think of the dark box buried in the sand.

Sometimes the women's voices were nothing more than the burbling of a river. The sound was distinct but nonsensical. Other times phrases would rise up—like hearing the name of a familiar place embedded in the dialogue of a foreign movie—and he knew their meaning. Then there were times when he would reach out for words as if they were fish swimming by, but they would disappear no matter how hard he tried to concentrate and grab them. So, he lay exhausted more and more, letting the present moment wash over him and sluice away into the past.

"You want to go trick-or-treating, baby girl?" Clive said straight into Nix's eyes.

She was startled for a moment. "No, Clive. No, I don't. Don't have a good costume."

"I'll give you mine," the sick man wheezed, then closed his eyes.

"IS THAT OLD fool dead yet?" L.P. asked Nix as she came in the door.

"No . . ." Nix sighed, picked up a pile of old magazines off the straight-backed chair, and moved them to the floor. She sat in the chair and propped her feet on the stack of reading material.

L.P.'s soft brown face had a maze of deep wrinkles. His gray hair was braided, and each braid was affixed with silver clips. He thumped the bass string of his old Gibson guitar, wincing with each note.

"He's taking his time then, isn't he?"

"Yep," Nix said.

"What do you mean, 'yep'? What you thinking about now, Maya?"

"I don't want him to go on like this." She picked up a *Harper's* with an image of a burning computer monitor on the cover.

"You want me to kill him?"

She didn't say anything at first, then sighed. "Not right now." She smiled at the man across whose massive rough hands lay still on the strings of his guitar.

"Christ, Mary on a crutch," L.P. said. "The world turned all to hell when white people started thinking they wanted to be Indians. Jesus. Please talk to me, Nix. Why do you think he's holding on?"

She flipped through the pages of the magazine. "I don't know, but I have a feeling I'm going to be told."

"You damn right you're going to be told," he said. "He's holding on because that's all he's got to do. He's holding on so he can look at that honey-sweet face of yours one more time."

L.P. smiled at her, but Nix scowled. Outside the house, the wind beat around the rocky anchorage, and she could hear it scour the trees that lined the beach, as if the wind carried ten million brooms trying to sweep them away.

She shook her head, and the old Lakota man started to reach for her hand, but she walked out of the room.

"I'm not going until it's all over," he yelled after her. "You can't get rid of me, you know. I see you let other people sleep here when I'm not around, but that don't matter." His voice had no effect on her as she walked down the stairs.

"White people!" he called out. "First you take our land and next you give your spare bedroom to the Tongans!"

FROM GLOOMY'S PERSPECTIVE, everyone lies about why they are in prison. The lies are so common they fall into a few recognizable patterns. If you asked your average convict, he'd say he's in prison for an unavoidable killing, like finding his wife with another man. These killings for rough justice are popular fables in jail, fables that reaffirmed the societal values of the place. No one was expected to believe them for their historical accuracy.

The truth is most convicts were trapped for violence against members of their own family. The others were a mix of drug dealers, mules, or low-level snitches, politicals, and posers, and of course there were a lot of sex offenders who easily could have been netted up accidentally for something else if they hadn't been serving time for that.

Gloomy Knob kept to himself and had stood behind Lester whenever he had needed protection. Gloomy had been convicted of second-degree murder, arson, and kidnapping. He had been political and this accounted for his life without parole. The politicals were sitting on the bench all day even if it was their first offense. Most of the politicals were black, brown, or red people from the South Bronx, Compton, or the Black Hills. Some were guerrilla boys who had mixed the jargon of crime with that of liberation, and, as such, found themselves out of the game permanently because the postwar government was not having any revolutionary rhetoric coming from black or brown people with guns.

There were a large number of Second Ghost Dancers who had cooked up a new independence movement. Lester Plays with His Face had little patience for their company. Those Indian men generally met in the sweat area that the government provided under the Freedom of Religion Act, which granted prisoners the right to access their chosen God while incarcerated. The Indians would burn sage and chant in a makeshift sweat lodge that was out of bounds to the white prisoners. Lester wanted none of it. "Wagon burners," he muttered. Then he added softly, "I don't think prison is the place to begin to be an Indian." Lester's eyes looked small and hot, like a wolverine's. He practiced the one-hand shuffle with his shaved deck. "You think if they had built Crazy Horse a sweat lodge in Fort Robinson he'd've adjusted better?"

These words had some emotional heft for Gloomy, but he liked Lester, if only for the reason that Lester seemed to like him. Lester had gotten a kick out of having a cowboy for a cellmate. But no matter how heated Lester's rhetoric had become, Gloomy hadn't thought Lester was really a political prisoner. Certainly he wasn't a guerrilla boy or a new warrior. Gloomy had a dim memory of the kind of anger he encountered in others, but he chose not to think about politics. He lived in the day-to-day, and the only politics that mattered to him was what was for chow and who sat where in the hall.

Gloomy had read about repressed memory, and he didn't believe in it. He could feel what happened seven years before, his mother buried in a plywood box and the beautiful yacht that exploded with his sister's dead body on it. Gloomy remembered pictures of famous people in silver frames, and he remembered the smell of gas. He thought he even remembered the dirt on the carpet, but he had to admit he couldn't be sure what order his memories came in.

As for the rest of it—the fire and death—Gloomy could feel it as if it were a block of ice lodged in his chest. The memory was there, in his body. Gloomy simply didn't want to think about it. He didn't want to talk about it. He knew he could remember if he wanted to, but even if he tried just the slightest bit, say, if he began to follow the dirty footprints across a green carpet in the main saloon, he would grow anxious and stop. Then the ice would drop to his stomach and he'd get sick. Too much of this jerking around, he knew, would finally turn his chest into a sop of shards and bloody meat. Memory of that day didn't make time pass any easier or any faster.

Maybe it had been the same with Ghost. Everyone believed Ghost had killed Lester and Ghost was fine with that. Ghost claimed to be a guerrilla boy, but that wasn't true. Everyone in the section knew Ghost was a bitch for someone high up in the prison system. Ghost liked to brag that he was on the bench for the rest of the day because he killed a black drug dealer in Idaho. But the word was Ghost had struck out on three chicken-shit charges. Strike one had been the botched robbery of a taxicab in Tacoma when he was seventeen. He was tried as an adult because the cabdriver was a paraplegic after the gun had gone off. The second strike was for beating and raping a pizza deliveryman in Everett. And the third was just for robbing a taxi driver in Seattle, a young woman with a small bundle of cash and a little dog in the front seat. The bad luck of it was the driver was white, and her parents were members of the same church as the congressman from the district— not that it really mattered. It didn't take much political heat to get Ghost his life sentence.

Ghost claimed Aryan Nations affiliation and had only done that to outrun his snitch jacket by working for the drug cops in McNeil. As long as he told them about the drugs coming in, they would keep the fiction of his political-killer status intact. Ghost was about as much fun to be around as the Ebola virus, and like the Ebola virus, once you were within the circle of Ghost's influence you were in danger of dying for no good reason.

Gloomy walked down the stairs from admin, quickly skipping three steps at a time. He was long-legged, with a cowboy's stiff-ankled gait and an awkward limp. He remembered that Lester had said he looked like a Native Gary Cooper, with his chiseled jaw and blue eyes. Lester had said more than once that he was going to try to get a cowboy hat for Gloomy. "Not some drugstore shit with a string under his chin but a Texas oilman's four-X Stetson." Lester was always trying to get Gloomy to show some style.

Two men who were not clients pushed through the door—men in civilian clothes: slacks and polo shirts, leather shoes—but neither of them were wearing their badges. Ghost was with them.

"Sorry." Gloomy backed away from them. He looked at the door behind them. He assumed these were visitors. The black man wore a burgundy polo shirt, as if he had just come off a golf course. Gloomy had never seen him before, and he could get written up if he were found in unsupervised contact with a visitor. It worried him that these men were not wearing badges. Everyone had to have some kind of badge, particularly now when all the prison employees seemed edgy. But it worried Gloomy more that these men were in the company of Ghost.

A tanned and well-combed white man, a large black man with a thick neck, and Ghost. Ghost had crooked teeth and was skinny; his shaved head was bumpy and slick as wet bone. The handsome white man looked like a movie star and had a disarming smile.

"Sorry," Gloomy repeated, and he stepped farther back into the stairwell.

"That's okay, bud," the handsome white man said, and he reached out and took Gloomy by the elbow, pulling him close.

"Now, what were you doing upstairs?" he said softly to Gloomy. His breath was warm and scented with spearmint gum.

"I had a slip," Gloomy caught himself saying, and then, worried he would be asked for the actual slip, he stammered an explanation. "I mean, I had an appointment to see the CO. I'm headed back to my unit right now." Gloomy looked at the two unfamiliar men without badges as they pressed in close. The black man was reaching into the pocket of his tan slacks, and for a moment Gloomy thought he was going to show him the scorecard from his last round. Movie Star pushed his thumb into the nerve just above the elbow joint, and Gloomy's arm jerked back with pain and then went numb.

"I didn't ask you that, convict," Movie Star hissed. "In fact, I'm not asking you anything. I'm here to tell you something."

The black man smiled and held his hands low. The skinny white man looked up the stairs and blocked the door behind him with his foot. Ghost sniggered and sucked snot back down his throat.

"I'm telling you that you should give this parole chance a pass. You keep your fucking mouth shut. You understand?"

"Just kill me now." Gloomy stood up straight and was more than a head taller than Movie Star.

"No such luck, bud," Movie Star said, and he motioned behind him to the black man. The black man held up his right fist, sheathed in a pulse glove. There was a sizzle and a blue spark arced across the knobs of each knuckle.

"No such luck, bud. You have to keep your fucking mouth shut. You talk when we tell you to talk. You understand?"

Movie Star let go and the black man swung with a hard jab up into Gloomy's stomach. Gloomy slumped over and felt the jolt of power surge through his body.

Night came and his mind sparkled with angry flies. Fire ants crawled on his skin. Movie Star bent over him, lips moving, and eventually words came to him as well.

". . . and just to be clear. You are not going to apply for parole. You are not going to fill out form one. Are we absolutely straight on this, convict?"

Gloomy nodded. The black man leaned down and rubbed the metallic covering on his fist against Gloomy's forehead as if he were checking for fever. The molded plastic was hard and warm. Then there was a sizzle, a jolt, and night seeped in with the mysterious smell of burning flesh like a trash fire somewhere beyond the walls. He was warm somehow and sleepy.

GLOOMY KNEW HE was still alive, there in the dark. He could not feel his body. He could make out no light. It was as if his mind were a black pebble growing a black shell around itself, inside of which he could hear or see nothing. He felt the darkness of unconsciousness come over him until he felt nothing at all.

Eventually he began to feel his fingers and the burn on his chest near where his stab wound was healing. He felt the concrete floor against his back. His sadness turned to fear, and he tried squeezing his eyes shut in an effort to go back to the dark. Why was his hair wet? His wound was stitched up. But it was no use to put the sequence together. Memory and time were jumbled. He was coming back into the world and to do otherwise would be like changing directions mid-dive. He was waking up in the prison hallway and no one was around, neither the men who wanted something from him, nor the people who seemed to want something from him. He had no idea who any of them were, and this made Gloomy sad. He had no memory of the last few hours but he felt strangely good.

Chapter Four

Torture or "enhanced interrogation techniques" began to fall under the same legal analysis as pornography when Justice Ditto commented during argument in the case of *United States v. Muhammad S. Muhammad* (US Supreme Court, 2020) that he "would have to say that [he] would know it when [he] saw it." Then after reading the briefing and hearing all arguments, the Supreme Court laid out the most current findings on enhanced interrogation techniques, essentially saying that if a detainee would voluntarily submit to the procedure, the interrogation could not be considered "so coercive as to rise above the standards of behavior laid out by any national or international convention or agreement on treatment of prisoners, no matter the techniques used during the interrogation." This brought in the "happy ending" era of torture techniques and the strategic use of psychotropic and analgesic medication, which allowed the manipulation of memories left behind in the interviewee's brain after the interview. Essentially, as long as they were happy afterward, everyone was happy. If there was cause for concern that officials were dabbling with the veracity of the memories they were uncovering, that was left to the experts back in the labs as

they unhooked the water hoses from the breathing apparatus and the electric cuffs from the genitals.

AS IN MOST black sites around the world, this work
was done in what looked like an old shower room on
Olympus. Green tiles with bright lights in a sealed-off
room. There was really nothing much to see, the lights
were only for helping the detainee climb into the sus-
pension tank. The tank itself was a black box filled with
salt water for additional buoyancy: essentially a modified sensory deprivation tank used by physiologists in
the sixties to experiment with early dream studies. But
in this case, the detainee wore a modified diving mask
as a breathing apparatus, which had oxygen and salt-
water intake hoses, as well as a gas intake, for various
infusions of smells and even drugs like nitrous oxide, if
necessary. Of course, there was a microphone, for talking
back to the interrogators. The detainee had a watertight
shunt site in their forearm with two in lines that were
ported directly through the walls of the tank with stain-
less steel fittings and long and flexible enough lines that
the detainee would be unaware of the tug against their
arm. The chemical cocktail would be constantly monitored and changed as needed as the interview progressed
as ordered by the debriefer in charge, who was always a
colonel or above, if the subject was a military asset, or a
specialist in the case of civilian subjects—usually, a man
of undetermined ethnicity, in a midpriced sports jacket
and no tie, soft leather shoes, and a haircut that always
looked as if it was several months removed from military
service.

Of course, the subject was given drugs for relaxation
and disorientation. Sodium pentothal used to be called

a "truth serum," which was an oversimplification. That would be like saying that all your dreams are "true." Surely they are, in some way, but what are they telling you? This is the task of the interviewer debriefing specialist. As was the case with a small-time private investigator looking for a runaway kid, you never look for the kid, you look for the person who will tell you where the kid is. This is much like digging the truth out of a brain; the brain belongs to someone who is desperate to hide the truth, so you do not look for the truth itself. Instead, you need to find the thing, the emotion, the power inside the person's psyche that will cause them to give that truth up.

Fear and pain often induce anger and resistance, particularly in someone who has been indoctrinated using pain and a kind of humiliation. Problematically, some subjects take a kind of pride, or even pleasure, in pain. Likewise, the threat of death may not be concurrent with fear, but with a kind of dreamy pleasure of release, which can lead to creating the "plausible lie" that can get the pain—once it has become too much to bear—to stop. Humiliation has been tried as a tactic as well, but often it was useful only as a recruitment tool, as was discovered based on how much US soldiers love to take pictures with their flip phones. Prisoners love to talk, and nothing can stop them from talking about some bad-ass bomber signing up to go back and voluntarily take a drug bath (the chosen shitbird term) for the new debrief, for a second or third time. Word gets around that the sheik is giving it out and that is disheartening to the rank-and-file suicide bombers and true believers.

In the drug bath, the interviewer, sometimes a lower-level psychologist or even a student intern, digs around in the detainee's psyche, looking for the right combination of hot-button emotional topics, something to use as leverage or something that will cause high stress levels. For most subjects, what works is a combination of emotional, religious, and philosophical triggers, sometimes involving unresolved childhood trauma—everything from child rape and abandonment to having walked in on their grandma in the privy. All these emotional hot spots were rated, described in context, and given a score. Sometimes all they found were mysterious reoccurring images, which were left for the more experienced debriefer to interpret. Everything went into an electronic file, not kept on-site but sent off to some federal office.

Eventually a colonel or a sports coat man, or, more often now, a woman, would come out to Olympus by boat with a laptop and backup drives and request a tank for two or three days. At the end of those three days they would sometimes leave with the prisoners. But often, the prisoner would spend two weeks in the hospital ward with the meat pumps, and several times the prisoners left on an amphibious plane, in a zipped-up rubber bag with a metal tag stapled to their foot.

So, the drug bath became the hot ticket. It *was* torture, experts agreed, but the memory of the unpleasantness was wiped out, in most cases leaving the detainee with the memory of a happy ending. The truly pious were left with a religious experience; the more worldly remembered something more akin to phone sex. Some subjects were left with something in between, something that reassured the manliness of the prisoner, as well as his godliness. Whatever the case may be, the subjects were always left with a bracing feeling of well-being and a willingness to come back, even if they also felt a burning sensation in their nose and lungs.

HERE IS AN example of a transcript from a happy-ending interview:

REDACTED TRANSCRIPT OF INMATE
#20046 02736 7/12/26 # 18

Folder marked "GENDER FLUID"

Acclimation time: 15 minutes. Baseline questions and pharmacological efficacy established.

You . . . you . . . you . . . are rising up into the body you have always known. Your real body. Shed this false weight. Do you feel your old body sloughing away? You are rising up out of the weight of the old body you were born into. Feel your real self. Feel your smooth skin. Tell us, what does it feel like? Tell us, who are you now?

[Murmuring. Unintelligible.]

Go back now. You are at home in your childhood bedroom. Look under your bed. You have your secret trunk. Your mother knew you had it, but your father never knew. Did he? Take it out now. You look so pretty in those clothes. How do they feel on your skin now? Can you smell the perfume? Can you feel how it felt to wear those shoes that made you feel so much taller, but unsteady? At first you couldn't walk in those high heels. But you were brave and strong and the more you practiced, the better you got. You could close your eyes and imagine your real body. Imagine yourself with your teacher's body. Imagine yourself sitting down on the toilet to pee. You know how it would feel to wear dresses every day. The underwear so soft against your skin. Do you remember wearing them to school before you had to go to gym class? How it felt to have the silky fabric rubbing against your thighs?

In your trunk was your perfume, your dolls, your clothes, your magazines, the one old blond wig you stole from your grandmother when she got sick, and some of her jewelry you took after she died, your old Polaroid camera you would set up on your desk to take timed photos of yourself from across the room so you could make those collages of your done-up face on all those bodies cut out of the magazines.

We all know . . . it's wonderful . . . it's right . . . it's wonderful . . . it's right . . . it's who you are . . . It's who you . . . you . . . you . . . really are. It's perfect. You are safe here with us. You are safe here being who you really are.

Rise up as you really are now. Feel the soft skin and how your body curves. Feel the smoothness of your crotch, where your pussy waits for you. Your family knows all about your body. They always knew, and they always loved you, and they love you now. They love their daughter. They love the woman you have become. They were at your wedding when you married the strong man you worked with. That man who rolled you into bed. That man who took care of you, who loved you completely. The man who saw through your ugly old body and saw the princess he knew you were. Remember before he went to jail? Remember when he was going to get the money for your new body? How he rolled you in bed? How he held you in his arms? Don't struggle now. You are starting to sink . . . Your father is not coming in. Don't worry . . . You are not drowning. You are not drowning . . . His breath smelled like cigars, and his beard was scratchy against the soft skin of your stomach. His breath was hot against your pussy, wasn't it? He would touch your sensitive spot. He would say your name over and over again. He knew how hard to rub you. He knew how to fill your empty space at the same time. He would cover your mouth with his, and his weight would fill you. For a moment, you would lose your breath and you would slap his ass, and he would jut his tongue into your mouth, and you would bite his lip and slap him again, hard enough to make him wince. He would fill your empty space with his finger and pull on you hard enough to make you cry out. He would pull your hair and go down on you. His wet mouth was full of you then, licking you, and his finger pushed in and out in your tight, tight hole. You would arch your back as he bit you, and his tongue flicked and sucked your most sensitive spot. His hand reached up on your woman's body and twisted your nipple until it made you cry out.

You pulled his hair, and his body rose up above you, and you scratched him as his cock stretched you wide and filled you up. It hurt you at first, but he kept pulling on your sensitive spot, and you spanked him hard with each thrust. His breath was hot and

*sweat dripped down on your sweet woman breasts,
and he licked your nipples as he thrust, and you kept
slapping him so his skin was rosy red, and he told
you how much he loved you. He told you that he
would put all the money from the bank, every dollar,
he told you that it would all be for you, and he told
you where he would put it. Didn't he? Didn't he
tell you, just then? Didn't he tell you? Before you
could come, he stopped and held your face in his
hands. His breath in your face. He stopped pushing
and he took his hard cock out of you and lay it up on
your belly, he told you because he loved the woman
you are, he told you where he would put the money
for you, didn't he?*

[Inmate responds in the affirmative.]

*What did he say? You are starting to sink. Don't
you want him to finish fucking you now? He wants
to fuck you. He wants to come. He wants to kiss you
while he comes. Don't you want to come? Don't
you want to have him come on your belly? Don't you
want to kiss him all night and wake up with him in
the morning and shower with him saying your real
name over and over? Don't you want him to wash
your hair and comb you out while you sit in front
of the open stove in that pool of sunlight that comes
between the buildings in the morning?*

[Inmate answers in the affirmative.]

*What did he say about the money? You are sink-
ing away. He is leaving you. His dick is getting soft.*

[Inmate gives address and description. Medication adjusted. Confirmation of address and recovery team dispatched. Sexual scenario is completed.]

———

Interview #16-2302317. 12/26/2020 TSFP
DECLASSIFIED and REDACTED

Note: Every mention of the Prophet is followed by the proper "blessed be his name" often omitted in transcript.

   You are here now. You . . . you . . . you . . . are like the Prophet held far away from Mecca and Medina in the other place. You . . . you . . . you . . . are rising up now and returning to the east over the gray-green waves of the seemingly limitless ocean. Do you, you, you feel your body rise? Do you see the waves rise and fall beneath you? The birds swirl and circle below you . . . you . . . you . . . you . . . travel faster than the eagle and the gulls that only skim the edges of the earth . . . See them turn to specks and the light turn to darkness and the stars funnel you . . . you . . . you . . . toward the east. Do you feel warmer now? You are nearing the Holy Land and the home of the Prophet, the desert of brown and gold, the long, straight paths and roads where the Prophet trod. You are no longer separated from your people. From your home. Can you see your home. Tell us, tell us, tell the Prophet where you are. Do you feel the joy?

[Response.]

   Tell us who is in this righteous house? This

observant house? This house that is clean and sweet smelling? This home that does not smell of other man's sweat and pig fat but of lamb, and wood smoke, of cinnamon and turmeric. Who is there?

Tell the Prophet their names.

You are leaving them now? How can you stay if you resist? We show our humility and our devotion. How will you if you do not show obedience to us? You must come back across the ocean. That is the ocean. You cannot rise if you resist. You will sink. To rise . . . your heart must rise with happiness. With our happiness, with the happiness in this holy house. Where is it? What are their names? The woman reaches out to you. You are drowning. Let her save you. Call her name. You are drowning. Reach out your hands. She will save you and lift you up. Say her name, and she will lift you out of the water. She will not let you drown. Do not let her watch you die.

[Inmate says a woman's name.]

I cannot hear you.

[Inmate repeats the woman's name.]

That is not her name, why would you say another woman's name? Why would you not say her real name? You are sinking.

[Inmate sputtering, crying. Inaudible. Clears airway, breathing hard. Inaudible.]

Why would you make up a name?

[Inmate explains the relationship of the woman, apparently a maternal aunt, and analyst checks background information, then further clears airway and administers analgesic gas.]

Of course she is. We knew that all along. All along. You . . . you . . . you . . . are at your aunt's house. You had been keeping that from us, but we knew her. This is where everything happened, isn't it? Tell us . . . us . . . us . . . relax . . . now you are floating again. Who was that beautiful girl you knew there, when the aunt was not there?

[Inmate responds.]

That girl, you knew her before her teaching was complete. She was a virgin. She wanted to please you because she knew you were a soldier of the Prophet. That was where you met her, right? You can tell us . . . us . . . us . . . Only we are here. When you lay on the pad near the balcony and the curtains were drawn, only the two of you were there, and the doors were locked. No one was going to come home until much later that night. Your aunt had taken the bus to visit her son. You were alone. What was her name, the girl?

[The inmate pauses.]

You are not sinking.
[Inmate says a woman's name.]

You kissed her first and she shivered, didn't she?
She smelled of strange perfume, and her skin was a
beautiful almond color, not sickly white.

[The inmate agrees, his respiration increasing.]

You, you, you sit beside the Prophet, blessed be
his name. His light, the warmth of his body is the
warmth of the sun. You are part of the Prophet.
You, you, you feel the voice of the Angel as he speaks
through you, through you and into the Prophet,
blessed be his name, "I shall ordain My mercy for
those who are conscious of God and pay the prescribe,
alms; who believe in Our Revelations; who follow the
Messenger, the unlettered prophet they find described
in the Torah that is with them, and in the Gospel—
who commands them to do right and forbids them to
do wrong, who makes good things lawful and bad
things unlawful. The Prophet relieved them of their
burden, and the iron collars that were on them. So it
is those who believe Him, honor and help Him and
who follow the light that has been sent down with
Him, who will succeed . . . " Who has paid more than
you . . . you . . . you? You know all the wisdom that
is taught by the messengers and now by the Prophet
. . . you, you, you can feel it now in your chest . . .

[Increased levels of 198652.]

Tell us what is needed. You are losing the
knowledge.
[Buoyancy decreased.]

[Inmate affirms.]

[Inmate affirms.]

Phone rings in the inmate's headset. Asks him in a mechanical voice as if a phone operator, in Arabic. "Quick interruption. Is [gives name of target] still living in your apartment in Munich?"

[Inmate responds in the negative.]

Where then?

[Inmate gives name and current address of target.]

You . . . you . . . you are living in the light of the Prophet. Blessed be both your names. You are dissolving into Him now. Dissolving into the Word, into the Book. She, too, the young virtuous woman, is part of the light, the smell of cinnamon and wood smoke, the taste of honey wine and lamb. You . . . you . . . you . . . are one with your people in the one Holy land . . .

[Drug course shifts and hallucination continues. Inmate has full buoyancy and relaxation of all doubt and insecurity. Inmate reports "religious experience" upon revival.]

THESE SCENARIOS PASSED legal muster because of the drugs used. As in surgery when a patient may be awake but have no memory of the procedure, the painful parts of the interrogations are kept to the middle section, and as the drugs change and gradually wear off, the only memory left is the memory induced by the scenario, which is established by the officer in charge of the interrogation.

This dabbling in the fabric of witnesses' memories becomes an important part of not only the evidence of the defendant's case but also the shared reality of their world, not to mention the legal framework that was the basis of *United States v. Muhammad S. Muhammad,* and the status of US interrogation policy. But most important, there turned out to be thousands of human beings walking around with memories that they had never actually experienced, and not just sexual experiences but entire relationships, remembered human beings and religious ecstasy that never actually grew from experience but were created whole cloth by the US government.

Take our Gloomy Knob and Ishmael Muhammad: interrogators had searched and hunted for the emotional anvils they needed. Sex was one anvil they used at first, but they miscalculated with our Gloomy. Gloomy was wired differently than were the other men the specialists had encountered. For one thing, having grown up in Cold Storage, Gloomy shared a computer—and a computer history—with his sister . . . and so as strange as it sounds, Gloomy had never seen pornography. His only sexual experiences had been lived. The first, when he was young, was puppyish and prepubescent. The second, with his wife, was tender and emotional. So when the military debriefers started bombarding his psyche with images of what most military-age men were used to in the late 2020s, poor Gloomy was quite frankly fried. Sex was not the anvil they could use after they sex-shocked his brain.

No matter how much he missed the woman he loved,

or how sexually alone he felt, he would not give in to anything more than an erection. Gloomy hid his erotic feelings deep down. They did not define him. For many male inmates, it was in part a kind of sexual energy or at least manhood that motivated their crime. Clearly many also had a religious fervor, but that fervor was fueled by testosterone in some part. Manhood, the identity as a man, the expectations of masculinity, had caused many of them to seek money or power, or to strap bombs to their bodies in service to their God.

After the missile fell apart over Alaska, the young men found a warhead half sunk in the muskeg up near the unnamed lake where Gloomy had fished as a child. Ishmael had an idea to sell the warhead. Life in their little town had become chaotic. Helicopters worried the air like bees, and military men pounded up and down the boardwalk day and night. Ishmael did not trust the US government, particularly at that time. He and his cousin didn't tell any friends or family members about what they had found. Gloomy wanted to turn it in to the proper authorities at once. Quickly there were some buyers on scene as well as the US military. The buyer whom Ishmael had settled on was working off a large yacht called the *Moondancer*. But instead of the easy hand-off Ishmael was expecting, what ended up happening was that US authorities got word of the transaction, infiltrated the scene, and captured both Gloomy and Ishmael onshore. The yacht they had been on sank, but divers recovered both NoNo's body and a warhead from the wreckage. Nix was also recovered from a box buried below the tide line, just before Ali Wild Horses was rounded up walking down toward the dock from the dump. The Jamaican fled the country and was never seen again.

GLOOMY STOOD NEXT to the gate that would let him pass into his unit. The buzzer sounded loudly, but he had his arms draped through the bars to hold himself up, and the door would not open.

A mechanical voice from the tiny speaker screeched: "One . . . seven . . . ready for access . . . Stand away, please . . . Stand away, please."

Gloomy woke up from the second layer of the drunken haze his life seemed to be becoming, stood away from the door, and it slid open almost soundlessly on its rubberized track.

"My head hurts," Gloomy said to himself.

After the confrontation with the men in the hall where the black man hit him with the Taser glove, Gloomy made his way back to his cube. He was ten minutes late for dinner. He had six minutes to get through three gates before he would be locked out. Not going to chow was fine, but if he started and got locked down in one of the hallways, he ran the risk of being written up, or worse: locked inside a passageway where he might not be safe. He stripped off his red overalls, which he wore when he left the perimeter, and quickly found his prison issues in his footlocker: blue shirt and tan pants. Just under his shirts was his box. He had no time, but he fumbled for his key anyway.

Each prisoner was allowed one eleven-by-fifteen-by-four-inch lockbox. This was the only private space they got. It took a search warrant issued by the prison magistrate for a corrections officer to examine the contents of the box. Those warrants were not hard to get, and there was little if any probable cause required to get one, but it was a punishable offense for a convict to open another convict's lockbox, and a prison guard still had to file the necessary paperwork before they could toss a box in a search. Now

Gloomy had just under four minutes to get through the gate and would have to run to make it. He fumbled with his key as his hands shook. He scraped his knuckles on the edge of the lid as he opened it. He looked down and was out at sea.

There was a photograph of a beautiful young woman, dark hair tied back, smiling up to the lens. She held her fingers out for a toddler to grip. The clothes were nondescript, she wore jeans and a T-shirt. The child was in diapers on a stubble of grass, and a green house was in the background. It could have been taken in 1979 or last week. Gloomy didn't know.

A buzzer sounded, and he threw the picture back into the box, locked it, and ran for the gates, hoping he wouldn't call attention to himself if he made it to his table before everyone finished.

WHEN HE GOT back from dinner there was a paper on his bunk from his CO: the form to apply for parole. Gloomy was alone in his unit. He wondered if anyone had seen the form. He wondered who knew about it. He undid the box and placed the folded paper on top of the photograph of the woman and child. He did not look at the photograph this time but hurriedly hid the box and then lay on top of his bedding with all his clothes on until he heard a voice in the speaker next to him.

"Lights out in ten, got to get stripped down."

Gloomy had no idea whom the voice belonged to but knew it was looking out for him. He could be written up for having street-style shoes on when lights-out came. All convicts had to be barefoot or in issued slipper socks by lights-out. The voice didn't need to warn him, but it had. Someone was watching him carefully.

Gloomy stripped and placed his clothes in the white bag hanging over the toilet. Then he lay down under the one blue blanket and the stiffly starched fireproof sheet. After five minutes, a buzzer sounded and the lights all over the building dimmed one level and then went out with the clunking sound of a breaker being thrown. Darkness jumped on him and rubbed down through his eyelids.

THE NEXT DAY Gloomy stood at the second gate. There was a light rain, but he hadn't put on his rain gear. He stood shifting from one foot to the other in his bright red jumpsuit. Tommy was nowhere to be seen. Other convicts stood in the lockdown area. Periodically a name would be called from the tiny speaker, the lock would buzz open, and a convict would walk through the gate. He had been standing there fifteen minutes and all the other men on outdoor work details had gone through the gate, leaving him alone.

Finally the metallic voice addressed him: "What's up, bud?"

"McCahon. I'm in the off-site construction crew," Gloomy said. There was silence. A gull carved the air overhead in a quarter circle and then disappeared from view. The drops of rain grew a little larger, splashing in a puddle at his feet. Gloomy draped the hood of his rain gear over his head.

"Don't have you down, bud," the voice finally returned. Gloomy stood there and looked up into the camera mounted on the pole inside his lockup. He knew not to say anything more, but he lifted his tag from around his neck, predicting the next move.

"Run your tag through the slot," the voice instructed.

Gloomy took two steps forward and ran his tag through a slot next to the lock on the metal gate.

When the tag was scanned, the operator could read the files directly off the encoded information. They were reviewing his jacket now. Gloomy had never seen his jacket. Most of it was historic information that was not of much use to a gate watcher, but in one stroke the gate watcher could call up daily instructions, work orders, warnings, or any special limitations. This was mostly conjecture on Gloomy's part. Convicts loved to talk endlessly about the prison computer system. There were stories that had entered lore: convicts who had hacked into the system and changed their jackets. There was the inevitable story of an eighteen-year-old kid who had changed his release date and walked out three years early. There were stories of inmates hacking the Island 3000 system and gaining access to teenage chat rooms, and even being allowed to score sex tests for pornographic sites. None of those stories were true.

Lester had snorted at all those stories. "Whatever happened to tunneling out under the fence with a spoon? These fools put all their hopes on beating the machine. You can't beat the machine, baby. They want you to believe that you can beat the machine, so you keep punching the buttons like a fucking monkey." Which *was* undeniably true.

A raven perched on the fence above Gloomy. The gate's voice was silent. The raven raised the fine black feathers on the back of its head, opened its beak, and began cracking out some emphatic abuse on Gloomy. The bird shook and a fine spray of water rose off her feathers. The raven sparkled in the gray light like a pool of crude oil. Gloomy shivered, stamped his foot, and waited.

Finally a guard approached the other side of the fence and pushed a combination into the keypad. It was Movie Star. He wiped rain off the brim of his cap and looked in at Gloomy. "Well, hey there, Gloom. Sorry to keep you here. We'll be going now." The door swung open, and the raven stopped screaming and flew away to the north landing on top of an antenna near the central tower.

Movie Star had an overly friendly edge that caused Gloomy to back away from the door he had just opened. Was this guy really even a guard? Guards could be friendly but not in the way this guy appeared to be. Most of the guards were nervous, with kind of a loose friendliness that was really only an awkward attempt to hedge against that day when everything went wrong and a convict would hold a loop of wire around his throat. There was nothing to worry about from those guards, but the ones with the stiff, authoritarian friendliness were usually hard-asses or freaks: the kind of men who would sexually brutalize convicts in the dark areas away from the cameras. But Movie Star had something else in mind. He was on a mission.

Gloomy walked down the dock just a step ahead of this new guard.

"Come on now, fella." Movie Star turned and spoke over his shoulder as they both walked quickly to the work skiff. "They can't burn that garbage without you." At the dock, Gloomy put on the extra-large life preserver before Movie Star snapped the manacles and leg irons on.

Gloomy sat on the metal bench in the stern of the crew boat. He was the only prisoner going out, which was not unusual. This job was not part of the regular prison rehab and control system and had been created only in the last fourteen months. Sometimes it seemed to Gloomy as if this work detail had been created especially for him. He never inquired about it. In fact, he never inquired about much of anything. Gloomy had been a model prisoner.

The boat was moored in an iron shed, and as the boat moved there was an area in the prison anchorage domed over with galvanized fencing. The sky was blocked out into tiny squares. But as they moved out of the cove, Gloomy could see the sun coming through the cottony gray clouds. Light streaked down through the clouds, landing finally in a sparkling pool on the calm gray water. He could smell the salt tang of the beach through the engine exhaust, and whatever it was in his body that weighed him down began to lift. His shoulders relaxed, and he took two deep breaths. The engine throbbed underneath him, and he closed his eyes and saw an image of his father moving away from him. *Headed to bed*, Gloomy thought. It was just an image of a hickory shirt moving past a brown door and some cheap paneling. But that image carried the feeling of others as if it were an encoded chip that were being inserted into his memory bank.

THEY DOCKED AT the women's prison site. Gloomy noticed a civilian tugboat in the anchorage, which seemed strange. There were civilian workers at the site carrying tool kits and materials in and out of the work site as usual. Tommy was not there. None of the usual security team was there. Something had changed but that in itself was not unusual in corrections, things always changed. But he was worried about Movie Star, who had his rifle pointed directly at his chest.

Gloomy looked down and saw a red dot on his shirt. He knew it was the outrider of a copper-jacketed lead round.

"Let it come, Gloomy. You know you are ready," a voice in his head said.

It was when he heard those words that he relived a strange moment of homecoming with a family he couldn't quite remember.

But everything shattered as the building fifty feet away exploded, sending a pressure wave rolling over Gloomy's body. He was dizzy now, and he tumbled back in a giddy recognition of the sensation that he could only assume was his death. He opened his eyes to welcome it, and he saw the flat gray sky. He could smell a fine dust, which surprised him. What surprised him more were the huge spiders of concrete and iron reinforcement flying through the air. Wires and pieces of pipe were dripping down from the sky, burning like sparklers. Finally Gloomy could hear men screaming through an intense heat.

Movie Star was on the ground. There was a three-foot section of iron rebar sticking through his shoulder. His weapon was six feet from his right hand, which was another six feet from his torso.

Gloomy crawled across the cobbled beach, trying to get away from the blast site. There were about three acres of slick gray-green boulders the size of large pumpkins all the way to the water. But now there was also smoking concrete and shredded aluminum. Convicts wearing coveralls that appeared to be on fire ran, stumbling down the beach, to dive in the water.

Gloomy's ankle chains snagged under a barnacle-encrusted stone. He could not move. He tried to lift himself upright to get the chains free, and he looked down. He watched as his own blood dripped into the water, forming tiny clouds in the tide pool beneath him. Dozens of sheet-metal screws had cut through his shirt and were embedded in his chest. He touched his face and felt a small cut running down his cheek.

He sat on a rock and pulled at his leg irons. He was grimacing and coughing, and his eyes burned.

Stranger things certainly could have happened to Gloomy. He could have been transported back in time to go fishing with a grandfather he had never met, or an ice cream truck could have fallen out of the sky and he might have discovered he had just enough money to buy a double-fudge cream and had time to eat it all before it melted in the heat from the fires. None of those things happened, but this did: a woman's face appeared in front of his eyes; a blond woman with a strange and severe haircut.

"Are you Christopher McCahon?" she asked in a pleasant but rather urgent tone.

"Yes," Gloomy said through his tears, expecting her to be an EMT or part of the prison response team.

"The same man who was convicted of setting fire to the *Moondancer* back during the war?"

Gloomy looked at her carefully. He had never seen her before. He remembered women. She was not in prison admin. She was not in catering or medical. She was a civilian.

"I am Christopher McCahon"—he fumbled for his tag around his neck—"072353. I'm housed in suite E-4. I am part of the White Unit and would like to return there. This is not an escape attempt."

"You don't need that now." The woman grabbed the tag and put it into one of the many zippered pockets she had on her insulated gray jumpsuit. She fumbled in another pocket and took out a small ring of keys. She knelt by his waist and started trying keys on his leg irons.

"Now, *that* was a little overkill, don't you think?" She was addressing someone else as she got the leg irons off

Gloomy's ankles and stood up. "For a diversionary blast, I mean, that was a little bit of an aggressive display, don't you think? Boys and their toys. There is no such thing as a small bang with these guys." She slung the leg irons over her shoulder and started pulling on Gloomy's elbow. "We have a little more time, which is a good thing because we almost killed him, you know what I'm saying? I mean, what good is breaking him out of jail if we kill him?"

Gloomy stopped and the young woman almost fell backward. "I can't go anywhere," Gloomy said, so softly he barely recognized his own voice. "I've got my job. If I miss the horn for the boat, they'll write me up for an escape attempt, and I'll never get my job back. I can't go."

The woman looked up into Gloomy's face. She grimaced. "The Iranian agents inside the prison are trying to kill you. We know that." She looked at Gloomy with more concern than he could remember seeing in anyone's face.

"You're injured," she whispered. "Just come with us." The young woman pointed down the beach where the isthmus over to the planned employee-housing area was narrow enough that they could easily walk over to another anchorage. "Just come with us, you have some injuries, and we can help you." She looked at him, this strange young woman who now seemed vaguely familiar. Her eyes were bright, and her expression bespoke hardened commitment. "Mr. McCahon, we are your friends," she said in a voice that betrayed no irony at all.

Sincerity . . . Gloomy thought to himself, *without a threat attached to it seems so strange.*

Gloomy turned around and started walking back toward the burning shell of the new women's prison. Men were calling for help. Someone was running around with a large orange first-aid kit that had broken open, trailing bandages and gauze pads. Everyone was checking on each other and no one seemed to be looking for him.

In the distance he heard a helicopter. The blond woman spoke into an old-fashioned handheld radio. Gloomy could not tell what she was saying. She ran up to him and stood directly in front of him. "Mr. McCahon, you've had a serious head injury. Let me just cover that now. Later, we can take care of it properly." She placed a small mask over her mouth and nose. Then she held up a small aerosol can and sprayed a mist into his eyes that burned like acid at first, but in seconds the pain fused to numbness that soaked inward and Gloomy slept.

SOMEONE WAS SLAPPING Gloomy lightly on the cheek. There was a strange pressure around his head as if he were wrapped in a thick rubber sheet. Now there was a voice, a man's voice, urgently cutting through whatever strange new atmosphere Gloomy was waking into.

"We don't have to overdo everything. First we blow the crapola out of the building and now you put our guy to sleep. What kind of dose did you give him, Norma?"

Gloomy opened his eyes and saw the face of a young unshaven white man. He could not see the woman.

"He was going back to the prison. I had to stop him. If you think you could have done it any better, Rocket, then maybe you should have been here helping me." There was a pause and the woman added, "Rocket!" as if she had just turned his name into an obscenity.

Gloomy looked down at his body. He had been zipped into a Gumby-style rubber survival suit designed for mariners when they have to abandon ship in northern waters. Only his face was exposed through the tight hood. The rest of the suit was loose-fitting and bulky. There was a large inflatable yoke around his shoulders and behind his neck. The suit was designed to float him faceup in the subarctic waters off Alaska.

"I've got to get back," Gloomy said finally.

"That's exactly what we're doing, brother," the man said. "We're going to get you back in the world. We're here to protect you. We are with you now."

"Stop fooling around, Rocket," Norma's voice cut in.

Gloomy turned his head so he could see her. She wore a beret and a fisherman's pullover under her rain-gear bibs. Rocket was wearing a wool jacket and had battered poly gloves on each hand. Gloomy awkwardly lifted his rubber-mittened hands to his own face and could vaguely sense a bandage taped across the cut on his face. Rocket and Norma squatted down and faced him.

"Listen, we don't have much time," Rocket said. "The helicopter is making its passes over the building. It's ferrying emergency crews to the site. They'll be busy with that. It was chaos when the explosives went off. Yeah, I'm sorry about that. They're probably more concerned with perimeter security back on Olympus than they are about a hard count looking for just you. They don't know which way to shit right now."

"That's colorful," Norma interjected.

Gloomy looked from her face to the young man's like a sick child might look from his mother to the doctor, both on the edge of his bed. He had been a model prisoner, Gloomy kept thinking. In the years of his incarceration he never remembered stepping out of the routine, and he had been rewarded with the fire tender's job. Now everything seemed to be blowing apart. The thought of losing his job, of not getting the boat ride off the island for a bit of time every day, made him frantic.

"All right, then. As soon as they get everything locked down, and they do their count, they'll start surveying the scene, and then they'll double the patrol boats. That's okay, but we need to get off this beach, and quickly." Rocket said the last bit in a strangely stilted way, as if he was trying to impress the woman with a kind of military bearing.

"Where's my tag?" Gloomy asked softly. The tag was his prison identity. Without it he was nothing. No, worse. Without it he was a running ghost outside of any protection.

Norma put her hand up to his cheek and flattened down the tape holding the bandage. "I went back and threw your tag in the blast zone. If, in fact, they can still trace your tag, it will show you in the blast zone. They won't show you AWOL until after the blast area is secure and the hard body count is done in the whole facility. We've got another . . . maybe ten minutes. We've got to get you rafted to safety before we answer any more questions." They lifted him to his feet, but Gloomy found himself too weak to walk. He stumbled and Norma held him up.

"My gosh, how much did you give him?" Rocket asked impatiently.

"Enough! Leave me alone," Norma spat out her words. She turned to Gloomy. "I sprayed you down with Dropen. It's a corrosive sedative, like mace with sleeping pills. It incapacitates you first and then the sedative takes effect. The effects won't last too long."

"I hope," Rocket threw out. "He's got to be awake, Norma, or he'll drown. We damn sure won't get paid the second half if we kill him," Rocket said, his voice peevish.

"You just hold up your end of this log stunt," Norma spat again.

The two of them walked as fast as they could, pulling Gloomy along. They crossed through the trees, onto the sandy isthmus. There was a tiny log house sunken into the sandy beach fringe. It could have been an old dollhouse or maybe a cache.

"We cross over just past the old sauna," Norma said.

Gloomy saw a work skiff out on the water. Tied to that was a large hemlock log. On the sand, a camouflaged tarp was draped over what looked to be two small kayaks. Both Rocket and Norma looked quickly at the sky. There was the sound of a helicopter in the distance but nothing above the beach.

"Now you've got to hurry. See that large hemlock log?" Norma held Gloomy's face in her hands. "Rocket found it a year ago over on Kruzof. It's perfect for this. There was lots of rot in the butt end, but he's cleaned it out pretty well. You're going to get inside. We have a plug for the end that matches almost perfectly with the rest of the log, and the whole thing is weighted to lie flat so you won't be spinning around in there, but"—they were walking quickly now, both Rocket and Norma pulling Gloomy down the sand—"but it will get a bit wet in there. That's why the suit. You will be in there for several hours. Maybe ten or twelve hours if they shut down all motion in the sound. There are two scuba tanks in there with you. Each has its own respirator. Like I said, we've tried it out. There are some small holes for air, but we couldn't cut them too big because it would have been too suspicious if we get a close inspection. Use the compressed air only if you have to. Remember, only if you have to, and try not to use the tanks if we have come to a stop or anytime you hear someone thumping on the outside. That means we're being searched. Breathing through the respirators makes quite a bit of noise. It may tip them off. Okay? Now I know this is sudden, but just get in."

The log was floating in shallow water, barely bumping the rocks with the small waves coming ashore. On the edge of the tiny bay, a few yellow cedar trees draped their wings down to the water. Eagles and ravens pumped their wings, flying away from the island toward some of the smaller rocks near the outer coast, where the waves built up and broke white across their full face. Gloomy's two keepers waded in the water to the tops of their high rubber boots and then some. They stuffed Gloomy into the butt end of the log. He was still groggy from the explosion and slow from the sedative, but he tried to crawl out.

Norma gently pried his fingers away from the lip of the opening, saying sweetly, "I know this is tight, but don't worry. The regulators are hanging there above you. There will be some rolling and a little bit of water. Rocket has promised that this will work," she said with some irritation in her voice. But then her voice softened again as she looked down at Gloomy's panicked face. "You'll be home soon, Mr. McCahon."

Everything went black, and someone hammered a plug into the end of the log. Then Gloomy heard the sound of a power screwdriver tightening down some fastenings. He could not move his shoulders. He could not lift his arms. He was pinned inside the log, unable to move. He rolled and felt the bumping of rocks and sand scraping across the log. He could hear the engine of the skiff howling as it struggled to pull the giant log free. Finally the log bobbed into deeper water. His feet seemed higher than his head. He still could not move. The survival suit was bunched up underneath him. His breath came harder and faster, and he felt water easing up around his face.

Gloomy started to struggle and pulled against his right arm so hard it felt as if he were tearing all the muscles in his shoulder. He yelled and flailed his head back and forth as the water splashed against his mouth and nose.

Then he stopped. *Now* he was going to die, he thought, and this relaxed him. He thought of the universe when all the light in the world was trapped inside the skull of God and things knew each other only through touch. The stones' secret movements were set then, the sliding and the slow rubbing back and forth—all of this was there before there was light, when there was only here and nowhere. When the light issued forth, the possibility of the ambiguous "somewhere else" opened up.

Inside the dark box of the floating log, Gloomy knew he was going to die and that he was going to disappear. He would be stone: his body in the here and eventually dissolving into the nowhere.

He found this comforting. His breath slowed expectantly and his body relaxed, waiting for his life to bubble out of his chest in a curling plume. But instead, his arms freed themselves, and he was able to move freely in the log. His hands naturally found the air regulators, which he quickly put in his mouth. He drew in three good deep breaths and sadly recognized he was going to live.

Then the voice came back and was all around him. "Hush . . . hush now," it said, as if it were his parent. "There is nothing to be afraid of," and Gloomy knew then it was true. The inside of the cedar log smelled good to him, and the roll of it through the water was somehow comforting, along with the distant sound of the water lapping against the bark of the old tree. For a few moments, Gloomy thought of how many hundreds of years this old tree had grown in one spot on these islands, how many hundreds of years it had stood with its limbs out to the Pacific winds, bending its back into the storms and creaking into the icy winter weather. Long before he was born and long before there were Europeans on the continent, this tree had been a living, breathing presence. Now here he was breaking out of jail deep inside of its body. Gloomy's head was spinning and he was getting sleepy.

The blast site was a continuing squall of chaos. There was little fire; only some of the cribbing around the forms was burning, and a dozen storage boxes were consumed in flames. Injured convicts tried to attend to each other the best they could while the guards stood over them with guns.

Inside Olympus all the gates swung shut at once, and the entire facility was cut into secure lockdown areas. All three shifts were rousted out and sent up on the catwalks to Heaven. The computer count took almost two minutes, but there also had to be a hard body count from Heaven. The computer count had Gloomy over at the blast site. He showed up as "Unconfirmed," as did a new fish who was thought to be in C-3 but turned up in a stairwell in admin. He was not under Heaven, for Heaven only included the security apparatus of the prison. Ghost, who was supposed to be in the kitchen, was also listed as "Unconfirmed," following the manual search.

The civil authorities and the coast guard were notified. The motion sensors in the perimeter were checked and debugged. Patrol boats were launched. Dogs were let loose on the high side of the island and dog trainers cleared all of the patrol boats before they were allowed to leave the dock. All patrol personnel went through two hard body confirmations and conducted a pat-down inventory of all possessions.

The correctional machine was turning more and more

quickly now. Inside the facility they switched to emergency power and the emergency lighting flashed, letting all inmates in the lockdowns know they were to sit on the floor and wait for a direct order to stand. Anyone found standing would be in danger of being "tagged." There was no siren because studies had shown that sirens on island facilities did little good from a command-and-control standpoint. Everyone needed to hear and speak clearly into their radios. In C-4, a convict took the opportunity to stab his suite mate with a mechanical pencil. In D-6, a group of Christians from an April 19 group broke through a doorway and took over the common room of their suite. They were seen on the security screens on their knees praying, and the monitoring officer heard them reciting from the book of Revelation. Other than those two incidents, the officers were happy with the progress of the lockdown.

Rocket and Norma pulled the log slowly from the bay and were beyond the three-hundred-meter perimeter of the island before the first helicopter flew over. Their tug and a larger log raft were anchored in an exposed little reach near the entrance to Green Top. The copter flew low over their skiff. There was a loudspeaker slung underneath and a male voice boomed over the din of the rotor noise. "This is Stevens Correctional. Please slow your engine and go to channel sixty-eight. That is VHF channel six . . . eight. Failure to do so will put your craft in danger."

Norma worked the radio and disconnected the antenna slightly so the interference would keep her from being fully understood. They listened to the transmissions on their other scanner. She yelled into her intentionally broken VHF: "Hello . . . this . . . proceeding . . . happening? Okay?"

They continued on toward their log raft. The current was pulling them sideways in the channel now, and they had to increase the throttle to maintain headway. Rocket stood near the bow, waving and pointing to the log raft. The crewman at the door of the helicopter waved and acknowledged their progress.

"Asking . . . headway to keep off rocks . . . okay? We'll not . . . area? Over," Norma transmitted.

The helicopter pilot responded, "Tow vessel, you are breaking up. I understand you need to clear the channel. Go to your support vessel and wait there. The tug cannot move until cleared by prison authorities. If you copy, key your mic twice."

Norma keyed her mic, and they powered to the log raft. The helicopter veered away to the southwest, continuing its pass around the island.

"Stevens . . . we've got a salvage vessel near the point. One log in tow. They have been contacted and will hold by their support vessel. Send K-nine patrol for clearance."

When Rocket and Norma approached their tug and raft of about thirty logs, they looked skyward again and made sure the helicopter was out of sight. Rocket reached a line with a pike pole and pulled the line aboard. He fed the line through his deck winch on the skiff and began cranking. The log raft pulled apart in the middle as the line worked against the blocks on board the tug and against a block underwater on the anchor chain. With the section of logs apart, Rocket secured the line, hopped out, and pulled the single log containing Gloomy into the center of the raft and set it adrift among the other hemlock logs. Norma attached a loose hemlock log very similar to Gloomy's log, which had been secured to the outside of the raft, to her tow line. Then Rocket took the skiff around to the other side of the raft and clipped a carabiner attached to a net full of beach rocks to another line fed through the blocks. Then he pushed the bundle of rocks off the log it was sitting on. The net fell through the water and pulled the lines, forcing all the logs back together in a nice tight bundle. The rocks sank away and eventually pulled all the lines through the blocks and free of the raft. When the rocks came to rest on the bottom, Rocket coiled the line back up into the skiff. Norma secured the boom logs around the stern of the raft and it was done: Gloomy was in the log in the middle of the raft and the tow log secured behind their skiff was a solid piece of hemlock.

"What are you doing?" Rocket yelled at Norma. "Get your lunch out, for God's sake." Norma slapped her forehead and pulled herself over the bulwarks of the tug as the blue and white patrol boat came around the point. Norma took her lunch, jumped across the raft, and walked the logs, eating her meat loaf sandwich with the drippy mayo and ketchup.

The patrol boat pulled up next to the tug. A correctional officer in a float suit wearing a gun belt and holding a clipboard stepped quickly over the bulwarks without being invited. There was a woman officer holding two large Rottweilers on a heavy leather lead.

"Hello, Skipper, this is a routine inspection of your vessel. Do you have any contraband on board today?" The officer started off on a series of questions. Rocket answered his questions politely and watched carefully as the officer checked off items and looked around. Finally the officer paused. "Right now, Skipper, I'm just going to take a look around, and I'm also going to ask the dog handler to give your vessel a once-over. I'm sure that's going to be okay with you."

"Of course, it's fine with me, Officer, but I've got to tell you that I'm not the skipper." Rocket pointed over to Norma, who waved gaily.

The officer scowled and signaled the female dog handler, who stepped back over the bulwarks onto the raft. Her footing was bad, and, as a log rolled, she slipped, falling into the water up to her knee.

"Madame, could you come here, please," the officer yelled over to Norma.

Norma jumped up quickly, danced across the logs, and breathlessly answered all the officer's questions. She showed all her paperwork, including her commercial tonnage license and even her radio licenses, which no one had ever asked for. The dogs sniffed through the galley and the small forecastle bunk area of the tug. Another officer walked over the raft to the skiff. He pulled the tow log over and began thumping on it with a long-handled hammer. The dog handler with the wet leg now put away her clipboard and, in a blatant shift in tone, tried to ask Rocket and Norma a list of friendly, nonthreatening questions about the weather and their schedule. Both Norma and Rocket had easy and well-scripted answers. They were salvaging logs. They had a small sale for green logs down near Redoubt. They just came across some old beach-run logs. No, they had not been onshore near the institution. No, they had not been near the perimeter. Yes, they heard the explosion and had come in close to see what was happening. Yes, they went to shore at the women's prison site to offer first-aid assistance to some of the wounded. No, they didn't see anyone leaving the island.

The chief of the boarding party came up from below and signaled the handler to take the dogs over to the skiff. The dogs sniffed out the skiff and the tow log behind it, and as the handler was signaling the boat to come alongside, one of the Rottweilers lifted his blocky head and sniffed the air. He spun and pulled against the lead. The handler shot an urgent look over to the leader of the boarding party.

"Let her go," the chief told the handler, and she unclipped the lead. The one dog bounded off the skiff and clumsily ran toward Gloomy's log. Silently the dog sniffed and worked directly toward the hollow log as if being pulled by a string.

Norma turned sternly toward the captain and her voice rose in agitation. "That's it now, Captain. I know the rules as well as anyone. I am in waters outside your perimeter, and I have not given you formal permission for your search. I'm going to hold you liable for any damage to my gear or my cargo. Do you understand? I repeat myself, Captain, do you understand?"

The Rottweiler lurched across a log and stood squarely on top of Gloomy's log. The dog barked twice and then buried her head into Norma's lunch bag.

"Kathy," the dog handler barked. "Back now!" The dog lifted her head toward her handler, now with the remains of the meat loaf sandwich in her mouth.

"Now then, Captain," Norma said softly, "that means you're going to have to buy me lunch back in town." She patted him on the shoulder and left her hand there for half a beat longer than a playful gesture.

The dogs were boarded and the captain gave Norma a yellow carbon of his search report. He told her to tell any officer in the future to refer to the report number on the top of the form. The dog handler allowed Norma to stroke the head of the search dog across the two boats. Then the engines started, and the patrol boat pulled away as Rocket began the hydraulic winch to pull the tug's anchor. Everyone waved as the boats pulled away and the helicopter set down behind the hill inside the perimeter of the institution. Deep inside the hollowed-out log, Gloomy had heard only muffled voices and the strange clicking of the search dog's toenails on the wood.

NORMA HAD BEEN born in New York City. Her father was the son of a silk importer, and her mother did volunteer work at the Metropolitan Museum in the twentieth-century painting permanent collection. She lived in Manhattan at 200 East End Avenue, across from Gracie Mansion, where the mayor of New York lived. Paul Simon had once lived at 200 East End. Walt Kelly and Jimmy Breslin used to drink in the bar of the Chinese restaurant on the first floor. There had been no celebrities in the building when Norma was growing up; at least Norma hadn't been aware of any. Mostly there were young professionals with expensive clothes and leashes for their toddlers. Norma wasn't impressed by celebrities anyway. The culture of the famous was a virus propagated by the captains of industry.

The fact was that Norma's family had been rich in New York. They had moved to Sitka, Alaska, when she was getting ready to go to college. Norma had liked New York City. It had the wildness she found in Alaska, only in a different form. She had liked being rich but didn't like what being rich had meant to her family.

Even on the east side of Manhattan she had been preparing herself for the wilderness. She wore canvas work clothes and discarded shoes from a bowling supply company she had found on Long Island. Norma had been proud that she had been suspended from classes at the

Chapin School for girls in the tenth grade, when she refused to follow the dress code, as liberal as it supposedly was.

Of course, Chapin was a good school that had prepared girls for the best colleges. Lots of famous people had gone there. Norma was aware of the school's reputation, as well as her status. She felt the full weight of it. It didn't matter that she was getting by with a B-plus average; she knew she could always get into her safety schools if she needed to, and if it was absolutely necessary, she could go to one of the smaller schools in the Midwest and then transfer after a couple of years. The big schools were all overrated.

In her senior year, Norma and her friends gathered at the coffee shop on Eighty-Sixth Street every day after drama rehearsals. They were preparing to do some scenes from *Our Town* for the spring production, and this had caused a small stir among the faculty. Norma and her friends discussed the play and their college choices around the cluttered table at the coffee shop. The four girls smoked Pall Malls and Camel Straights, filling the ashtrays with snubbed-out ends as they talked and made vague plans for the future. In one way or another, the burden of their good fortune was the theme that ran through all their conversation. Perhaps it was the weight of their privilege that made them swear like stevedores when they gathered in the diner.

Heather said, "I mean, fuck it, Monica. What were you expecting? It's really fucking hard to get into Barnard. I mean, you don't fit any of their target spots. You're not poor or anything."

"Oh, shut up! Just 'cause you got on the waiting list doesn't mean you have to rub my nose in it. I mean, fuuuuck."

Kim lit her cigarette with her father's treasured Zippo, clicked the cap shut, and slid it across the glass countertop to Norma. Kim blew out the first long plume of smoke and spoke with authority: "You know, I heard that if you let them know you're a lesbian in your application, you have a much better chance of getting in. I heard you get sorted over to their target student categories."

"Yeah . . . I'm so sure," Norma said.

"So your freshman year, what? Your freshman year you've got to be sleeping with your roommate, or they won't ask you back?" Monica said into the top of her coffee mug.

"Oh . . . sick!" Kim said, spilling her water glass. "I mean, who wants to go to Barnard, anyway?"

The subject of their application essays came up. Kim wrote about her cross-cultural sensitivity because her mother was Jewish and her father was second-generation Armenian. Monica wrote about her job as a camp counselor for kids with birth defects. Norma didn't say anything. She flicked nervously at her cigarette with her thumbnail.

"Well, what did you write about, N?" Kim asked. Norma had been called "N" since sophomore year. "Norma" was just too "country western."

"I just wrote about that thing with Bob."

"Yewww," the girls said together. "Where are you applying, like . . . Antioch or something?" Kim said, laughing.

Once, after a party up on Sixty-Second Street, Norma had been walking home up Madison Avenue. She had had an argument with her English teacher, Mr. Yough. She had become angry and stomped away from the party. Mr. Yough was a young handsome teacher who taught Shakespeare and composition. Norma had been one of his favorite students all sophomore year, but her junior year he had changed. Mr. Yough would often show up at the parties after official dances. He would drink a beer and then leave. Some girls thought he was a spy for their parents. Some thought he was looking for sex. But the girls were both flattered and irritated when they heard his voice come through the downstairs intercom.

At the party, Norma had been talking to Christine Dennis. They were standing outside the bathroom waiting for Tiffany Schecter to stop throwing up. Norma had said she was sick of all the phony posturing and cynicism among her friends and even among the teachers. If they didn't believe that one person could really make a difference, what were they doing being teachers anyway?

Mr. Yough walked around the corner from the kitchen, and, finishing the last of his beer, he tried the knob of the bathroom door and said, "Our cynicism isn't phony, hon. We're genuinely cynical."

It was his long, taunting laugh that had upset Norma so much. It reminded her of all the people on TV. It reminded her of her parents' friends, who loved to make fun of everyone in public office no matter their convictions. Norma was hearing Mr. Yough's laugh on loop in her head as she stomped toward Eighty-Sixth Street, where she planned to take the crosstown, but now she was enjoying the walk.

She had always enjoyed the walk up Madison past the galleries and the hair salons. That night, her mother's favorite dress shop had the grating pulled around the entire corner. The busses thumped across the iron plates covering the construction trenches and steam was rising up in strange little puffs around the edges. It was late and most of the doormen in the apartment buildings sat snoozing on their stools next to the intercoms, their long, double-breasted coats bunched up over their chins. When she got to Eighty-Sixth, she looked up at the sky, and the night seemed to be rushing past the tops of the buildings. Out at their country house she could hear the wind blowing through the plantings and the stiff little pines that bordered the pool. In the city, the wind was a rumble in her ears. Up high, the clouds were fused with light, pushing past the antennas and elevator sheds, curling and rolling through the sky so quickly it made her dizzy as she stood shifting her balance from foot to foot. Something in her chest rose up. It was her "Dorothy feeling," she called it—a willingness to fly, a lightness that she felt whenever she recognized the power of the world beyond her little route to and from school. She wanted to fly away from there. From Mr. Yough and her friends. She tried to imagine a place where people actually said what they meant, and then tried to act on it. It wasn't Kansas, she knew, but maybe it wasn't Oz either.

She took the crosstown and got off on York and started to walk north toward Eighty-Ninth. She passed a dark doorway and heard a man groaning in pain. Her first instinct was to walk faster. She had done it before when she sensed danger of any type. Maybe it was the "Dorothy feeling" in her chest. Maybe it was the weather or the irritation with Mr. Yough, but she looked back into the darkness, for the source of the groan.

"Hello?" she said.

From the shadow came a weird gurgling sound, human, but from deep down in the chest and stomach.

"Are you all right?" Norma walked near the edge of the doorway.

"No, I'm not all right." The voice was strangely clear.

There were a few lights under the nameplates near the buzzer, and she could make out the form of an older white man in a long wool coat with vents up the side. The coat was out of place on the bum and appeared to be meant for a mounted policeman. The man waved a hand across a matted beard. "Isn't it quite apparent that I am not all right?"

"Are you bleeding?" Norma called down to him, not sure really how to begin assessing his situation.

"Yes," he said softly. "Yes. My brain is bleeding."

Half an hour later she was walking down the street, half carrying and half steering the lurching man in the long coat.

"I'm actually quite dangerous, don't you think? I'm Bob, by the way. I'm Bob and apparently you're not," Bob said, and laughed.

The smell of his body was powerful. Norma had never experienced anything quite like it. It was the combined smell of a crowded subway car, vomit, red wine, urine, and feces. Underlying all of that was the wet wool of his coat. The coat was relatively clean, and Norma considered the possibility that Bob had recently stolen the coat. Bob had his left hand deep in the pocket of the police coat as he wheeled down the sidewalk, clearing pedestrians off the sidewalk and into the street with a stiff right arm. At the curb on Ninetieth, he stumbled hard and sprawled into the street. Norma had let him fall, not wanting to be pulled down with him. She looked up and down the street to see if any traffic was coming, then quickly bent over him. The left hand, which had been buried in the coat, was flailing around now, and she saw the stub of knuckles clipped off like cigar butts where his four fingers and thumb should have been.

"Leave me alone!" he roared up into the streetlight. "Turn it out! Turn it out!"

Norma had no idea what she was going to do when she helped Bob up. But now, she was self-conscious and painfully aware that she couldn't just walk away and leave him in the street. She didn't think there were any shelters in her neighborhood but didn't have enough money for cab fare.

"Where do you want to go?" she yelled at him.

Bob didn't answer. He closed his eyes slowly, as if falling into a sound sleep. He lay his head down easily on the pavement in the middle of the street.

Norma started to walk away. Down the block she heard the rumble of a truck and saw it was coming toward Bob. Norma kept walking. Bob did not move, and the truck came down the block and passed Norma, and she did not look back.

She heard the truck's horn blare. She heard the air brakes. She heard men yelling and swearing, and she turned the corner. There was a blast of cool air from the East River. Her apartment building was lit up like a war memorial and the mayor's mansion was decorated in small white lights around the iron fence. She was two hundred yards from her apartment. Her parents were in the country. A tug moved slowly down the glittering river; the lights rippled in jagged streaks across the water. A woman with a Doberman on a short leash turned the corner, away from her. Norma looked up and saw a gull riding in the light from the apartment house. The bird was stationary in the cool wind, its head moving back and forth, scanning the street. Norma took a deep breath and walked back to get Bob.

She knew the doorman would snitch on her to her

parents. He almost wouldn't let Bob in the building, but Norma started making a scene, and a couple of heads waiting at the restaurant turned, and the doorman ushered her into the elevator with Bob.

"You keep him in your apartment then, miss. I see him without you, I'm putting him out, you understand?"

Norma assured him she did. The doorman, who was from Eastern Europe, had been good to her, particularly when she had had parties in the past. But she wasn't counting on any help from him now.

Bob sprawled on the parquet floor in the hall. She tried to take his coat off but then reconsidered when she opened the coat and there was a smell she couldn't stomach. She buttoned him up again and left him there. She went upstairs and found her old sleeping bag from camp, the flannel one with cowgirls on it. She found the old pillow she had used for their puppy before her mother had gotten rid of it for peeing one too many times on the carpet in the front room. When Norma came downstairs, Bob was in the living room standing in front of the Japanese silkscreen. He pointed his wobbly finger.

"That's nice," he said in a voice of hushed surprise. Then he fell through the glass tabletop.

There was no blood. A lacquer cigarette box had also broken, contributing to the diamonds of broken glass from the table that lay scattered across the floor. Norma pulled Bob into the pantry and laid him out on the linoleum, then she covered him with the sleeping bag. She pressed a chair up against the knob of the pantry and went upstairs, locked the door to her room, and went to sleep.

In the morning, Bob was gone. As was a bottle of Chivas

Regal and all the contents of her parents' medicine chest: her father's heart medication, the mouthwash, the unused antibiotics, the half-used tube of foot cream, the nose hair clippers, and even the tiny bottle of cream rinse taken from the Ritz Hotel in Paris.

In the broken glass of the tabletop lay a note written on a long strip of paper from the little roller of message paper next to the kitchen telephone. It was curled like a streamer thrown from the deck of an ocean liner. The handwriting was chaotic but legible. Some words in cursive, some printed out in uneven letters. It read:

> *You showed uncharacteristic sensitivity toward me. There are sparks going up through the hole in the ceiling. I will not bother you. I did not take anything. Goodbye —B.*

In the pantry, the sleeping bag was slung between the shelves like a tent. In the middle of the floor, there were ashes. Norma looked around and saw all the labels on the soup cans were missing. Bob must have scraped them off, piled them under the eaves of his shelter, and lit them on fire. There was a faint sooty cloud on the ivory-colored ceiling.

Norma looked up at the stain on her parents' ceiling and started to cry. Her chest heaved twice and she covered her eyes.

Years later she met Rocket on the ferry coming to Sitka and became a liberation Christian. She supposed it all stemmed from that experience with Bob back in New York when she first wanted to rescue someone but couldn't.

Or at least that's what she told herself when she instructed the man with the English accent over the phone to deposit one hundred thousand dollars in her Mexican bank account as a first payment to break Gloomy Knob out of Ted Stevens Federal Penitentiary.

GLOOMY COULD HEAR his heart beating in his ears. The tight hood pressed against the side of his head. He thought the log had stopped moving. After the water had stopped rising inside the log, he had been able to wedge one hand behind his neck to prop his head out of the water. He had used all the compressed air in both tanks. At one point he thought he had fallen asleep, but he wasn't really sure. The bandage had rubbed off his cheek, and he could feel a crusty trail of blood leading down into his hood. The log rolled back and forth steadily in the water but without the porpoising movement that indicated forward motion.

Suddenly there was the mechanical whirl of an electric drill, followed by the rattle of a chain and a crunching sound as the wooden plug was pulled from the end of the log. Water and air rushed in around him, the sound of waves against sand, but not like the beach where his fire was. These waves were different—a small breaking wave on sand: long inhale, short exhale. Hands reached in under his shoulders and pulled him from the log out into the night, dragging him through the shallow water of a wave running back down the beach. He could see stars through the open arms of the trees. He was laid down near a small gas heater under a shelter. Norma's face was now in front of his.

"You're almost home now, Mr. McCahon. It won't be long."

Gloomy couldn't think of a thing to say, but he looked over the young woman's shoulder to where the tops of the waves sparked with a fine speckle of phosphorescence.

"Home?" Gloomy asked, as his eyes caught sight of the sparks of a fire just under the trees. "I need to get back to my unit," he said as he took an unsteady step in the dark.

Chapter Five

"We are playing for the life of Clive McCahon," L.P. said to the three women in the room. The wind continued to wail and pull at the metal roofing as the old Indian brushed his thumb along the edge of his shaved deck of playing cards.

All of them knew the deck was rigged and that the old man knew the position of every card just by the feel of the edges. He had keen eyes and extraordinarily sensitive fingertips. L.P. knew each card that he dealt as he dealt it, but that didn't change the nature of the game because it would have been easier to predict the deal of a straight deck than it would be to try to understand the thinking of this strange gambler who had remained loyal to Clive McCahon, the old man whose body was about to give itself up to the cooling world of stillness.

Lilly had only known Clive McCahon as an invalid. To her he occupied the same space in her heart as her grandfather who had died three years before back on the islands. She had not been with her grandfather at the end. She thought of him, back in the village, and could almost smell the steamed vegetables and boiled chicken that had been staples at her grandfather's house and the warm breeze that was perfumed by the sweet night-blooming flowers whose name she no longer remembered.

Lilly's heart ached and that aching was in her hands when she attended to people in that cold place. She didn't like that Native American man L.P.; he came when he wanted, and he never seemed to bring food but always ate plenty. He seemed too familiar for a stranger. She never said a word against him because Nix loved him, and that was enough for Lilly to keep her thoughts to herself. Lilly looked at the card L.P. slid in front of her. It sat facedown. She never considered picking it up. It was evil; the Indian's talk of death seemed to sit patiently in the room, like the prospect of death itself.

L.P. riffled his fat thumb, bulbous and pink on the tip, down the edge of the deck. His hands were gnarled and broken, the color of cherrywood, both clumsy and nimble at the same time. Like all the others, Lilly knew it was fruitless to guess what he was up to. He loved sleight- of-hand tricks, and he had delighted her with them before, the ladders of rigged decisions and the illusion of free choice. Everything about him was distraction and disguise, which was why she suspected that Nix loved him so much.

"The high card can either kill him or stop the next-highest from killing him, and"—he paused and smiled at the three women—"and . . . you don't have to play."

Nix remembered the close smell of her own breath in the darkness of the box buried in the ground. The screaming fear as the waves came closer to the air hole. The ammonia-laced hysteria as she wet herself, kicking hard against the sides of the box until the earth started pouring in and she quit, worried that the earth would collapse in on her.

Then she remembered her life that came after: numbed and sleepy, slowed by grief, her son in prison for life, her daughter dead. She had gone from a free-spirited artist and builder of the community into the stunted observer of the rest of her life.

Clive McCahon had clarified Nix's life. She had been smart and brave before they met, but Clive had made Nix's goals and values crystal clear, even the values they didn't share. No matter what card trick the old Indian did, Clive would be dead soon, and her heart was weary as if she were still holding up the weight of the earth and trying to will back the waves from her only source of air.

She looked down at the card that had been dealt to her and decided to play.

OUR PAST IS the country with no borders, and no ports of reentry. All of our keepsakes, the trading cards, the shell paintings, and the old correspondences are a foreign currency we will never spend. Gloomy knew he wanted to go back to prison, yet he felt an urge to go to his grandparents' cabin down the inlet. They would surely tell him the right thing to do. Didn't he just think of them? Didn't he just talk with them? He was confused, yet he felt like a child when he stood on the beach fringe so far from Olympus. All he wanted to do was lie down in some quiet place where he could float away from the weight of his body and rest for a moment.

There was a fire set back from the trees, and the sparks rode up toward the canopy of limbs. There was no wind, but there seemed to be a rustle of limbs coming through the woods. It was the breath of the forest, distinct from the waves on the sand. The period of gusts of wind in the trees was longer than that of the waves on the sand. Gloomy thought about the explosion back at the prison site, wondering if it was going to push back the construction schedule. This would mean he could extend the work detail and his job might last longer. Then Gloomy remembered he was off-site and would not show up in the count. He would get punitive segregation if he were lucky. They might transfer him out if things went bad. This frightened him. Even if you only believed a third of the stories coming from the Mexican co-op prisons and the gladiator schools of Texas and California, he knew he would not have so much as a good day in any of them. White men over twenty-five were good for nothing but targets in the southern gladiator schools.

The gladiator schools were the last of the remaining old-style prisons, built and maintained on the model of Dante's *Inferno*. Those prisons enclosed the circles of hell and the inmates were allowed, in fact expected, to dole out retribution to one another. In the apartheid of the American penal system that had developed at the end of the twentieth century, these prisons were mostly filled with the poor and uneducated, mostly nonwhite, now that people of means could pay to serve time in private facilities.

But after the California riots and the new federal incarceration strategy there were fewer and fewer Inferno prisons in the federal system. With new community-based corrections, prisons became the culture centers of the most ravaged communities.

The prison populations were reaching across several generations and creating a true culture of crime that radiated beyond the walls and into the streets and homes of the free communities. Entire extended families were finding themselves inside, and these families became the core of small militias, and their branches extended out onto the street. The prison culture was now feeding the violence on the street instead of the other way around. There was a need in the new prisons for a different kind of isolation and control, where family members could be separated and monitored. In short, since the prison system had determined the culture of the American poor, the prisons were becoming their natural home. More and more children were born in prison each year and thousands of people died in confinement. The women's prison that Gloomy had been building was slated to have the largest maternity ward and daycare facility ever designed by the Department of Corrections. Children of these federal prisoners were to be kept on-site until they could be relocated with foreign-born refugee and terrorist children.

To counter this feeling of community, the federal designers tried to make the newest prisons mechanical containers with no sharp edges. Instead, there were rounded cubes where prisoners could be comfortably isolated. In a sense they wanted the new prisons to function more like air travel: a state of bored numbness where convicts could be kept like perpetually delayed travelers.

Gloomy had a good idea of what the system was becoming, and yet, he still wanted to go back to Olympus, for many reasons he didn't quite understand. Maybe because, as with most of the prisoners, institutional poverty was all he could hope for on the outside now. Or maybe the state had compressed his mind into the neat shape of a small rectangle.

Gloomy was standing on a wild beach by a fire. He was a free man among free people, and he still wanted to go back to his unit, where he knew with an institutional certainty that he would fit.

Norma ran over to Gloomy and, without an introduction, tried to unzip the rubber exposure suit he was still wearing. Gloomy pulled back, startled.

"You must be getting hot and slimy in there," Norma said as she pulled down the cord tied to the thick zipper tongue.

Gloomy sat on a log as she tugged the suit off his shoulders. The cool air felt good on his clammy skin, but the instant he pulled off the rubber suit he began to shiver. "Christ," Gloomy said to himself as he hunched his shoulders and dug his hands between his legs for warmth.

Norma bent down and looked up into Gloomy's face as Rocket placed a blanket over his shoulders. "I know you must be eager to get going," Norma said.

"Going?" Gloomy looked at her as if they were both speaking in a strange language. "Going . . . where?" he finally said.

"Well, I figured you must want to go see your daughter," Norma said.

"Daughter?" Gloomy said, and he rocked back on the log, as if he could duck away from her words. He nearly lost his balance.

GLOOMY HAD HAD few visitors during the years he was in jail. A couple of lawyers would come by when they had to see other clients. There were a few ministers and people he didn't remember from his old life. Gloomy rarely even responded to the visitor notices anymore—just when his father came to see him.

Nix had never visited him in Olympus. None of Gloomy's family members but Clive had; he had come just a few times, and it had agonized Gloomy to see him through the glass wearing his stiff brown church suit. His father, still fit and muscular, was somehow made frail in the prison visiting room. The few times he had visited, they had tried to talk on the phone through the glass, but they could think of nothing much to say. Both men had stared at their hands mostly, the old man tapping his massive fingers on the glass out in front of him and Gloomy wanting to reach out for him but being too embarrassed and ashamed to do so. The last time Clive came, Gloomy did not go to the visiting room and his father hadn't come back. And now he was sick. Gloomy had been informed of his father's condition by the prison authorities via an electronic message he received at the work station in his cell. They had also sent along the funeral policy for inmates who wished to attend the services of loved ones, but it didn't really apply to Gloomy because of his sentence classification.

"You need some food," Norma murmured.

"You've got to get me back," Gloomy pleaded. "I don't know what in the hell you think you're doing but . . . I've got to get back."

"Just have something to eat." Norma gestured to someone near the fire and a plate of food was brought. Norma helped Gloomy up and moved him in by the flames, where he could be warm. Someone put a round of firewood near him and set the porcelain plate near Gloomy's hands. There was grilled venison steak, salmon, fried potatoes, and a fresh tomato sliced with oil and vinegar.

"Ya want a beer?" Rocket called out, and Gloomy nodded vaguely. Rocket gave him a cold long-necked bottle, and Gloomy watched the beaded water slide down the neck onto the tops of his fingers. Tasting the beer was like experiencing his first teenage kiss.

Gloomy chewed the salmon. It was hot and flaked off on his tongue. He recognized the flavor of garlic encrusted on the lightly charred outer flesh. He closed his eyes and gave his mouth over to the oily, sea-soaked flavor of the fish.

Norma dug a small book out of the deep pockets of her cargo pants. She looked at it carefully as if deciding something, then set it down on his knees.

Gloomy opened his eyes, looked down at the book, and saw that its leather jacket was rustic and could have been made by hand. There was a globe embossed on the outside with a raised fist holding a handful of wheat. By balancing the volume on his knee, Gloomy was able to open it to the title page. When he read the words, he pulled back so quickly his fork fell to the rocks near the fire.

The book was entitled: *To the Waterline: The Burning of the Moondancer*, by John Hartley.

"I wasn't sure if you'd seen this before," Norma said.

Gloomy leaned over for his fork and his food spilled onto the ground. He lifted up the book and on the inside of the front cover was a grainy photograph of a burning yacht. On the facing page beneath the title there was an epigraph: *Consider the ravens: they have neither storehouse nor barn, and yet God feeds them. Luke 12:24.*

Gloomy flipped the page and saw a photograph of himself, almost unrecognizably young. He tasted the beer from the long-necked bottle, and the cold liquid bubbled down his throat. He thought about the taste, and he thought about the popping fire, and a strange thought came into his mind that surprised the heck out of him:

I'm just a goddamn good-looking American, he thought.

LESTER PLAYS WITH His Face grew up in his grandmother's house near Lodge Grass, Montana. He wore his hair short. He didn't like fry bread and he didn't play basketball. His grandmother didn't drink and she wasn't particularly in touch with her heritage. In his memory, she was always an old Indian woman, but it wasn't until he moved away from the rez that he began to understand what it was that made her Indian. He remembered she liked to watch Mary Tyler Moore and Carol Burnett. She worked in a dentist's office and liked to eat at the VFW hall on Saturdays. She loved going to Crow Fair, and for weeks before, she would work on the costumes for her nieces, who were some of the best fancy dancers at the fair.

Lester's cousins were two years older than he was, and they were such beautiful girls that there was never a chance they would like him. Denise once asked him to walk with her to the gas station soda machine, and a sparkler of delight was lit in poor Lester's heart. But a few days later, he had seen Denise at JV baseball practice and she had laughed out loud at him when he asked her how it was going. She had laughed like a white girl, loud *ha ha ha*s, and had never covered her mouth, unlike all her girlfriends, who tittered behind their hands. They all had laughed at him, then they turned and ran to the gym like startled fillies.

Lester's grandmother died when he was seventeen. She was hit in a crosswalk by a white truck driver from Idaho. The litigation went on for years, going back and forth from tribal to federal court. As far as Lester knew, no one ever got any money, except the lawyers.

Lester's mother had given him over to his grandmother when she was seventeen and had then joined the air force. The last anyone knew, Lester's mother was stationed in Alaska, but when George White Man Runs Him tried to contact her about her mother's funeral, George was told that Lester's mom had mustered out of the air force in Anchorage.

So, Lester got on a bus to Seattle with one duffel bag and his toolbox. He had just turned eighteen and had never been that far from the Crow reservation, but he wasn't particularly scared. He was thinking of going to a technical college in Tacoma and getting the complete GM auto mechanic's training. He had written to the school and had three thousand dollars tucked into the flannel lining of his canvas coat. He wanted to learn the new ignition systems and even hoped to buy some of the diagnostic equipment for the newer cars. If there was too much competition for setting up a shop on the West Coast, he'd go back to the rez. The prospect of a new life on the rez didn't scare him either, but secretly he was hoping to make a new home somewhere else.

Lester liked the band Nirvana, which was part of the reason he went to Seattle. The singer Kurt Cobain was dead now, of course. Lester had listened to *Nevermind* incessantly in the four months after his grandmother died.

There was a bus to Tacoma leaving in two hours. Lester stood on the curb in Seattle, and was thinking of walking around and maybe going to a record store, when a white Jeep pulled up in front of him and a tall Indian man with shoulder-length hair rolled down the curbside window.

"Long way from home, in't?"

Lester didn't acknowledge the stranger, who now slid over to the passenger seat and hung his skinny arm out the window.

"Hey, Holmes, you can't stand there looking like some country Indian. Someone is going to rob you. I'm telling you this as a friend, you know. Spokane, that's me. You got family?"

Lester shook his head. No, he didn't have family.

"You come with me then, cousin. We'll go gamble and meet some women."

A light rain was beginning to fall. Another car pulled up behind the Jeep and the white driver tapped his horn tentatively. The Indian man opened the passenger door and waved frantically for Lester to get in.

Lester got in and they drove up to the Indian casino north of Seattle. He missed his bus that night and gambled with all of his three thousand dollars. In the morning, he walked out into the parking lot with thirty thousand dollars in plastic buckets. Security guards from the casino escorted him to a rental car the casino had provided. Both the guards were black men, and as they held the door of the Toyota Camry open, Lester gave them each a hundred dollars and they all laughed. Lester never went to technical school.

Years later, Lester would tell his cellmate, Gloomy McCahon, that bad luck could take many forms and both men believed it.

That first evening, driving down I-5 to Seattle, Lester thought the thirty thousand would never run out. He thought of the garage he would build there in western Washington. He thought of a well-painted, clean shop floor where he would never let a drop of oil spill from the pan of the foreign cars he would work on. It was one of the most amazing things in Lester's life to learn how fast a person could piss away thirty thousand dollars. He lived in a hotel and ate in restaurants downtown every night. He bought a stereo system, which the hotel asked him not to play. Then he bought a small Discman with expensive German headphones. He went to clubs and bought drinks for his new friends. Lester never drank alcohol himself. He had gotten drunk a few times in high school and didn't like what had happened, the sweet sickly taste of vomit in his throat and the dry mouth and headaches.

Six weeks later, Lester had developed a dependence on money. He had fifteen hundred dollars left, went back to the casino, and promptly lost that. When he tapped out, the security guy took him back to the office, where he met a middle-aged white woman who ran the floor, and this was the beginning of Lester's career in the gaming industry.

He grew his hair and began to wear the braids. He dealt blackjack and later ran a craps table. Eventually he became a pit boss and he bought Italian evening clothes: jackets with padded shoulders, thick linen shirts with high collars, and silver pins in place of a tie. He remembered the pictures from the library at the Crow Agency and styled his hair in the massive pompadour of the old Crow warriors. He plaited red thread in his hair and got his front teeth capped.

He would describe himself during this period to Gloomy and tell him truthfully, "I looked fucking great, like the original good-looking American."

Lester worked the good rooms in casinos all over the west. He was smart and quick with numbers. He could manage a table of boat people washed ashore from Los Angeles or Salt Lake City with a gentle wit and authority, never stumbling or arguing. He could ease nervous railbirds into a game and get them to double their buy-ins and enjoy doing it.

Lester liked the gambling life. He loved the atmosphere of the casino: the never-evening, never-morning lights falling evenly on the bloodred carpets, the girls dressing for work in fishnet stockings at eight forty-five in the morning. Most of all, he loved the packs of anxious white people sitting for hours at the tables or in front of the machines while they fingered their good-luck charms. There was something in their expressions that drew Lester's attention. They had tired eyes and all seemed to be asking themselves the same question: Am I deserving, tonight, right now, am I deserving of good luck? He loved watching them ask this question even while they were losing. Money and hope bled from them like a gutshot bear, but they kept coming back week after week.

Whether these people drank or not, they were like alcoholics in that there was not enough good luck in the world to convince them they were worthy. Good luck was the fluke they kept running toward, but bad luck was the norm, at least eight times out of ten. None of these people got unexpected love letters. None of them were surprised or delighted by good news. Fate, left to itself, would only bring them bad news. The casino gave them two chances out of ten to win. It was sad, Lester thought, that all it took were the casino's two slim, well-managed chances to cause a sane person to loathe their own life and wish for a better one.

Once, on the way to the break room, Lester saw a young white man buying candy bars and cheese cracker snacks from the vending machine near the pay phones. The man had a drink on top of the machine and he steadily pumped quarters into the candy machine, pushing the buttons on the front. The candy would drop and without looking, the white man would push in another set of quarters. As Lester Plays with His Face walked by, the man smiled a wobbly drunk's smile at him and said, "Big . . . winner," as clearly as he could manage.

It was often said and repeated that there was less corruption in Indian gaming than there had been in the early days of gaming in Las Vegas. Lester didn't really know what that meant. The Indian people he worked with largely liked their jobs and didn't want to mess up the deal. Here was a business where you could build a windowless building in the middle of a hunted-out forest and white people would come by bus to drink watery drinks, eat foot-long hot dogs, then leave behind 80 percent of the money they had brought with them. There was no need to steal in circumstances this strange and favorable.

Of course the line between sanctioned greed and criminality can be blurred by anyone. Lester never quite shook his love of wealth and the feeling that his intelligence could bring him luck. He was a good gambler. He knew what games to play and when. He never gambled at his own store but could slide into white casinos dressed as if he had just come off the rez. He could fake drunkenness and count cards all night long. He knew how not to call attention to himself and to win small and slowly, easing around different clubs and never getting rounded up or thrown out.

But he had a secret vice that surprisingly was the most common vice among the sheep he felt superior to: Lester began to think he was deserving. Lester thought he was deserving because he didn't drink. He thought he was deserving because he didn't take drugs, and he paid attention to the details. He thought he was deserving because he had grown up a poor Indian and his grandma who raised him had been killed in a crosswalk. As much as he wouldn't want to admit it, Lester thought God was going to reward him for his suffering and his virtues by bringing him a little extra good luck. It was that tiny bit of faith that pushed Lester Plays with His Face just over the limits of his natural good fortune and caused him to stay in debt to the gangsters who employed him.

Lester was not a gambling addict. He was simply a goddamn good-looking American, and this was the seed of his bad luck.

GLOOMY KNOB GOT up from the fire and started to walk toward the dark trees. "I've got to get back for count," he said, and stumbled over a bottle thrown by the fire.

Norma and Rocket stood up and touched Gloomy on the shoulder and he shucked them.

"You people are crazy," Gloomy said. "I don't want to see any daughter. I don't have a daughter. If anyone, I want to see Slippery and Ellie. I didn't ask to be taken from jail. I've got to get back."

"Mr. McCahon," Norma said, turning toward him, "you do have a daughter. She lives in town. I will take you there once it is safe."

"Besides," Rocket said from over her shoulder, "the news is all over the radio. There's been an attack on Stevens Penitentiary. They are searching for you in the wreckage. There is no undoing that now. And Slippery Wilson is long dead. Ellie, the anarchist? She died before you were born."

"You people are crazy. Who asked you to plan a life for me?" Gloomy blurted out.

"You're right." Norma tried to push Rocket away with her back as she spoke slowly and evenly to Gloomy. "You're right, Mr. McCahon. It was presumptuous of us. But I know what happened back in 2020. I know the truth, Gloomy. I know that there were men who were trying to kill you in prison, and I couldn't let that happen."

Gloomy sat on a stump. The sparks from the fire rose up and momentarily stuck to the damp hemlock boughs some twenty feet above their heads before winking out, never igniting a thing. Gloomy knew that this woman would never understand. She would never understand that he was not afraid of those men. He preferred dying, in fact, if he couldn't get his old job back. If he were captured now, he would serve time in a hole. He would be watched and never allowed to die, never, even if he insisted upon it. He would be kept alive until every bureaucrat in the system had forgotten him, and then he would languish for another twenty years on a gigantic ward hooked up to a meat pump. Only after everyone who had ever thought about him had died or forgotten him would he be allowed to slip away to the death that he had longed for ever since the day when the beautiful boat blew up. Whoever these insane foolish people were, they did not understand what they were sentencing him to.

"Just who are you two?" Gloomy asked, as he held both hands toward the fire so as to shield his eyes a bit.

"This is Rocket," Norma said formally. "He's an old friend and he agreed to help me with this."

"But you?" Gloomy said, straining to look at the woman. "Do I know you?"

"I'm Norma Hix," she said almost apologetically. "I work for your mom at the bar." She moved around behind Gloomy, who was facing the fire again, trying to ignore the people around him. Trying to will himself back to his unit, back to his bunk.

Gloomy stood up and began walking toward the waterline. He would swim back to Olympus if he needed to.

Rocket and Norma ran after him. "Let us show you a little more before you make any rash decisions. We only want the best for you," she said, and then turned to pick up something at the base of a large spruce tree.

"I'm sorry about this," Norma almost whispered, and held up a large canvas bag. "I'm sorry, Mr. McCahon, but you're going to have to ride in this for the next little while. We just need to keep you in the dark."

Gloomy started to pull away, but Rocket grabbed his arms as Norma held up the aerosol spray. There was no use in fighting them. If they could blow up a building and break him out of Olympus, then they would have no trouble stuffing him in a bag. And they didn't.

Chapter Six

The mildewed pillow smelled like failure to Gloomy now. Failure, boredom, and painkillers mixed with vodka.

All he had ever wanted to be was a logger. He had worked a few years in the woods of Alaska and several on the west side in Washington, making good money falling second growth on Indian land, but he worked in the Oregon woods for only one day as a cutter. He had gotten the job through a friend who was the foreman on a helicopter logging outfit flying near Bend. Gloomy had bought a new Swedish chain saw and an automatic grinder to keep all his chains sharp. He spent one day in camp getting settled, and early the next morning he hiked through the cut to begin his strip. He cut the face to control the direction of the fall. The big ponderosa pine, teetered a bit and as he began the back cut, and the tree ripped up the middle then split halfway up, as if on a hinge. Gloomy tried to pull out the saw, but the massive tree fell and pinned him to the ground, crushing his left hip. Fallers call this a Barber's Chair when a tree splits that way, and Gloomy thought about that term as he lay on the dusty cone-covered ground with his face butted up against a rock. He shut his eyes and wished he could take his mistake—the bad cut or the miscalculation in the tree's weight—take it all back, but the three-hundred-year-old tree lay on him like history, and he could not get up. The pain burned up his waist and through his entire left side. The boys hurried over and blocked up the tree, running their saws to remove the limbs that were in their way. Once the trunk was stable, they dug in the earth around him and dragged him free. Gloomy remembered the chattering of the saws, the chips from the chains, and the sappy smell of the green wood on the ground.

For six weeks, he stayed in different hospitals, and when he was discharged, a friend who had been a hook tender on his crew drove him to the basement in Seattle. Gloomy didn't tell his father what had happened. His mother had recently written to him, and Gloomy didn't have the heart to write her back. He just lay in the basement for five months watching TV, eating multicolored painkillers, and washing them down with vodka. He read the Bible and tried to pray for a different kind of future, one he was starting to imagine as he breathed in the mildew and studied the water stains on the sheetrock.

Gloomy hadn't really felt the sting of any kind of remorse in that damp basement room. He knew he was in trouble. He knew his injury was serious. He would walk with a limp if he was lucky, but working in the woods would be painful. But he was aware that he was becoming a drug addict, chewing endlessly on painkillers. As a boy Gloomy had known old men who lived musty bachelors' lives above taverns and bars. These old boys had been injured in the woods and lived off the kindness of barmaids and church ladies who brought them plates of food. They were drunks mostly. Gloomy couldn't bear the thought of this future.

For the first time, he put his mind to real, purposeful prayer—not the kind of religious meditation he had done as a teenager, but the desperate transactional kind of "You do this, and I promise I'll do that" kind of praying. He poured out his fears to God. He made promises he wasn't sure he would ever be able to keep. Gloomy remembered rain falling off the eaves of the house and puddling on the eaves of the basement windows. He watched the water leak down the walls in forked tracks. He asked Jesus for help. He imagined the vision of God. He imagined Jesus standing on a mountain. He imagined Jesus on the cross, but all the images seemed distant and painted in, as if Gloomy were recalling movies he had seen rather than having the vision itself. Gloomy's head swam with imagery from the Bible, and he pledged his love. His fear had the heft of honesty, but of course it wasn't. His fear was the screen on which he was projecting the image of God—God of the movies and of cheap Bible illustrations. In his heart, Gloomy knew this and prayed for the screen to drop, but it never did.

His hip healed slowly, and he had to force himself to cut back on the pills. Eventually he felt different words, different verses of the Bible in almost every breath he took. He imagined the Holy Land to be like the dry hills that surrounded Karen's trailer in the Methow. He imagined the hot days of summer and the dust coming up from the side of the road when a hay truck blustered past, and he imagined Jesus walking up to him, but he could never put words in His mouth.

Without the pills and alcohol, Gloomy was leaning toward despair. He was running out of money. His friend who had been paying the rent was leaving for a job in Colorado, and Gloomy was going to have to move. He knew he was going to have to tell his father eventually. Gloomy began toying with the idea of killing himself, but he could not bear the image of someone finding him dead. He didn't want anyone to curse his body as they lifted his corpse onto a gurney, so Gloomy worked on the problems of suicide and faith at the same time.

Then on a day when he least expected it, he stayed up all night and prayed as hard as he could. He prayed and cried. He admitted all of his pride and weakness, and still he could summon nothing more than some strange Hollywood Jesus. When he finally went to sleep, Gloomy had resolved to throw himself off a bridge near Anacortes where the current was strong, and hopefully his body would never be found. But in the morning when he woke up, he found fifteen thousand dollars in his boot and decided to go on living. As he reached for the money, he saw that his wife, Karen, had left a note and a picture of herself. Her beautiful black hair hung down her face, and her eyes focused on him. There was a phone ringing so loud and insistent it gave him a headache and made him short of breath. He reached down and grabbed the heavy old receiver off the cradle: "Hello?"

"You put those expensive boots on yet?" said a familiar woman's voice as sweet and sharp as a rum and Coke. "Get yourself straight, buster, we've got to find that second bomb you squirreled away."

THEY HAD TAKEN him out of the bag and laid him somewhere in the dark. His head hurt, but he was bored by the pain by now. His hair was wet. He had not opened his eyes yet, and he didn't know where he was. He wasn't even sure how long he had been in the bag, but he could make out the scent of a mildewed pillow, and instantly his brain bloomed with a memory of being back in the basement room in Seattle where he had been laid up for six months while recovering from a broken hip. The memory closed in on him like the dark. He was there in a Seattle basement listening to the radio and staring up at a water-stained ceiling. But he wasn't. He was in Cold Storage.

Gloomy's eyes stung when he rubbed them; his face felt rubbery and numb. Something in his body knew he was not in prison—maybe it was the sound of the wind or the slight ticking in the distance that tipped him off. Or perhaps the body knows more than we give it credit for. Maybe it's the body that orients itself and informs the brain and not the other way around. Whatever it was, Gloomy knew he was in Cold Storage, Alaska, because Cold Storage had always felt this way, from the first moment he had set foot on the wet boardwalk.

The town itself was one rain-soaked avenue of wooden buildings along a boardwalk, with trails and stairs running down to the beach and up a steep path into the hill. Kids rode their bikes up and down the length of the town, and old men sat on the benches in front of the bar and the post office and the cold storage. Everyone either knew your business or thought they did. When Gloomy had fallen in with angry friends, the clerks in the stores knew he was in trouble before he did. Rain fell on black garbage can lids, and ravens sat on the edge of them scolding anyone who would listen, but Gloomy had stopped listening by the time he set foot on the millionaire's yacht. He had spent most of his time in his skiff traveling to the bluffs, dodging the rangers and interpreting scripture in a way that upset his parents.

As he lay there in the dark he could hear rain on a window somewhere. He might have heard some voices

above him, but he wasn't sure. One voice he recognized
and others he didn't. Gloomy remembered the dark-
haired woman who visited him in his prison dreams. Just
as Gloomy knew he was in Cold Storage, he knew she was
present somehow. He loved this woman, but when he tried
to call her up in her entirety, ice rose in his throat and he
felt as if he was going to vomit. The woman had high color
to her skin, as if she were an Irish girl drinking red wine.
He had been in this town with her and had even watched
her work at a job in a store. Gloomy turned his head, and
there, through the gloom, he thought the dark-haired
woman must be sitting in a favorite chair. He thought he
heard her breathing.

"Hello?" he finally said out loud. "Hello?" He heard
nothing.

When he finally woke up completely, Gloomy could
barely make out a square tank, maybe a septic tank near
his feet. There was salt water on the floor and he tasted
salt water in his mouth. His hair was still wet. His brain was
fuzzy, as if he had been asleep a long time. He could smell
urine and wood chips. He heard a rustling in the dark. When
he sat up, a large gray rat rose up from the sawdust on the
bottom of the cage and sniffed the air near Gloomy's left
foot.

Gloomy needed to make his way back to Stevens, somehow. He wanted to turn himself in, but he knew it had to
be to prison authorities. Local law enforcement would
likely kill him. Some rent-a-cop in town would cap him for
sure just to get their story online.

Gloomy was no longer in his prison jumpsuit. He had
on old sweatpants and a T-shirt that read: *Cold Storage Hang
Gliding: Don't just stand there, get some air!* Gloomy could just
read the upside-down print through the gloom, and he

could make out the drawing of a large-breasted woman kicking her legs underneath a kite-shaped glider. On his feet he was wearing broken leather pull-ons, the kind his father had called ranch Romeos and what some in Alaska called boat slippers. He heard honking outside and the vague sound of music.

When he stumbled in the dark and finally found the basement door, he pushed against it and was met with a heavy kind of immobility. Nothing sagged. No hinges creaked, no wood gave. This was not an old basement door but one that had been reinforced somehow.

Light seeped around the edges of the basement windows, which were on one side of the room at about head height. They had plate steel screwed over the frames. There was not enough room around the edges to insert his fingers.

The rat ran on a loose-jointed wheel. Gloomy could see its pink nose bobbing in the thin light. Just beyond the rat was a fireplace. He knocked his shin against a table getting there and reached up inside the sooty opening. The damper was shut and there was a new padlock attaching the handle to a bolt in the wall of the chimney. Gloomy had had enough. He lay on his back and kicked the damper handle. After three good kicks the lock had not moved, but the bolt had pulled out of the rotted firewall. He opened the damper and looked up to see a tiny square of daylight, and he crawled up the chimney. His face filled with soot, and he quickly shut his mouth and eyes. He shimmied like a worm up the dirty dark cave, pushing his feet, sliding his elbows and lifting. Using his chin to leverage his head and neck when necessary, he finally forced his arms out the top of the chimney and pulled himself onto the steep-pitched roof of the house.

Acting fast, he slid down a gutter spout and landed in a rosebush.

He was covered in soot and smelled of creosote. He spat and gagged. The rosebush had cut his hand but not badly enough to slow him down. An old dachshund stood by the picket fence sniffing the air, much as the rat had been doing. The dog's stomach sagged limply and was scarred as if he had been dragging it. Based on the blue haziness over his eyes and the way he sniffed, Gloomy figured he must have been blind. He barked weakly, more of a gag really. A man came to the door of the house Gloomy had just escaped from. Gloomy lay flat on the muddy ground behind the rosebush just outside the fence with the barking dog.

"Hogan! Hogan! Get in here now," the man yelled, but the old dog obviously could not hear a word of it, so the man lumbered off the porch and walked right toward Gloomy.

Gloomy buried his head down into the mud and he could feel the man's footsteps vibrating along the soggy lawn toward him. Luckily Hogan must have been attuned to the vibration, too, for he spun and dragged his belly toward the doorway, causing the man to stop before Gloomy came into sight on the other side of the fence.

He lay there feeling the footsteps going away and listened as they clattered up the steps, disappearing behind the crunch of the closing door. He lay there another thirty seconds. He tried to wipe the soot off his clothes by tearing a chunk of grass out of the fringe of the lawn through the fence and scrubbing himself with it. It didn't help much, but he stood up and walked briskly to the street as if he had a right to be there.

Gloomy stood outside on the boardwalk where a set of

stairs went up into the woods. He had stood here some fifteen years before. He remembered the confluence of memories of family members and a brown bear running up those stairs. It was a series of memories Gloomy had left behind almost a lifetime ago.

He had left the rain-forested fishing town, an old board-walk town of drunks and eccentrics. The forest and the ocean pressed in on each side, giving the town a close and easy feel in the bad weather and the kind of giddy atmo-sphere of a beach town on those rare warm days when the flags popped in a dry wind.

But where he stood just then was something else. Some-thing that didn't match his memory. It was lightly raining. He saw the old cold storage with a new coat of paint and a new sign advertising it as a convention center flashing in neon on the side of the soggy wooden building.

The small boat harbor was where it should be, and the boardwalk was oriented to the sea and to the moon as he remembered. But there was a strangeness about the town, unsettling and dreamlike. Gloomy looked to the west where the mayor's house had been on the little island with the causeway and immediately noticed a long deep-water dock with metal pilings and a deck that ran the length of the harbor. The little houses that had lined the causeway had transformed into shops, and there was an open-air café with a strange geometric rigging of fabric over aluminum scaffolding. Gloomy could hear music com-ing from the dock area. There were no boats tied at the dock, but people crowded the area near the community center. The music was an electronic steel band playing "Margaritaville."

The sun was setting and white people in brightly col-ored rain gear were walking down to the dock with drinks in their hands. Gloomy rubbed his eyes and shook his head. He had lost a day from the time he had stood with his kidnappers on that unknown beach near Ted Stevens Penitentiary. He had lost a day from when he had crawled out of the log. The music swelled and throbbed as Gloomy started walking toward town. There was a kiosk at the old store with a sign pointing to the ticket holders' line. There were signs along every section of the boardwalk near the harbor for different forms of "flight-seeing" and hiking, Jet Ski adventures, and whale song tours. There were dozens and dozens of children walking with backpacks offering to sell "local lures" and plastic abalone shells.

The crowd was intimidating to Gloomy, and he walked toward the old town hall, where there was a cottonwood tree and a totem pole. All the buildings were now taller than the church and each had shops and restaurants on the bottom floors and apartments with terraces on the upper. These buildings could have been dropped in place from Key West or Maui. There were "island casuals," as one of the rental signs read on the front office. From a side street, he could see down the causeway to the cruise ship dock. There was a large neon sign advertising the Cold Storage "sunset tradition." At the end of the dock was a man with dreadlocks breathing fire. A woman in tights was riding on a unicycle, juggling the stuffed cloth fish she sold from the "Just for the Halibut" stand.

An electric police cart pulled around the corner and stopped some thirty feet from him. A young officer stepped out of the driver's side. As he walked toward Gloomy, he spun his baton like Charlie Chaplin.

"Hey there. Aren't you a little off your beat?" the officer said to Gloomy.

"I suppose so," Gloomy said, his heart beating faster

than he thought possible, a new ambivalence about capture surging through his veins.

"You're not wearing a bracelet, are ya?" The cop shined his light on Gloomy's face and down at his dirty clothes.

"No," Gloomy said, thinking of bolting.

"I guess I don't know you. What's your name?" The cop turned off the light and slipped it easily back into its holder with one hand as he continued to twirl the baton.

"Gloomy McCahon," he said slowly, and although the young cop didn't notice, Gloomy was holding his wrists behind his back, waiting to be cuffed.

"Yeah, right! And I'm Jesse James," the cop guffawed. "You look good for a dead guy."

"Dead guy?" Gloomy stood straight and pulled up his dirty sweatpants.

"Oh yeah. They blew his ass up out on the rock. Weird, huh? This big famous terrorist gets capped when some joker tries to blow up the new women's facility." The cop looked at his fingernails and then absently at the fire-eater on the end of the docks whose spumed flame sent weird shadows down the street. Then he looked up and stuck his hand out to Gloomy to offer him a greeting. It had been so long since anyone had done anything of the sort that Gloomy was taken aback slightly, but he responded.

"I'm Terence Younger," the young cop said, and he held Gloomy's hand for a long time, waiting for him to speak.

"Oh," Gloomy blurted after a moment. "Bob. I'm Bob," he said, and smiled too broadly.

"That's it? Bob?" The cop looked up and down Gloomy's frame, scanning for bulges or straps that might secure a holster.

"Oh, sorry . . . Bob. Bob Hand," Gloomy said as he kept shaking the soft white hand.

Down the dock, people were clapping as a kid played Russian songs on an accordion and a dog in a pink tutu started to climb a makeshift tightwire.

"Well, Bob, I tell ya, you're looking kind of rough. I bet you got off work and are looking for some tourist fun, huh? But you know how the merchants are. They don't really want us, you know, us local types, down around the sunset activities. I know, I know, it kind of pisses me off, too, but what are you going to do? They bring a lot of money into town. Some guy at that new stuffed fish place near the old radio station, he had the nerve to tell my kid to go get music lessons before he played his harmonica downtown." The cop was clearly excited now and gestured wildly toward the sunset festivities. "And that's not all. Someone from the chamber told me I had better not come down to the party in sweats. Or they had better be matching sweats, you know? What's a guy to do? Well, let me tell ya, why don't I give you a ride back out to housing and that way you'd save on the car fare." The cop took Gloomy by the elbow and put him in the backseat of his silent cart.

The cop was right about one thing. Nothing about Gloomy's village seemed the same. There were huge houses that had been built close in on each side of the trail at the end of the boardwalk. The trail was now in fact a gravel road. The road itself had been widened to accommodate the gated parking areas for the beachside houses. Every sixth house or so, Gloomy recognized an old wooden house from his era, dwarfed by the modern island homes. Terence Younger prattled on about building and the new rules of the community as he drove south on what had been a clamming beach in Gloomy's day.

"So . . . Hand. I don't know any Hands. You new to town?" Terence looked into the rearview mirror.

"Uh . . . yeah," Gloomy finally said.

"You got family out at Stevens?"

"Yeah, that's right. I was hoping to get a chance to visit. I just landed a job cleaning out a chimney for a guy. Kind of lucky. I need the dough," Gloomy said as easily as he could.

"I figured," Terence said, and he turned down the squealing radio so he could speak above it.

"They've got a visitors' barracks out at housing. That is, if you don't have the money for one of the temporary apartments. How long you figure to be around?"

Gloomy watched the water side of the road. Through an opening in the trees he could see out past the islands where the waves were breaking on the outer rocks. The sun was down behind the horizon now, and the sky was a silver-gray streaked with smeary red lines. To the south-west, in the direction of the wind, was a glow in the clouds over the shining prison searchlights.

"Just a couple of days, I guess."

The police cart rounded the last corner, where Gloomy was expecting to see the old sawmill site come into view. Instead there appeared to be a small city.

"Okay . . . housing . . ." Terence said, and turned his radio back up to report in.

Housing comprised three large apartment complexes attached by covered walkways. The deep-water dock and the sheds from the old sawmill were still in place, but instead of the main tanks up behind the plant, there was a playground built on old hog fuel chips. At the foot of the slides were deep muddy puddles, and the rings on the end of the chains swung back and forth listlessly.

The apartment complexes were newly painted but had the monumental blockiness of structures from the Soviet era—cinder blocks stacked one on top of another in a monotonous progression. Above them, the mountain was a wild tangle of trees and rocky bluffs. To offset the bulkiness of form, there was a type of concrete molding on the outer walls of the apartments. This molding was painted and outlined smaller town houses around the tiny balconies facing over the deep-water port.

Terence pulled up under a covered entrance beside the north building. He turned around and spoke to Gloomy through the holes in the bulletproof shield.

"Just head down that hall and ask for the meeting. That's where you'll find the person who can book you a room in the temporary visitors' barracks. Go to the meeting, they'll fix you right up." Terence hit a button on the door beside him, and the back door Gloomy was sitting next to opened automatically. Gloomy got out and looked around at some kids who were leaning on the handlebars of their bikes. The light washed out their skin so the kids looked almost dead under the fluorescents.

"Take care now," Terence Younger said. He pulled away, waving as if he were in a parade. He continued waving to the kids in baggy pants on bikes.

The kids looked dull-eyed and expressionless as he passed, and as he rounded out of sight the youngest one, with a black stocking cap pulled down almost over his eyes, spat on the ground and said, "Ten-four, Officer Friendly," and the others laughed.

Gloomy walked down the hallway. He turned the corner to where a woman was sitting at a desk surrounded by narrow shelves of filed paperwork and key rings hanging on brass hooks. She had a yellow correctional badge with her photo ID on the front. As he turned and looked at her, Gloomy was almost sure her eyes widened with alarm. He wasn't sure, but he thought this woman had been out at Olympus.

Gloomy turned quickly and looked at the bulletin board. He started scanning the notices tacked there.

"Can I help you?" the woman's voice cracked out from under the protective glass.

"I'm . . ." Gloomy scanned the board until his eyes landed on a handwritten slip of paper. "Yeah, I'm here for the meeting. I'm here to see . . ." He squinted his eyes to read the block printing. "I'm here to go to the meeting." Gloomy put his finger on the slip and looked over at the woman with part of his forearm covering his face.

"That's in the basement of the next building down. Out the doors and to the left."

She appeared to go back to her comic book and Gloomy quickly made for the exit.

The room was down a flight of concrete steps and through some heavy doors with meshed glass inset in the middle. About fifty chairs were set up on the painted concrete floor. In the corner were some washers and dry-ers. One dryer had the door open and the room had a warm, linty smell that almost cut the layer of fresh paint and heating-oil fumes. There was a card table with a bowl of flowers and a full water glass next to it. Most of the seats were taken. There was a tired-looking woman with brown skin wearing a waitress's uniform. She had a little girl spread out on her lap. There were six or eight older women sitting together. They wore flowered housedresses and slippers. They passed a box of chocolates back and forth. A couple of young men with skinny arms and intri-cate tattoos sat next to each other, and behind them a prosperous white man in a jacket and tie spoke with a young woman holding a baby. There were two older men

whom Gloomy recognized as guards from the prison. They
didn't look up at him, but when Gloomy tried to back out
to leave, he felt a warm hand on his back and a gentle push
forward.

An older woman wearing a blue pantsuit walked behind
Gloomy and closed the door after him. She reached
directly behind his back and turned the dimmer switch,
bringing the lights low in the room. Then she flicked the
next switch, which illuminated only the area of the card
table.

"Welcome," she whispered, and she motioned toward
the folding chairs with her reed-thin arm. "Welcome . . .
we will be starting shortly. You may want to have a seat. The
refreshments will be served after." The guards looked up
at him but the lights were lower now and they showed no
indication of recognizing him.

Gloomy thanked her, and the woman set a bag of
prison-industry cookies on a back table next to a large
plastic jug labeled JUICE, APPLE, FROM CONCENTRATE in
governmental lettering.

Gloomy sat toward the middle of the room, at the end
of the aisle with the woman and her sleeping little girl in
the same row. The woman smiled at him and then nodded
solemnly to the front.

A man with gray hair and a neatly trimmed beard
stepped around the corner back by the washer. He wore a
gray jacket with a military cut but no insignia. As he walked
into the pool of light next to the card table he paused and
scanned the audience with clear blue eyes. He made eye
contact with each person in the audience. If a person did
not look him in the eyes, he would pause for perhaps ten
seconds or more, waiting until that person met his gaze.

He slowly drank half the water in his glass and sat down

in a folding chair near the corner. The lights dimmed almost to darkness, and a single spot came on the lectern in the front. The speaker walked to the lectern. He stared intensely at Gloomy and nodded slowly.

"Whose world is this?" he asked the crowd.

"Our world!" they answered in unison.

"And whose time is this?" The gray-haired man leaned forward.

"Our time!" they said back.

The speaker paused and smiled at them. "I am grateful that we can be together tonight," he said, "on this particular night, in this particular place. Though it may not be the perfect place we once imagined. And this may not be the times that you wanted as a child. I am grateful to be here with you . . . right now because, yes indeed, it is our time."

The young men with tattoos settled into their chairs. They folded their arms across their chests and watched the man in the front of the room. Gloomy looked around and started to stand up to go just as Norma and Rocket walked in the back. Rocket pointed toward the guards and shook his head with some urgency.

The man in front continued to speak. "We have all been heartbroken in our lives. It may have started when we came from our mother's womb. We struggled to come into the world and after that doctor slapped us, we started crying"—he paused and scanned a moment—"and I don't think they were all government doctors either." This brought a chuckle from the woman down the aisle from Gloomy.

"It is old news by now that ninety percent of the world's goods go to one percent of the population."

The crowd nodded.

"And it is old news that the earth now belongs to the

rich. Not satisfied with bigger houses and cars, they now own the beauty of the earth . . . think about that a moment. The rich own beauty."

"That's right," someone in the crowd intoned.

"Now they own the natural beauty of the world."

"Yes," someone said.

"The rich own the clean air and private hospital beds, where they can die without fear of leaving their children penniless." The speaker's voice was building, yet he stepped away and lowered his tone to one of smiling confidentiality. "But as I said, that's old news. What I want to bring you tonight is some *really* old news."

"All right then!" the tattooed boys called out.

Gloomy stared down at the floor. He slumped in his seat and tried to hide his face in some of the literature left on the chairs. The woman near him, rubbed her child's back slowly between the shoulder blades. She smiled sweetly at Gloomy as if to comfort him as well.

"Do you remember Luke 12:24? 'Consider the ravens: they neither sow nor reap, they have neither storehouse nor barn, and yet God feeds them.' Now, why *ravens* in Luke? Why ravens at all? Others talk of birds of the air and the lilies of the field. Why ravens, my good friends? Well, here is what I think: ravens come for the bodies."

He stopped. Outside the gears of bicycles clicked by the basement windows. A boat's horn sounded in the distance. Gloomy did not look up from the floor.

"That's right. Ravens come for the bodies." Here he sped up slightly. "Back in the time of pestilence, the ravens fed from the bodies laid out on the side of the road waiting to be picked up. If you saw a raven, you knew death was at hand. But anyone who has ever hunted knows the raven will take you to the game. They want your scraps, of course, so a good hunter knows to listen to ravens when he is out stalking game.

"My friends, we know ravens come at the time of great questions. They come at the crossroads between life and death, between the sane and the crazy. That is why we are here now. There was a time when Christian men and women started on the right road and then veered off. Where once they wanted to bring light, now they want to bring death. These people want to kill you." The speaker paused and stared straight at Gloomy. A kid somewhere tumbled on a bike, sending a clatter down the covered walkways outside.

"These Christians have come to the crossroads and turned hard in a direction all their own. These old friends have turned away," he said slowly. "What does it say in First John? 'In the beginning was the Word, and the Word was with God, and the Word was God. He was in the beginning with God, all things were made through Him, and without Him was not anything made that was made. In Him was life and the life was the *light* of men!'" The preacher said this last part forcefully, then lowered his voice to a stage whisper.

"Tonight—right now—we have come back to that fork in the road, friends. We have come to that place where life meets death, where sanity meets insanity and *freedom* meets *imprisonment*. It is just now that we need the light. We need the light that was stolen, my dear friends. The light that was stolen from *you*." His words hung in the old laundry room. The boys with the tattoos rocked slightly back and forth and the woman with the chocolate box sat stone still, taking in his last words.

"Yes, that light was stolen from you, *and God wants you to have it back!*"

Gloomy heard a whoop and a short clap come from behind him. He turned and saw the man in the coat and tie stand up briefly, before nervously sitting back down. Then he saw two new people were in the darkened back of the room. They were both clapping. He squinted to get a better look. Norma and Rocket moved up to sit in Gloomy's aisle to block the guards' view of him.

"Let's go back to Luke a little bit. 'But woe to you that are rich, for you have received your consolation. Woe to you that are full now, for you shall hunger.' And of course, 'Blessed are the poor, for yours is the kingdom of God. Blessed are thou that weep now, for you shall laugh.' And, 'Blessed are you when men hate you and when they exclude you and revile you and cast out your name as evil.'"

Norma nodded at Gloomy and smiled. Rocket walked toward the front of the room, acknowledged Norma with a nod, then turned back to face the speaker. Gloomy looked around, trying to decide which door to run toward.

"God wants you to have your light back. Your old friends have turned against you, and want to send you to heaven sooner than you may want to go. We know this and here is what I think. Here is what I believe. There is light enough in heaven. We know that. God wants you to have this light *right now!*" He slapped his hand. "God wants you to live on this earth bathed in the light of the Sermon on the Mount. For if Jesus is the light, where does it shine? I'll tell you. It shines on this earth. It shines on our bodies as well as our souls. It shines on our children's bodies as well as their souls."

Gloomy heard a tinkling sound and he looked back at Norma and saw she was holding a pair of handcuffs down at her side. The guards looked at her. Looked right at the cuffs and at Gloomy. Smiled at him, in fact, but did nothing but continue listening.

"There is enough light in heaven. The light needs to shine on earth and the rich have to take their rightful place of *humility* among us."

"Speak, brother Daniel!" a tattooed boy called.

"Have we felt the stink of our poverty?"

"Yes!" the women called out.

"Have the rich felt the prick of their conscience yet?"

"No!" came the call.

"No, they have not, but soon . . . soon the new light will fall all over this country and the rich men . . . the prison contractors . . ."

"Yes," someone said.

"The wardens . . ."

"Yes."

"The doctors and administrators . . ."

"Yes."

Daniel paused and smiled at his congregation, drawing out the moment.

"Did I mention the wealthy prison contractors who become millionaires based on the suffering of your families?"

"*Yes!*" the entire congregation called out.

"Well, all of them, my friends, my dear friends, will come to know the meaning of the Sermon on the Mount just as we have known, and just as we have felt our blessing, so they will know their woe."

The tattooed boys stood up together and waved their fists in the air. "That's right. That's right. That's right."

Norma came around the side of the room toward Gloomy. Rocket looked back toward the exit, where a large man in green army fatigues stood with his arms crossed in front of his chest.

"These billionaires have a duty to God, and when this

new light shines on the world, we will be able to see the ugliness of what the rich have wrought. This light will shine on the prisons and in the sweatshops and housing complexes all over the world . . ."

Everyone was on their feet now, guards included, yelling and holding their hands palms up to the fluorescent lights. As Gloomy stood up to run, Norma moved in close to him and discreetly snapped a handcuff around one of his wrists. The other she locked around her own.

"The light will shine on the garbage dumped on the ground. The light will shine on the toxic waste dumps. The light will shine on the diseased and dispossessed animals . . . and I'm talking about all the animals, friends, all the animals who have been burned by the sun and made toxic by greed. This light, this glorious light, will light our way back."

"I'm not letting you go again," Norma whispered, and she tugged Gloomy toward the back of the room. When he tried to jerk away, Rocket's hand closed in around the biceps of his right arm and firmly held him. With Rocket on one side and Norma on the other, Gloomy was led out through the door and to a white van, where they dumped him through the back door.

"We have a stop to make and then you will take me to that second bomb, won't you, Gloomy?" Rocket said to him, in a voice that didn't seem to be his own.

Gloomy sat on the bare floor of the van with his back against the metal side. Rocket fished for the keys in his pocket and started the engine. Norma, who was still cuffed to his wrist, was sitting next to him.

"Mr. McCahon"—Norma cleared her throat and her voice was patient—"someone is trying to kill you. Will you take me to the second bomb?"

The van pulled away and the passengers' shoulders

rocked as the axles tackled the potholes. There were some kids building a fire in a metal drum down on the beach. One of them threw a soda can full of gas into the flames, and the other kids scattered. As the flame blistered out into the darkness, the van turned the corner onto the dark road back to town.

"I'm going to show you something," Norma said. "I think it will give you some hope."

Norma fiddled with the handcuff on her wrist, lifting both her and Gloomy's arms up to her eye level. Then she took the key and undid the cuffs.

She turned to look at him. "Listen," she said, "I know what happened on the *Moondancer*. That knowledge has put me in danger. I've been under the same kind of death threats as you for the last seven years. I had to do something about it."

"Why now?" Gloomy asked.

"We need to find the rocket before anyone else. We need it before the prison authorities get their hands on it."

"Just come with us for a little longer," Rocket said from the driver's seat. "There's gonna be a risk because there'll be cops all over the house. But we're going to show you something."

The city's all-purpose truck bumped along the road toward town. The boardwalk of Cold Storage, Alaska, was crowded with strange people in wildly colored rain gear out on the tideflat and in front of the bar. Music streamed down the streets from small speakers tucked back under the eaves of buildings or in the trees near the abandoned phone booths. Happy music, upbeat but not interruptive, meant to push people along their way with a spring in their step.

They pulled in behind a store, picked up two large boxes, and put them in the van. The boxes were big enough that a large adult could fit inside each one. Norma took a jackknife and cut a small hole in each box and the van sped off down the road to the north.

"I'm trusting you here. I could keep you cuffed but I'm not," Norma said. "I just ask you not to try to run. Take the scope and look down the hill at about two o'clock. It's a green house."

He lifted the spotting scope. At first he saw a blur of alder trees and light reflecting off the water. They were out near the ferry terminal and the old barge landing. Gloomy recognized the small island offshore and the shallow cove where herring liked to spawn in the spring. He aimed the glass at the house.

The light from the large windows was like milk spilling out onto the grass in front. The drops of water on the alder leaves sparkled in the light. Through the window he saw a woman sitting on a couch, reading a book. It was a large book with pictures, perhaps a children's book, but Gloomy could see no one else in the room. The woman had long black hair and must have been in her late forties. She was wearing a long nightshirt that covered her legs. She reached up absently and scratched her calf. Her back was toward the window.

Red and blue lights flashed on the water and on the window.

"Shit!" Norma blurted out.

The woman in the window turned to look out into the dark, and Gloomy sucked in his breath and dropped the spotting scope, then grabbed it and held it to his eye, his hands shaking.

Someone you love has gone missing and you reach out for them. You have felt the body of a loved one,

the firmness of muscle and the close intimate smell.
You have known the sadness of their disappearance
just as you tasted the delight of their skin. You reach
out to them through your companions. You reach out
through memory and through desire. You walk an
imagined bridge across a golden landscape. You
walk that bridge without any assurance of finding
the loved one, but you walk toward them nonetheless.

THE WOMAN'S JET-BLACK hair framed her square jaw. Her wide lips drooped slightly on the left. Her cheeks were pink as if she had been drinking alcohol, and the glitter of her eyes cut through Gloomy's chest. The woman stood up and stared out the window toward the flashing blue and red lights.

Something felt broken to Gloomy now. He could actually feel his past moving and shifting around. His eyes ran wet with tears, his head ached as thoughts swirled. This thing in his heart, this frozen river cracked and groaned, and it hurt him just as it exhilarated him.

This could not be his wife. He knew that with certainty.

And yet a voice in his head said, "That is my wife."

"It is time for you to tell her everything, Christopher," Norma said gently.

Gloomy walked down the stone steps of the pathway, and the door opened. His lungs hurt now; he was breathing hard. He drifted inside, and Norma's voice was like an angel's behind him.

"That is the mother of your child, the woman you love, and now we've got to sit you down, so you can tell her everything. Everyone thinks you're dead; they're saying so on the news, but everyone knows that's not true and this place is covered with the worst kind of law."

The hood slammed down, and Rocket got into the front of the van and started the engine.

Gloomy looked at the beautiful woman who stood in front of him. He smelled the coffee she held in the mug in her hands. She set a mug before him and she leaned over to kiss him.

Gloomy felt the warmth of his wife's kiss being replaced by the thick flavor of blood in the back of his mouth. There was a warmth in his body that he had never felt before. This was his wife. He was out of jail and he knew he could finally let her into his mind. He would not be imprisoning her along with him.

"Karen," he said. "Jesus . . . I'm so sorry."

"Christopher," she said, "honey, we don't have much time. The police will let you stay here with me. I will bathe you here. I will heal your wounds. Just talk to me now. I'm so confused about what is happening."

"I am, too, Karen . . . what do you know about what is going on? Who are these people?" Gloomy asked, and he cried as the woman he loved but had been afraid to think about began to speak.

"We know the Ghost Movement has been monitoring you throughout your imprisonment. We know they tapped into your file and knew you were being considered for parole as long as you gave a full statement. We know the Iranians have been trying to have you killed."

Gloomy raised his hand to his eyes. He rubbed them and the numbness began dripping away from his body. His chest was burning, but he was able to prop himself up against the chair he was sitting in. It hurt a great deal to start speaking, but as he did he felt a lightness in his chest. He felt something in his body rising up and floating out of him toward the woman smiling there.

"We don't have much time, honey, just tell me what you remember."

Gloomy started softly. "Ishmael had been getting more and more angry as the months passed. He was angry at the president and he was reading more radical literature. He was busy installing sheetrock at the bar. He was making a good living, but it never seemed to be enough for him. He always talked about what he had given away. He said he had made sacrifices for his beliefs, but he didn't seem happy about it. I kept going to prayer meetings, and I had been thinking about not going anymore.

"Then, that day when the boat burned NoNo wasn't around. She had spent the night at a friend's house, and hadn't come home yet. I wasn't worried. I was about to head up the road to meet her when Ish pulled up to the house and asked me to go out in the skiff with him. I told him I couldn't, but he insisted. He said the men on the boat had done something to Nix. She was safe but she needed me to do something. I didn't know what he meant, but I knew something was wrong—seriously wrong. I was worried he was going to get involved with something crazy—so I followed him.

"He was tense, and I don't know, he seemed angry. We drove to his skiff and then went out into the channel where this beautiful boat was anchored. Ishmael said he had something he wanted me to do. He said it was a test of faith.

"We got up on the boat and walked into the main cabin below. It was a seagoing tug style, but a yacht. I remember I considered taking my boots off before I walked in."

Outside, a man ran by the house and yelled a string of numbers into his headset, but Gloomy was focused on his story, on his wife's face as she leaned in close to him, listening.

"Back behind the chart table was a counter and bottles. I remember thinking I had never seen a bar like this on any kind of boat. Then a tall Native man stopped and looked down, and I saw the body of another man."

"A Middle Eastern man?" asked his wife—was it his wife? "A Middle Eastern man?" she asked Gloomy again.

"Maybe, I can't be sure," Gloomy said. "I didn't recognize him. He was shot through the head, and there was blood smeared all down the side of the wall and the bar. I couldn't believe it. There was a bucket and some water the color of beet juice. Ishmael must have tried to clean up the mess. But there was blood everywhere: on the leather chairs, on the thick green carpet . . . nothing was going to get that blood off."

Gloomy paused. He was breathing hard, almost gulping for air. "Then Itchy told me that he wanted me to destroy the boat. I started to walk out the door, telling him he was crazier than all get-out, and I was going to the police. Then he asked me again, and this time he told me about what had happened to my mom. He told me that the terrorists had taken her and buried her in the tideflat. We had to do what they said. I said we had found the warhead that had separated from the Korean missile and we were going to turn it over to the authorities. He asked me about the warhead and where it was, and I said I had just come from there. Then Itchy just stared at me like he was thinking. He said we had to hurry or Nix was going to drown. There was no time. No time left. Look at the fricking time. That's what I remember most. He was panicked, I remember his crying. 'I killed a man, Gloom, I shot him trying to get him to let your mom go, I tried everything . . . we have no time left.' That's when NoNo got on the boat. She had taken her own skiff and followed us out. She knew about Ishmael's plan to turn the warhead over to someone other than the government, and she wanted to talk him out of it."

The noise of men yelling was growing louder, so the beautiful woman had to raise her voice to be heard. "Before we get to that, Gloomy, why did Itchy choose you? Why didn't he do it himself?"

"I don't know . . . I swear I don't know. The only thing is I had used dynamite before. Itchy had stolen some plastic explosive from the Forest Service bridge job. It was a river enhancement project. He stole two cases, while unloading them. He said it was for the cause. But he didn't know exactly how to blow it up. I had used it before when we were building logging roads."

Gloomy looked up at the black birds in the black ceiling. They were still trailing strands of shimmering pollen from the tips of their wings.

"Why'd you help him cache the explosives?" the woman asked.

Gloomy stared up again and this time the dark birds were gone. His head was clearing and he suspected that whatever painkiller he had been on was wearing off. His chest now felt like a bonnet of flame.

"Haven't you ever wanted to blow something up?"

The woman shook her head both up and down and side to side, not knowing how to answer.

Gloomy was sure he could smell fire. Boots pounded on metal grates. He heard a creaking and a whining. The floor shook. Through the window to his left he could see lights ricocheting around the sky.

"My Lord, it was a beautiful boat. Ish said we had to destroy the boat and go get my mom. Ish said he wanted out. Or at least he was confused. He was mad. They messed with my mom. They had their bomb. They cut him out. They didn't need him. He wanted out of the deal. He was going to sink the boat. 'Fuck them. Fuck the professor,' he told me. You know, there was a piano in the main saloon? There were old paintings of lighthouses and pictures of celebrities in silver frames on the walls. Someone had uprooted a potted plant, and I found the dirt all over the nice green carpet. NoNo looked around for a broom, but then she saw the body, and she started screaming at me. I was already down in the engine room wiring up the detonators. I was going to wire the explosives to the bilge pump switch and open up a valve to let water slowly into the bilge. Once the water was high enough, the pump switch would kick in and the boat would blow, hopefully after we were a safe distance away. But really, I didn't know if it would work.

"NoNo kept screaming after she saw the body. She said she was going to the police. The police could make Wild Horses tell where they had put Nix. He was there and he had a gun, but he was quiet. He seemed stunned or drunk or something. Like he couldn't handle the chaos.

"NoNo came down to the engine room and started pulling on my sleeve, which was scary because I was wiring up a bomb, you know. I told her to quit it, and when I looked up there was Itchy standing behind her. I reached over and unhooked the detonator from the pump switch, and Itchy took a gun out of his pocket. It was a big shiny pistol with a long barrel. It was Clive's .44 that he carried sometimes for bear protection when he didn't carry a rifle. I don't know, I took it away from him. I don't know how. I just walked over and took it out of his hand. I don't think he really wanted to shoot me so close to the explosives. It was a big-caliber gun.

"Then he pulled NoNo around in front of him. This engine room was big, you know, it was a fancy tugboat, but with the three of us, it was getting cramped. I had the wires in one hand and the big wheel gun in the other. NoNo started laughing kind of hysterical, and she said something like, 'Let's go home and get something to eat.' She was laughing like that, trying to make a joke and ease things up. But Ishmael took a piece of wire—no . . . it wasn't wire; it was a belt . . . like a fan belt or an alternator belt—and wrapped it around her throat. He pulled it so tight NoNo's face turned red and then dark blue. She wasn't making any noise. I don't know what I was thinking. All he said was that I had to sink the boat. I don't know what he was thinking. I just shot at him. I wasn't thinking . . . I was angry and—"

Gloomy heard the cracking of small-arms fire. He could make out the voices of men screaming.

He sat up and tried to reach out and grab his interrogator's coat but he could not reach her. "I shot my own sister. I killed her. I didn't want to testify at trial. I'm guilty."

The lovely woman smiled but backed away.

"Itchy ran up on deck. I just stayed there. I held her in my arms. I tried to reach in and take the bullet out with my hands. I slapped her and gave her mouth-to-mouth. I don't know, I just went crazy, I guess. Then Itchy started pouring gas down the companionway. I stayed there a while and then I left her. I went up on deck and Wild Horses had taken another skiff and was halfway back to the dock. His name was on the lease for the boat. He had arrived on the boat. He was seen around town with the skipper and with Ish. That was all they needed for his arrest. The inside of the *Moondancer* was covered with gas. Itchy must have poured at least ten gallons of skiff fuel all over the yacht. I couldn't figure out what to do. I just sat there, leaning against the rail near where I had tied my skiff. It was a sunny day with a few clouds and not much wind. There were skiffs coming and going, you know. Helicopters in the air, but nobody was paying attention to us. I don't know for sure how Itchy set the spark, but in a couple of seconds I saw a little flare back on the stern just before the concussion and the thump. The whole boat filled with flames and then died down for a moment.

"By that time I was in the skiff, black smoke had risen up like a mushroom cloud. I took off. I saw the people on the fishing boat coming to help. I waved at them and told them I was going to get help. I don't know what happened with the explosion. One of the experts later told my lawyer that the fire burned some of the wiring on the panel near the pump switches and a stray charge must have popped off the cap and the whole thing blew. As far as I knew the warhead . . . the bomb was on board because the divers found it with the wreckage of the boat. I know I was worried when the boat blew that it was going to ignite the device and I remember watching it, thinking that this could be the end of everything.

"When I got to the ramp, someone pointed to the burning boat and asked if I hadn't just come from there. I told her I was going to get some help. I ran up into the woods and lay down. I didn't know what to do. I tried to make it home. The authorities had my skiff, of course, and they arrested me that night when I tried to get back to make sure Mom had been released."

Someone grabbed Gloomy then, and he heard someone scream. He reached for her. Was it his wife? Was it her? His chest hurt and he had a coughing fit. The next thing he remembered he was back inside the van with Rocket and Norma, inside a cardboard box. Prison personnel were running up and down the boardwalk, and the night was electric with violence. Gloomy braced his back against the side of the van and kicked through the box against the van's door. Somehow the door opened, then tires squealed, and hands grabbed for him. Gloomy rolled twice on the pavement, kicked free of the torn box, and took off running.

Rocket ran to catch up with him, grabbed him by the coat, and pulled him close to his own face. Rocket spoke clearly and urgently. Gone was the dumb sidekick countenance, gone was the fool's errand, this was the voice of some kind of professional. Gloomy knew the tone from being a convict for seven years.

"Listen, you are about to have your tag lifted. You understand what that means? You are going to be killed. Either by us, or by them. I'm done dicking around. Tell me where that second fucking warhead is." Rocket stared into Gloomy's eyes.

And the poor confused convict was only able to mumble, "I don't know where the other rocket is. I swear to God."

Chapter Seven

Ishmael Muhammad had been born Roberto Ortiz. His father had been born in Arizona and was an Acoma Pueblo Hopi man, he had served in the army in the First Gulf War and married a Lakota woman from Montana. Itchy's memories from childhood were centered in Montana. Dreams often involved the smell of wood smoke in a musty trailer house.

Ishmael thought back to one of his most vivid memories. He was buried deep under a warm quilt, and he could hear his father building a fire in the stove. He knew he had a few minutes before he had to rise. The sun was not up yet. He had no idea why his father was up. Soon he smelled ham cooking.

"Hey," his father said flatly, then he whistled a little bird call. "Horses got out . . . get up, okay?"

"Yes," Ishmael said, as he dug his feet deeper into his bed.

"You finish making us breakfast," his father said. "I'm going to go catch up Little Molly, put her in the truck. You okay to ride your rigging?"

"Yes," he said, and he wiped his eyes and threw back his old flannel quilt, yawning, stretching in the dark. He had an old rodeo bareback rig with a couple of old cavalry stirrups strung on latigo leather from the O-rings and a padded leather banana bicycle seat sewn onto the handle, which allowed a small rider to carry the rig a long way on foot and then use it as a saddle after catching a horse in the field.

Ishmael shivered into some dungarees and a T-shirt. His socks had holes in the heels, and he hoped he wasn't going to have to hike too far. He pulled on his boots and his worn felt hat as he fried some eggs in the ham fat and toasted some bread. His papa came in, and they ate quickly. Little Molly stomped in the back of their old truck and pissed enough to send a yellow stream out the tailgate. Ishmael remembered that his papa didn't finish his coffee but threw the last of it out onto the dust by the truck as he got in and set his mug by the transmission hump. Ishmael had it full to warm his hands around. His rigging didn't have a place to tie a jacket, so he didn't bring a slicker and just wore his jean jacket over his T-shirt.

It was fifteen miles up the river road to where the fence was down in a muddy spot near a sand spit. Papa had his gloves, a fencing tool, a wire stretcher, and a coffee can full of staples. They decided to fix the fence first before finding the horses. Pop crossed the river and told Ish to try to track the horses on foot and see if he could figure out which direction they went. There were about fifteen head—horses that his father was breaking for a couple of the local ranchers and one or two for some local dude families. Ishmael asked if he could unload Little Molly and ride her around, and Pop said that would be all right as long as he didn't mess around with the length of his stir-rups, because fixing the fence wouldn't take long and he didn't want to waste time dinking around.

Little Molly was green broke and restless. She crow

kicked and acted a little snorty when Ishmael climbed on, but she settled down when he gave her head a bit. He took her down to the riverbank and she fell right onto the tracks of the other horses near where the fence was down. It looked like all fifteen head had stomped the fence down, then crossed the river and gone up the hill. Ishmael scanned the area. There was an old logging road that crisscrossed the broad hillside, and there was good grass up there, most of it unfenced. Rich people had second homes with fancy little ranch houses up on the flats. There would be hell to pay if the horses got into some city man's vegetable garden or took a piss near their pool. Ish started up the road and saw scattered horse shit and tracks that showed they had been moving at an easy trot, but he couldn't see any of the creatures themselves.

He got off Little Molly and touched the shit. It was cool. He walked her back across the road and waited for his pop. When he was done stretching wire and stapling it to fence posts and onto stout trees, Pop tightened up the cinch, swung up in the saddle, then lifted Ishmael up behind him, and they went up the hill.

Sunflowers were just in bloom and as the sun rose in the sky, the yellow flowers lifted their heads toward it. Deer waded and occasionally bounded through the grass and rattled winter's dead flower stalks. White-tailed bucks flicked their rumps and disappeared. Coyotes came up the hill and slunk away from the sunlight and into the ponderosa pine trees. One peregrine falcon carved a half circle in the air and dropped down on a mouse in the grass. Ishmael was twelve now, his stomach was full, and he had his rigging and a light horse blanket over his shoulder. He loved riding close to his father and secretly hoped he could ride behind him all day, not knowing what horse he would be able to catch up high in this field. If he ended up only being able to catch one of the more rank, unbroken colts, it would be a hard ride back to the truck.

They passed a couple of the second homes along the road. A little white girl came running out and told them that the horses had come by a couple of hours ago and had kept going straight up the hill. Pop had nodded and kept riding along. The little white girl yelled out after, "Was that little one a pony?" with some breathless excitement in her voice, and Pop just said "No" and kept on riding.

Halfway up the hill they stopped and gave Little Molly some wind. She was black with sweat. Pop stepped off on the uphill side and loosened her cinch. Ishmael stayed hanging on to the saddle strings.

"Up on top there is a nice grassy ledge with a big old dead pine tree on it. Steep all around, they must be there. Not much feed farther up and hard as hell to get there."

"You think I can catch a good horse to ride down this steep hill?"

He looked at the boy. He knew he was nervous, and he knew he had good reason to be. "Yes, we will make sure you get a good horse. A green broke horse would buck you off for sure." He smiled warmly at his son. "They would buck me off, too, just because they could." Pop got back on Little Molly and they continued up the hill.

In a half hour they were to the shelf. Half the horses were down in a little swale at the north end and the rest were standing in the shade near the big dead pine tree. Broken limbs were scattered on the ground, the fat trunk of the ponderosa pine was thick with pitch, and the sharp ends of broken limbs ringed the trunk like spikes. The older horses dosed by the tree with their tails swishing around their haunches and their rubbery lips snuffling at flies on their legs.

Pop said, "Ease up around there and catch that black with the white star and the three stockings. He's a good one for you to ride. Put your rig on him. I'm going to go down there and slowly push those others back up this way. Easy . . . slow and easy. Okay?"

"Yes," the boy said, and his father nudged the horse and walked slowly down toward the swale some five hundred yards away. Ishmael took off his hat and put some pebbles in it. He still had his blanket and his lightweight rigging tied across his shoulders like a bandolier. "Hello, son," he called out toward the horses near the tree. "Hey, kid . . . got some grain for you . . ." He shook his old felt hat up and down, letting the pebbles inside thump around, and the horses lifted their heads. The black one took one step forward and Ishmael walked toward him. He peeled his bridle free and looped it over his arm. The black came nosing over closer and soon he put his nose in Ishmael's hat. Ish got the reins around his neck and soon the bridle was on. Ishmael cleaned off the black's back as best he could and then put on the blanket and tied down his own rigging. It looked a bit like a makeshift English-style saddle, though Ishmael had never ridden such a thing. He was tightening the latigo and pulling the cinch tight when he heard a commotion coming from the direction of the swale.

Up out of sight, Little Molly was running and snorting in front of the group of five or so horses. The other horses were not running after her but were watching, and one or two were twitching and shaking their heads. Ishmael couldn't put everything in focus at first. Little Molly kept ducking her head, and he was about a hundred yards away. She rubbed her headset and bridle against her leg. She snorted and bucked. Pop was hanging on and using his quirt to whip her to come ahead. Ishmael saw that she had something on her foot, something gray and round, odd-looking, like a ball or a river stone. She grunted, farted, and bucked. Pop quirted her to get her to line out and he tried to pull her head up to keep her from bucking. Then Pop started slapping himself.

"Hornets!" he yelled, and Ishmael could see them all around Little Molly. The thing on her hoof had been a piece of a hornets' nest.

Then she was on the run, a full gallop. The nest shattered, but still a haze of hornets followed and clung to the mare. Ishmael thought that once she was out of the hornets Pop could get her calmed down, but she was wild-eyed and frantic. Little Molly was running straight toward the other horses standing under the tree. Ishmael couldn't understand what he saw next. Little Molly was slowing down but still at a run. She was close to the tree and her front foot hit a dried-out four-foot limb: straight with a ragged tip. It flipped up, then one end lodged in the ground and the other went right through her chest. It stopped her immediately, and Pop flew right over her head and into the tree.

Ishmael kept his eyes on Little Molly. He thought he heard running water as if a faucet had been turned on. Little Molly's legs were shaking. The stub had gone through her lung and into her heart. Blood was pouring out of her onto the ground. Her eyes were wild and open. She blew hot breath through her nose like a bellows. He grabbed her reins. He patted her neck, said her name. He loosened her cinch as she went down on her front legs, then slipped the saddle off her as she lay down on the soggy wet ground and died.

"Pop. Pop," Ishmael said as he looked around, and for the first time he noticed that his father was impaled on the trunk of the tree, eyes closed, chest still, and forever dead.

FOR YEARS ISHMAEL Muhammad lived in a pie-shaped concrete cell with a window that faced the relentless sea that was far above his head. The electronically enhanced sound of the surf was piped into his cell upon the advice of the prison psychologist. Ishmael had not been fit for debriefing; for the seven years of his stay, he had not spoken to anyone. He prayed. He was allowed to do the ritual washing of his body, and most unusually he had carved a figure into the concrete wall of his cell.

The figure was a dead lion in repose, great muscles relaxed with a look of anguish on its face. A broken spear protruded from under its shoulder blade. When security experts tried to question him about this image and why he had spent years of hand-wrecking work chipping away at the wall with his pens and spoons, Ishmael had remained silent.

Ishmael had read the Quran as a child. His father had taken him to the mosque and had taught him the blessings of the Prophet. Ishmael was not militant until he started encountering the stupidity of American intolerance in the larger world. He started reading the texts of Ali Wild Horses and even some of the right-wing ideologues. He read the twentieth-century philosophers. Like a lot of young men, he spent time in questionable chat rooms. He hated the new young Nazis mostly for their blind stupidity and their assumptions about "whiteness." He and Gloomy used to discuss it for hours and hours around a campfire on the knob. "I can't believe they celebrate . . . essentially

. . . nothingness. I mean, really. I mean I can get behind celebrating Scottishness, or Swedishness, or even Germanness . . . but hell, whiteness? Just shows no imagination what-so-ever."

Ishmael loved his cousin. He believed that the Prophet respected Jesus as a teacher and often spoke with Gloomy about the points of intersection and divergence between Islam, Judaism, and Christianity. Gloomy simply appreciated the clarity of direction that the Quran gave him. He appreciated the spiritual overlay that he saw, the interpretation that Wild Horses had brought to the Northern Plains Indians and the act of unification and the search for universal, spiritual justice that had been denied his people. This was where, in the long evenings, Gloomy would want to talk about love and Ish would get grumpy. But there, around an actual fire face-to-face with each other, they conceded that the genocides of the past and present could not drive a wedge between them. They would allow the word of God to unite them on the earth, there on the hard rock surrounded by the goats.

Ishmael used to talk to Gloomy about how he thought Christianity had become too mushy and flawed by love. He told him about how Nietzsche had taken his girlfriend to a beautiful monument near Lucerne and twice asked her to marry him when she had already said no. "So, he took her to this beautiful monument honoring the Swiss Guards. It's of a dead lion with its head on a Christian shield. He asks her to marry him again. I guess she was an early feminist bohemian because she says she will never give her life over to the authority of a man. So, Nietzsche goes up into a guesthouse in the mountains and writes *Thus Spoke Zarathustra* and a whole bunch of other shit about an 'Übermensch,' a 'Superman,' and the will to power, and his crazy sister waits until he dies and puts it together as a little Nazi primer and personally gives it to Hitler himself."

The fire pops on the cliffs and sparks zigzag up into the star-dazzled sky above the inlet, where whales are blowing and nature writers are curled in their sleeping bags, going crazy with dreams of beauty, and Ishmael says to Gloomy, "Now, don't you think if Jesus were really the Lord he would have commanded that wild little bohemian woman to at least have sex with Nietzsche and spare us all the horror of the fucking Nazis? Could He have given that gloomy, future syphilitic bastard some love in his life and spared us the Holocaust? Come on, Gloomy?"

Gloomy shook his head and admitted it was a problem, though he laughed, and his cousin didn't shake his faith a bit. But Ishmael continued to read and finally began to correspond with Ali Wild Horses.

THE DAY THEY were arrested, Ishmael had been cleared to anchor the *Moondancer* in the outer harbor. The Jamaican skipper had gone ashore in a skiff from town. The winch lowered the anchoring gear toward the muddy bottom. Ishmael watched his color depth sounder and the digital readout on the anchor winch. He eased the engine into reverse and pulled the scope of the chain across the bottom until the anchor slid and dug down into the bottom. He let the engine strain against the anchor for a few moments to seed it into the bottom and then he put her in neutral and turned the engine off.

He loved that first moment of silence when coming to anchor, the silence eased up out of the water and all around the boat. He could hear possibility in it. He leaned back in the captain's chair and switched off all the radios and monitors. Later he was certain all hell would break loose, but for this sweet moment there were no alarms.

The town was alive with military boats, men in uniforms giving orders. Gloomy had already found a warhead he wanted to turn in to the authorities. He had talked with his cousin Ishmael about it and Ishmael had other plans for it.

The *Moondancer* flew a Canadian flag and had a Jamaican skipper, but the skipper did not seem to want to know anything about the goings-on in Cold Storage. The skipper was happy to stay drunk at the Love Nest. Ish came aboard the yacht by invitation of the skipper, walked into the cabin, and saw the raven hair of Ali Wild Horses, a man whose teachings he knew well. The professor and pious man stood up and shook Ishmael's hand and said solemnly, "My brother, you have a gift for me?" Ishmael had admired the professor for years, but when the killing started, when Ish saw the dark blood on the floor of the yacht, as he had seen on that day Little Molly had driven the stick up into her chest and thrown Pop off her back . . . after he saw that blood, he wanted nothing more to do with abstract ideas and betrayal. He wanted his family.

BUT NOW ON this dark night in Cold Storage, the confused Gloomy was running away from the two cops on foot. He rolled down a muddy bank through a thick tangle of alder trees. Above him, the slick leaves were puzzle pieces of flashing red and blue. He flopped down and lay on muddy leaves, looking up, and tried to stop breathing. The police car stopped and Gloomy could hear baritone voices as the big white man and a police officer chatted back and forth in a cautious routine. He could not make out the words, but Gloomy thought for sure there was not an arrest being made. The voices didn't have the sharp edge of commands and denial. From a distance it sounded like a relatively friendly shakedown.

The lights stopped flashing and the van pulled away. The police car stayed parked. This beach had the shallow hush-hush of small waves on a flat-cobbled beach. Gloomy did not move. He could see the red light of a channel marker off in the distance. There was a white light on the end of a dock. A heron squawked in a prehistoric scraping sound, and Gloomy could just hear the wing beats as it passed in front of the dock light.

Boots crunched on the gravel above him and two flash-light beams slashed around in the trees. He lay still. The beams broke apart in the limbs, searing the green leaves white. Two more footsteps came toward him and then he heard a sliding and spilling of small rocks.

"Ah, Christ," a man's voice called out. "Come on, Paul. There's nothing down there. Too damn steep to go crawl-ing around anyway. We'll send Eddy out here if we need to. Let's get back on post."

The beams of light lurched around and disappeared. Gloomy waited for the second car door to slam before he shook off the stones the cops had sloughed down on top of him. He stood up slowly and used the trees as walk-ing sticks to help himself down the hill. He came to an overgrown roadbed where dozens of tires were piled up against a fallen-in Quonset hut. Here there were salmon-berry bushes lacing through the trunks of the larger alders and beyond was the green house.

By the time he stood at the door, his clothes were muddy, and his hands and face were scratched from the berry bushes. He had tiny wet leaves matted in his gray hair and tucked down inside his shirt. He was cold and perhaps that was why his hands shook uncontrollably as he knocked on the door.

A large dog barked and he heard the scramble of long claws skittering across a hardwood floor. The knob turned, then paused, and a woman's voice shouted back into the room.

"Get down now. Go back." Then the door opened.

It was the beautiful dark-haired woman he had seen from the road. Her eyes arched wide and she stepped back, startled. He didn't think he had ever seen her before, but he knew her somehow. She grasped the collar of the large black lab straining and wiggling by her hip. Gloomy took one step toward her, standing directly under the porch light. She took a step back.

"Gloomy?" the woman asked.

"Yes, I am," Gloomy said, and then waited. Up the lane a dog was barking and a car rolled down the gravel away from where they were standing. The woman let go of the dog's collar and it lurched into Gloomy, sniffing and wiggling.

"You can't come in here. I'm sorry."

Gloomy pushed the dog down and it ran off behind him. "Who are you?" Gloomy asked. He felt as if ice were unclogging in his heart.

"You know who I am," she said, her voice rising and color coming to her cheeks. The woman's voice was kind. "You know who I am because you came straight to this house. You know who I am. I almost went to jail for you."

Gloomy closed his eyes.

AFTER SHE REACHED puberty, all Karen wanted to do was ride her chestnut mare. She rode the hills surrounding Winthrop, Washington. She had been a child when the highway had opened and tourists had started their months-long caravans through town. But there had always been places to ride even as the years wore on and camper vans started appearing at the trailheads and expensively clad recreational runners made it farther out into the hills than she had seen before.

When she was sixteen, she got a job riding along the irrigation ditch. She carried a short-handled shovel in a rifle scabbard on her saddle and would throw branches out of the waterways and clean the fish wheels when they were clogged. Karen saw snakes curled in the cool shadows in summertime and often would startle mule deer in the early mornings in the fall.

One summer she lived back up in the Cascades, riding herd on some cattle owned by a man named Lasamis, whom she never met but whose office would send her the single fifteen-hundred-dollar check she would get for the entire summer's work. The pay was bad, but she didn't care. Her girlfriends worked in town at the restaurant, and they would go swimming together in the lake on hot afternoons and talk about boys. Sometimes they would lie on the sun-warmed boards of a floating dock, nose to nose with boys from school, who would stay in the water hanging onto the side, splashing and watching the pebbling bumps rise on their skin when they began to get chilly.

But Karen didn't miss the days at the lake. She would ride all day and slowly move the cows around to better grass, pack the salt blocks when she had to, and call her dog back when he ran a bull too far down a hill. Her camp was set back from the lake. It was an old canvas tent dug down into the dirt, where she kept her clothes and her tack. She slept with her saddle to keep the porcupines from chewing on the sweat-soaked leather. At the end of the day she would feed pellets to the wrangling horse she kept in camp, and she would turn out the old gelding and the three mules so they could feed on the grass all night. The gelding had a bell on his neck and hobbled on his front legs, so the sound of the bell would never be far from her tent. She lay under the canvas tent and listened to her keeper horse eat the pellets. The mare nuzzled into the tin pan of feed with leathery lips, then chewed and rumbled the food all the way to her stomach. Karen found the sound of the eating horse and the distant tinkling bell the most reassuring sounds imaginable. Here she was sleeping on hard ground, being exploited for her labor, and not making enough to even cover half a semester at junior college, yet she felt herself to be the happiest person on earth.

Years later she would remember those times as a sort of "ground zero" of happiness. Nothing would ever compare—only perhaps the birth of her daughter, but that was a kind of happiness that dug in and had a faint hint of dread to it. Back on the hard ground of the Cascades, there had not been the slightest cloud on the horizon, and she felt vaguely sad remembering everything about that summer as she grew older.

She had met Gloomy McCahon one day as she was trucking horses off the mountain and back to town. She was driving down from Billy Goat Corrals and had kicked the old Ford truck out of gear as she coasted down across a creek drainage. When the truck slowed going up the short pitch of hill on the other side, she missed her gear on the downshift and the truck lurched wildly, throwing her horses and mules back, breaking the tailgate and scattering her gear and one of the mules onto the road. She had stopped the truck and run around to the back to see the mule flailing wildly against the halter rope, rolling on its back and trying to kick free of the tarps and ropes he was tangled in. She cut things loose and caught the mule, then ran her hands down his legs, making sure the little mouse-colored creature was uninjured.

It was just then that the crummy from the logging company came around the corner and stopped. The men piled out stiffly and started to help her pick up the mess. They were mostly blustery and solicitous over her frailty, all except Gloomy, who sat on a stump and ate a sandwich and laughed until he almost wet his pants.

"Well, I'm glad someone thinks this is funny," Karen had said, pulling her black hair back tighter into her rubber band, the scarlet flaring in her cheeks.

"I was just thinking it must have been a hell of a shock for that old mule."

"And you find that funny?"

"Welllll," Gloomy had drawled, "I just imagine he wished you had let him drive." He laughed and Karen did, too, despite still being mad at him.

Later they went to school in Wenatchee and shared a little house near an apple shed. Karen was trying to get all of her science credits so she could get into a pre-vet program at Washington State. Gloomy took some courses in English and history at night, but then he got work and supported them both by driving a rubber-tired skidder and a small Cat for a road-building crew.

They talked about the home they would buy someday. Gloomy wanted a big place with more affordable land, someplace down in the basin maybe near Malaga, where there was nothing much to see but grass and fawn-brown hills. The land was cheap there because the millionaires were far away in the more beautiful country. Karen had to be in the mountains and her first choice was back in the upper Methow. Land prices were steep there with all the speculation about a big ski hill going in, but it didn't matter to her. She was going to be a veterinarian and would be making lots and lots of money.

Evenings Gloomy would lie on the bed and read a book while he wore his clean long-handled underwear. He loved to turn the oil heater up so he could lie out on top of the covers. For a time, he was reading *The Great Gatsby* when Karen came home from school. Summer or winter she wore her tight blue jeans and tooled leather belt with the silver buckle and tip. He loved to watch her wiggle out of her pants halfway, then sit down and kick out of her boots. She would throw her books on the bed and jump on him, kissing him as he pretended to be reading. They would eat in bed those winters, the bedroom being the only warm room in the house. They would make sandwiches and drink tomato soup from white restaurant mugs. They would read and make love and linger with each other after. Sometimes she would sit astride him, rocking gently back and forth for long minutes with her eyes closed. Then she would roll off, turn on the small light next to her, and begin reading her physiology book.

She flunked chemistry twice and barely made it through her second anatomy class, so it wasn't much of a surprise to her when she got a slip from the counseling office to schedule a meeting. They gave her materials on veterinary assistance careers and other jobs in animal husbandry, but to Karen, all of it sounded vaguely like being a receptionist or a candy striper. She tried to tell herself it didn't really matter because Gloomy was going to make some good money cutting timber down in Oregon on the job his father had arranged for him.

Gloomy left for Oregon and disappeared for ten weeks. They hadn't broken off their relationship, but Gloomy didn't like to write. He had promised to come back with thirty thousand dollars for a down payment on some land. When Karen heard about his injury from a girlfriend who knew some of the boys on his crew, she went to Seattle and found him in an ugly basement. Gloomy was drunk and filthy. He could hardly speak to her and when he did it was in a groggy, self-pitying voice that made her want to cover her ears. She did a load of laundry and bought some microwave dinners, some steaks, and three cases of apple juice in aluminum cans. She wrote a note to him while he slept, then got back in her truck and drove over Snoqualmie Pass before it got dark.

Karen spent the next few months on a ranch in the upper Methow that was owned by a development company from San Jose, California. The manager liked her and rented her an old ranch house at the box end of the valley. From her front door she could look straight up the canyon walls. The air was so clear on most summer mornings it almost strained her eyes. She broke horses for a dude outfit down the valley and led day rides in the summer. She was good with the horses and the guests and made a decent living in tips.

She dated a couple of the wranglers in the valley and even hooked up with some of the ski racers who had settled there, betting on the explosion of land values when the new ski area went in.

One summer morning she was working with a two-year-old filly in the round corral when three expensive four-wheel-drive vehicles drove into her yard. The manager didn't talk to her or knock on her door. He walked onto the porch of her house with a thick book of blueprints and pointed up the ridge for the older men in the stiff new jeans. They all had perfect haircuts and tans. They wore expensive sunglasses with colorful bands holding them onto their faces. The men walked with the manager while the women stayed put in the vehicles with the windows up and the engines running.

Karen flicked the filly at the hocks with the buggy whip and decided she had to move. There was a place up the Rendezvous for sale with a small cabin and enough pasture to raise hay and keep her own stock. They were asking three hundred thousand dollars, but she knew she could get it for less if she had enough cash.

There was a man named Carl who lived down the valley who said he could help her. Carl had once fished in Alaska. He said he had been a film producer and that he had "several properties under option." Carl said he could give her a job that would pay seventy thousand dollars if she was willing to accept all the risk. Karen had a friend who was back from college watch her stock while she made the final arrangements with Carl.

All she had to do was pick up a camper van in the parking lot at Disneyland and drive it up to Vancouver, British Columbia. She would get five thousand dollars when she got on the plane. There would be ten thousand in the camper for her, and she would get twenty-five thousand dollars upon delivery and the rest after one year when everything was settled and clear. Karen agreed. She did not ask questions. She wanted to take her dog with her but thought better of it at the last minute and stopped the truck at the head of her road and told him to run home. The cow dog looked confused, but obeyed when she slapped the flat of her hand against the door panel. She reached under the seat of her truck and took out the thirty-eight special. She slipped it into the duffel bag she intended to check through.

She had never been to Disneyland and she was too anxious to enjoy it much. The castle seemed too small and the streets so clean she wondered where all the garbage had gone. Goofy gave her a big kiss, and she screamed loudly as she jetted down the track of the Matterhorn. But she never lost that icy edge in her blood even in the warm, smog-soaked air of Los Angeles, where the sky was a tangle of wires and signs and everything smelled like gasoline carried on the sea breeze.

At four thirty, she went to the parking lot and the camper was where it was supposed to be. The key was on top of the propane tank in the rear compartment. Her money was under the seat. She started the engine and pulled into the unimaginably long line of cars full of over-tired children.

She drove at the speed limit and would wave at police cars as they passed her. She slept in rest stops for no more than two hours at a time. Up near Mount Shasta she checked into a motel and took a shower. That night she bought a bottle of bourbon, drank most of it, and sat on the toilet with the barrel of the gun in her mouth. The next day she broke the hammer off the gun by hitting it with a tire iron and then threw the cylinder in a trash can and the rest of the gun off a bridge. She watched as it fell, catching the light briefly as it spun, finally landing in a fast-moving river with only the slightest splash.

She wasn't that surprised when, at the border, the customs officials told her to drive the camper over to the covered shed. The dogs crawled all over the camper and alerted only on the inside near the chemical toilet. They found two kilos of cocaine in the toilet's holding tank and later found the other eight kilos up behind the paneling. The bags were long and thin, taped to the flimsy aluminum sheeting under the insulation.

Karen asked for a lawyer, but they didn't give her one. The field officer cut her a deal right there: she could give Carl up, do a wired buy, and then go her own way. They believed she was a "blind donkey," the current term the feds had cribbed from the Zen Buddhists. She didn't have a gun. She didn't have any money. She was clean and healthy, and she was a white woman. She was too dumb to be a pro. But they were willing to train her to be a recruit in the drug war. If she insisted on asking for a lawyer, the deal would be off. This was a one-time-only deal: no lawyers, plus a get-out-of-jail-free card, and she took it.

Karen rolled Carl and together they rolled Carl's contact—a man who lived at a remote fishing lodge in Alaska who had his own secure satellite phone system, which he used in running a legitimate trucking business as well as the North American dispatching service for a Mexican drug cartel.

When the final bust went down, the drug cops celebrated with champagne and beefsteaks at a club near the Anchorage office. They had dope and money on the table. They were happy. Carl was in jail for a short stretch and Karen was waitressing back in Winthrop. She didn't tell them about a small suitcase of money she buried outside a rest stop near Grants Pass, Oregon. After all was said and done and the cops had cleaned up after their party and the press had moved on to other stories, she went back to Grants Pass and dug up the suitcase. She drove the last ten hours without sleep, drinking coffee from fast-food franchises. She stopped at the basement where Gloomy was laid up, put the fifteen thousand dollars in his boots, and

drove on without waking him up because she was still nervous about the possibility of being followed by the cops.
As long as she wasn't in possession of the money or near
it she felt better. She longed to be with Gloomy but she
didn't dare infect him with her crime. She felt the warmth
of a fast-food cup of coffee between her legs as she drove
away and laughed a little as she wiped tears from her eyes,
thinking of what he would do when he put his boots on.

The money Karen hid was used for Gloomy's medical
expenses. He needed physical therapy, which wasn't covered by workers' comp. He needed drug treatment, which
was not even arguably covered, so they were back down to
zero by the time Gloomy came into the restaurant where
she worked and ordered a steak sandwich off menu.

The place up the Rendezvous sold for two-fifty to a
software guy from Seattle. He built a thirty-thousand-
square-foot home overlooking the valley with an atrium
and an indoor swimming pool. His wife grew orchids in
the greenhouse and they donated ten thousand dollars
to the local arts group for their spring play.

Gloomy and Karen got married in the park by the river.
They didn't ask family to attend and they didn't go on a
honeymoon. They were saving their money for a fishing
boat in Alaska.

On their wedding night, Karen cried and cried in
Gloomy's arms. They were eating lobster in front of the
TV at the Riverside Motel. Karen said she felt old. She
didn't know how to explain it. This was her wedding night
and she was twenty-six years old, but she felt old and too
tired to make love. On their wedding night. Would he
ever forgive her? Gloomy turned off the TV and curled up
behind his wife, holding her until she stopped crying, and
he continued to hold her all through the night.

THERE WAS A heavy weight on the back of Gloomy's head, grinding his face into the gravel. Men were yelling and he could hear a dog barking inside the house. He opened his eyes and the red and blue lights were flashing again, this time on the gravel and on the black shoes that were scuffling around the house. From his position Gloomy could only see feet and tires. He saw a broom near the steps and the tires of a small bicycle. He pinched his eyes shut again when the officer on top of him jerked his arms behind his back and snapped cuffs down hard enough to make his hands go numb.

"You can back it off. I'm good. I'm good. Just back the bracelets off a couple of clicks," Gloomy pleaded with the unseen weight. The cuffs clicked down harder until he felt the bones in his wrist begin to separate.

"Knock that shit off, Charlie!" Gloomy heard a man's voice moving down the driveway. "I mean it now, Charlie. Back off on those things now. I mean right now!"

The pressure released and a pair of beefy hands grabbed Gloomy by the forearms and stood him up straight.

A woman in an expensive dress suit stood in front of him. She had her black hair pulled back, and her eyes were brown and sharply focused. "I'm Billie Shears. I'm an assistant district attorney, Mr. McCahon. You could have gotten hurt running around a town like this. I'm amazed someone didn't put a round in you. I know you are disoriented and confused. But we don't have time for confusion now."

The big hands steered him up the driveway toward a waiting unmarked car. In the distance Gloomy could hear a woman trying to calm the dog.

"Is she okay?" Gloomy asked.

Billie Shears was walking next to him. "Your wife back

there? Yes, Mr. McCahon, she's fine. I think she was scared when the boys rushed in on you so fast. You know how it is. They've been sitting waiting for you for a day now. They . . . well . . ." Billie Shears looked behind Gloomy at the massive officer holding Gloomy's forearms as if they were sections of garden hose. "These boys get excited."

"Sorry, Ms. Shears," the guard mumbled.

"Well, don't worry about it, Charlie. I just thought you were going to do some permanent damage, and you know how much paperwork that can be."

"Oh, brother," Charlie said under his breath.

Once they made it to the unmarked car, Billie Shears took the keys from Charlie and undid the cuffs. Charlie looked nervous and tentatively put his right hand on the butt of his pistol.

Billie Shears waved her hand dismissively. "I've got him now, Charlie. You can leave us alone. Hey, if anything goes wrong I'll let you know." She turned around and looked at Gloomy, as if he were a sick child, then spoke as if she were trying to explain a procedure she didn't really care if he understood or not. "Look, the man and woman who broke you out of prison might be well-intended Christian people, but they were paid by the Iranian government to find the missing warhead. That's okay; we don't care about that now. We don't have time to dick around with that."

Charlie turned quickly and called out for some help. Billie Shears opened the door to the backseat and Gloomy got in. Shears went around to the other side and climbed in next to him. There were four patrol cars on the narrow gravel road: one in front of the unmarked car and three behind. Officers in black uniforms that Gloomy didn't recognize were standing around, talking affably. All of them were stretching and shaking the stiffness out of their legs, obviously happy to have the surveillance duty done with.

"You know, Mr. McCahon—listen, can I call you Gloomy? You can call me Billie if you want. How about that?" She sat close to him and touched his arm. He could smell perfume. He was instantly aware of her touch. It felt warm, almost burning.

Gloomy nodded his assent. He was still looking down toward the house. "I didn't know what the fuck . . ." Gloomy said absently.

Billie Shears followed the prisoner's eyes to the back of the green house. "Yeah, yeah . . . okay. You have a wife. Her name is Karen. You have a daughter. You were just back at their house. Okay, that's fine. They actually live here in Cold Storage; they don't work for the Iranian secret police. It was those other people, Norma and Rocket, who work for the Iranian government. But I don't care about that now."

The two of them sat silently for an awkward moment.

"It's true then that you've never communicated with her, with your wife, about the warheads?"

"Yes, that's true," Gloomy whispered.

Billie Shears brushed her hand in front of her face as if she could erase the unpleasantness. "Okay, let's come back to the point," she said to Gloomy. "Do you know where Ghost is?"

Gloomy looked up at Billie Shears. "Ghost? I have no idea. Back on Olympus, I suppose."

Billie Shears was shaking her head. "No. He went missing after the explosion. There were those who thought you two went out together. I never thought so, but I had to ask."

"Ghost has gone missing?" Gloomy asked.

"I don't know. He may well still be on the island and rat-holed up somewhere looking for a little light. I'm not all that worried about Ghost. He's got bad luck, you know what I mean? Ghost is going to end up dead soon enough. He's only got a few friends that I know of and those friends are not going out on any limbs for Ghost. What I'm more interested in, Gloomy, is why you won't tell anyone about the second bomb."

Gloomy said nothing for a moment. He had been questioned enough to know not to start babbling. "I don't know anything about a second bomb."

"You do remember Ishmael Muhammad, don't you?"

Gloomy said nothing. His cousin's name atomized and surrounded Gloomy's head like flies. Gloomy could smell gasoline and felt a rumbling.

"I'm telling you I don't know anything about a second bomb." Gloomy sat up suddenly in the soft seat, nodding toward the house. He had his hand on the door handle.

Billie Shears put her hand on Gloomy's shoulder. "Think of what he said back on the boat. Think of every word he said." She had a firm hand on Gloomy's shoulder, pressing him to lean back away from the door. Gloomy was acutely aware of her touch. Aware of the smell of her, the intimacy of the leather and the dark car.

"Ask him," Gloomy said. His voice shook and now he saw banners of flame blowing out the portholes of a ship. He saw a plume of black smoke roiling up overhead. His hands sparkled with blood.

"Ah . . . yeah. Okay, we have tried that," Shears said.

"He didn't break, did he?" Gloomy finally looked at Shears.

Billie Shears reached up under the seat and pulled out a small computer. As she opened the lid, the machine instantly flashed awake. She brought up a document on a blue Department of Law background and looked it over.

"There are several groups that want to break both of you out of prison."

They sat in silence for several moments. The police lieutenant came and knocked on the window with his fingertips. Billie Shears waved him away. The upstairs lights in the green house went out. The black windowpanes looked like the empty sockets of a skull. Billie Shears picked a piece of lint off her wool suit pants with her fingertips. She settled into her seat and the leather creaked.

"Why don't you take me to that warhead, Gloomy? The people I work with believe it might explode any second."

Gloomy looked through the streaked window of the van and down the boardwalk. It was hard to get his bearings in this town, which had grown so much since he had last seen it. The warhead had been found seven years ago. He and Ishmael had talked about it. It was there in the muck in the lake. Men from the *Moondancer* had carried it from the lake and up onto the boat. What the hell were they talking about, two bombs? But just then, he looked through the dirty window and saw four men in prison uniforms marching someone between them, almost herding the figure like an animal. They had flashlights and a full complement of weapons. The most notable thing they carried were long Taser wands. The two men in front and two behind each carried enough voltage to put down a brown bear. Between them in handcuffs and foot shackles was his cousin Ishmael Muhammad.

ALI WILD HORSES, who later became the founder of the Second Ghost Dance Movement, left Boston for Saudi Arabia when he was twenty-eight. He had not booked the usual hajj package sanctioned by the Saudi government to ensure safety and comfort but had North American Native Muslims who were ready to escort him through the sea of humanity gathering in Mecca. He had prepared himself with prayer and exercise. He packed light and brought nothing with him that he could not afford to lose. He did not bring a computer with any important writings or a phone, just some cheap but good pens, cotton clothes, a blank notebook, and paperback editions of religious texts translated into English.

The flight was long, and he had used miles to fly business class, thinking he would especially appreciate it on the return trip. His plan was to curl up in the clean nest of his own seat, drinking mimosas and eating almonds from his trail mix, listening to his own hip-hop mix, and maybe watching some silly buddy-cop movie—all to ease himself back into the cruel imperialist culture of the United States. For the most part, however, he was bored on the way over. He read and reread the flight magazine and looked through sales promotions catalogs with their silly spyware gadgets for bored and decadent travelers. Feeling a bit self-conscious about being in business class on the first leg of the pilgrimage, he ordered the vegetarian dinner.

Once he arrived, there was noise, heat, sunlight, and crowds of people. The men sent to meet him gave him a head covering, which was quickly deemed not appropriate, until it was fussed over and adjusted. They bowed and exchanged traditional greetings, but everything seemed to be lost in the clatter and roar of the crowd. Even when they leaned in to give him instructions or told him of their immediate plans, he could barely understand every other word. Ali was not used to bumping into so many people—in American cities he avoided subways at rush hour for this reason—but this was not a temporary funneling of people into a tight box. This was an overflowing delta of humanity flowing to the sea, a cacophony of different languages and phalanxes of mixing colors of fabric separated by the dominant choice of white rolling in the same direction.

They boarded a bus that was so crowded, Ali Wild Horses felt as if he could not breathe, and he smelled every possible odor of human being, and what a human exuded. He closed his eyes and imagined the high desert plains of the American West. He thought back to a day when he and his father had ridden out to chase cows for an uncle. For hours, there were no trees and no human beings, as they rode past the grassland up a river valley, with only the sun tracking through a blue sky and the sound of their leather saddles and a rattling metal bit in the mouth of his father's horse. The boy rode with a braided hackamore snug around the nose and chin of the colt he was breaking in.

At about noon that day, they rode past a family having a picnic beside a lonely road: a boy and a girl, simply sitting on the grass next to their parents eating sandwiches and drinking pop. They had a black Mercedes-Benz sedan. Ali and his father passed without saying a word and without acknowledging the white people. Ali imagined they thought of them as "wild Indians" and considered their sighting as lucky as seeing a mountain lion, though they had the manners not to take their picture.

Ali Wild Horses completed the hajj and circled the cubical Kaaba in the Great Mosque, although the crowd was so dense there was no possibility he'd get close enough to touch it. The best he could do was point toward the black stone. They prayed their rakat prayers, but again they could not get close enough to the appointed spot.

They saw men in royal robes appear to get escorted by armed guards to the place of Abraham and the Zamzam well, but the Lakota men prayed wherever there was room and drank from water coolers set up around the mosque, in the same way the pilgrims had. They ran the seven circuits through the air-conditioned tunnel though in fact it was a jostling kind of race walking. They slept and prayed in a massive dormitory and spoke with families from all over the world.

It was on his hajj that Malcolm X is said to have had his genuine conversion of love toward all humanity. Wild Horses had a somewhat different conversion. Though he saw the strength and diversity of Islam, and he saw the openness of Islam: the love of the poor and the willingness to live close to the ground, the willingness to live in a dormitory, to rub up against others and subsume their individuality for a moment, Wild Horses also saw an army of the formerly colonized who were focused now and disciplined. Not the heartbroken Christianity that Nietzsche had described. These people did not follow a God who could be killed. They did not read a scripture sprinkled with metaphor, but a fully realized set of instructions given from an angel to the Prophet and delivered directly into the soul of his followers. As Wild Horses saw it, in Islam there is no subject-object duality . . . at least as far as the messenger, the message, the Prophet, and the Believer is concerned. All is sacred. These people loved God enough to lay their unimportant differences (race, and culture, even gender, some argued . . .) aside and get down in the dirt. It was here that Wild Horses saw an army, a horde protecting the peoples of the American West, the Northern Territories, and the Arctic. He saw them protecting the first people to be able to own their land, practice their lifeways, and love God.

When the Lakota men spent the night on Mount Arafat, they camped some distance away, they lay out under the stars, and they spoke of a new life for the American Indian. They spoke with Palestinians and Africans, Muslims from Pakistan and Iran; they prayed together and they sang their traditional songs. They all spoke of loving God in their own land, as the land allows, but each according to the Quran. The Lakota spoke of the Ghost Dance and the Palestinians spoke of jihad, and the misunderstanding of Sharia in the West, and they each collected stones to throw at Satan the next day.

Chapter Eight

As he was growing up, Lester Plays with His Face didn't really hate white people. Not that he knew any of them very well.

Lester had friends who blamed white people for everything: alcohol, poverty, and the lack of good hunting near their homes. Lester thought there was a good case to be made for these propositions but he got sick of all the talk. The Crows had mostly had good relations with white people. There had been six Crow scouts with Custer at Little Big Horn. Lester's grandma had known some of the old men who claimed to be on that raid. There had been a picture in her house of the old men sitting on gentle horses. There was Curly and Hairy Moccasin, and between them was White Man Runs Him, holding a pistol and wearing dark glasses.

The fact that the white people had waged war on the Indians didn't bother Lester as much as the fact that they hadn't ended the war honorably. All there was in the end was the big empty sky filled with a lot of squabbling. The Germans got better and so did the Japanese. But of course there were never many Japanese who wanted to live in Pine Ridge and take over the Black Hills. It was easier to rebuild Japan as long as the Japanese would just stay on their island. Lester didn't resent the white people for fighting the war; he just didn't like to be around any of the whites' guilt-ridden gloating or the Indians' meek, defeated pride. So it came as a surprise to him to learn he had become a soldier for a group of criminal entrepreneurs who also happened to be white.

Lester was working as a floor boss in Vegas at the time. He was driving a German car and had a Japanese girlfriend who was a travel agent for one of the big law firms in town. They skied in Tahoe and partied in Los Angeles every other month or so. Lester stayed in debt. He had been working in a new casino that, while not Indian owned, was managed by a tribal group from Connecticut. The place was called Sutter's Mill. It had a kind of an Old West mining motif. The service crew wore cowboy clothes. The barmaids and servers wore net stockings and dance-hall-girl getups. The dealers had puffy striped shirts with garters and bowler hats perched on top of their heads, and they were encouraged to grow facial hair. Thankfully none of the Indians had to dress up in feathers or anything. Lester was wearing Italian suits and braids. He wore a couple of grand in silver.

From time to time guys on the gaming crew would do favors for the bosses in the front office, so it was no surprise when Lester was called in the back to talk with Frank. Frank had been his boss for three months. He had been brought in from upstate New York. He was Mohawk, but not identifiably. Frank was a numbers man and that was easily identifiable because of his glasses and his almost full-time presence in front of the office computer.

"Nice drop in your section, Lester. It's going good, huh?" Frank did not look up from the printout he was scanning. Lester nodded, knowing he wasn't expected to contribute any more to the conversation. There was an old white man standing near the video panel in the corner. Frank said he wanted Lester to meet "Mr. Wilson" and said it in such a way that Lester had the impression Wilson wasn't really his name.

Wilson was from New York and worked for their parent company. He wanted to know if Lester had time to go with him while he ran an errand. Lester looked at Frank and Frank took his eyes off the printout and looked directly at Lester. This had been the first time Frank had made eye contact with any person as far as Lester knew, which made the gaze all the more disconcerting. Frank stared hard at Lester and shook his head slowly, then he took his glasses off, putting them in his suit pocket. He patted himself down as if checking for his keys. He shot his French cuffs out past the sleeve of his jacket and clapped his hands together.

"Right, then. You can drive my car," Mr. Wilson said. He walked through the door ahead of Lester.

Lester drove the Lincoln Town Car down through the strip and out into the desert. An owl dipped down into the glare of the headlights. Mr. Wilson smoked one cigarette after another and leaned toward the door.

"You married?" Wilson asked.

"No," Lester replied as he leaned forward to look at the utility lines from where the owl must have dived.

"You serious with anybody?" Wilson blew a centipede of smoke toward the crack in the window.

"Naw," Lester said.

"You ever had sex with a man?" Wilson said with only the slightest change of pace.

Lester leaned back, gripping the steering wheel with both hands. "Can't say as I have."

Wilson twisted the gold ring on his left hand with his thumb. "Can't say you have . . ." Wilson was saying, slowly pushing the words out along with the faint puffs of smoke. "Pull out here on the left."

Wilson pointed to what could have been a wagon track: two lines etched in the packed sand. Sagebrush lay between the tracks, but the largest had been recently torn out and dragged a few feet.

"Down here a couple of miles. Won't be long," Wilson said. "Don't worry." He reached over and tapped Lester lightly on the knee with the tips of two fingers.

The track ended near a dark outcropping of rock. The lights of town flared up over the other side of the rocks, leaving the night sky streaming purple up into the blackness. Stars chattered down on Lester's shoulders as he opened the door and stepped out of the car.

"Pop the trunk," Mr. Wilson said softly, and Lester leaned back in and pushed the button. Wilson walked quickly around the back of the car and opened the trunk all the way. Lester stood by his door.

Lester watched as Wilson dragged a small Asian man out of the trunk who was tied with cord and had silver tape over his mouth. The Asian man's eyes were wide as a newborn colt's. He was breathing so hard his cheeks bulged out in time with his chest. Lester could hear the man's breath whistling out of his nostrils. Wilson had a silver-gray handkerchief he used to wipe his hands thoroughly after he propped the bound-up man against the fender. He waggled his finger at Lester.

"You want to kill him?" Wilson asked.

By now Lester, too, was breathing hard. He felt like running, but by now Wilson had a pistol in his hand.

"Naw," Lester said.

"Fucking faggots," Wilson said disdainfully as he held the long-barreled twenty-two pistol at arm's length. The Asian man began to shriek behind the silver tape. Tears sputtered down his cheeks, and his head cranked back and forth as if he could refuse what was coming.

Wilson paused, then threw the man down on the sand under the car. He stepped back four paces or so and shot the crying man in the head three times. Lester closed his eyes and walked backward away from the car.

Wilson wiped the gun with the handkerchief. The beams of a single set of headlights bounced up and down the desert night, and Wilson had the gun in the handkerchief as he walked up to Lester. "You better get rid of this." He slapped the gun into Lester's hands. A red Jeep came around from the other side of the rocks and pulled up fifty yards away with the door open. Wilson walked to the Jeep and got in. The Jeep pulled away, leaving Lester, the Lincoln Town Car, and the dead man to listen to the music of the desert: bugs chirring and cars hissing down the highway in the distance. A coyote yelped far off and a large prop plane banked high over the airport. The Jeep drifted away as if it were Lester's very breath.

Lester drove to town and threw his shoes in a dumpster. He bought flip-flops at a dime store. He gave the Lincoln Town Car to a hustler he knew who dealt in rolling stock. For some reason he held on to the gun. When he showed up at work the next evening, Frank said nothing to him. Lester asked if there was a bonus coming his way and Frank kept his eyes on the printouts and said only, "Wait until Christmas."

But Christmas wasn't going to come: the Town Car was registered in Lester's name and paperwork showed the gun had been purchased by Lester as well. The hustler was pulled over the next night as he was driving the car to a prospective buyer, and he gave up Lester without a fight.

Lester kept quiet for the first hour of his interrogation. He put in a call to Frank, and Frank suggested he call the public defender. The cops had photographs of how they found the victim; they were overexposed with blooms of light dazzling off the tape. The blood looked black, puddled in the sand. They had the tire treads, they had the Town Car, and the Town Car had blood spattered up under the rear fender; they had a cocktail waitress who remembered a handsome Indian in a nice suit wearing flip-flops walking out of a parking garage. By the time Lester tried to give up Frank and Mr. Wilson, it was too late. No one was prepared to believe his story—not the cops, not the public defender, and certainly not the jury of four retired white men, five white working mothers, two black former security guards, and one Hispanic grandmother. Thus began the days of Lester Plays with His Face's service to federal law enforcement.

SHEARS SIGNALED TO the four guards walking up the boardwalk. "In here," she said. She pulled him by the elbow toward a concrete building off the boardwalk near where the old community center had been. Now it was a communications center for the federal Department of Corrections. It was also a secure location for Billie Shears and her crew during the current hunt for the missing warhead.

Inside, uniformed personnel sat in front of computers with headsets on, perhaps a dozen in all, each engaged in a separate conversation, typing, pausing, speaking, then typing again. Some referred to pieces of paper; some referred to several monitors at once. One young man appeared to be in tears, as if he were a short-order cook on his first day at the grill. He was so stressed that he was sitting silently, punching the escape key over and over.

Shears walked over to him, placed her hand on his shoulder, and lifted up his headset. "Son, is your shift supervisor around?"

"No, ma'am . . ." the young man said in a slightly thin voice. "He got a memo, and he turned white and ran out the door."

"Just work your problem, son. Everything is going to be fine."

The young man looked up at her with tears running down his cheeks. "Is it true that a thermonuclear device is about to detonate?"

"No," Billie Shears said, and she smiled. "That would be a bad thing, right? So we are not going to let that happen."

She pointed to a small conference room off the coms center. "In here, gentlemen." The guards set the manacled Itchy down at the table, then Shears excused them.

Gloomy sat opposite his cousin and stared at him, while Ishmael looked down at the chains on his ankles. Before the door shut, a fat man in civilian clothes, belly spilling over his pleated khakis and coffee stains down his permanent-press shirt, walked in cradling an open briefcase overflowing with loose papers. Inside the briefcase was a laptop.

"Shears, did you actually tell one of my kids to just 'work the problem'?"

"Yeah, why?"

"Do you know what he is working on?"

"No . . . I don't really care either. He was melting down."

"He is calculating survivability figures if this fucking thing detonates in the next twenty-four hours."

"Well, fuck . . . why is he stressing? That's easy: zero. Tell him to write a big fat zero, and calm the fuck down."

"He's got kids on the island."

"Yeah . . . who doesn't?"

"You don't."

"Jesus, Jasper . . . but *I'm* here, aren't I? Can we get on with this?" She looked at the two convicts sitting around the table.

"Gentlemen, this is Jasper Jones, that's not his real name, so don't worry about it. He is supposed to be the leading expert in North America on these warheads you boys found. He now believes that one of them, the now-famous missing warhead, is likely to detonate sometime soon. That's right, isn't it, Jasper, that's your great time estimate? Sometime soon?"

"Soon-ish."

"Come on!" Billie said.

"Lawyer," Ishmael said.

Confused and sad, Gloomy looked over at his cousin. Ishmael looked angry. "We only found one . . . and you guys . . ." Gloomy sputtered.

"All right . . . listen." Jasper sat down. "It took years to get the specks from the Koreans, and it took more time to verify them. It took a hell of a long time to run the numbers down and for the recovery operations and disposal teams to double confirm them because, well . . . let's say some of them got antsy about destroying the warheads a little too quickly and one numb nuts tried to sell one to the Russians, and that's a whole other story, but at the end of the day we came up one fucking warhead short. I talked with the guy in Korea who built them himself. I saw an exact replica. It's a piece of shit, but it has three stages, and each stage has six little devices around a larger one:

that's eighteen babies, three moms. We've recovered all eighteen babies but only two moms. The mom is quite a bit bigger than the baby. This missing mom if it were to detonate here on the ground would blow a very deep and very ugly hole in this coastline. Frankly it's not as bad as it would be if it were in a big population center, and that's why you don't see a whole fucking army outside right now. That and I'm not sure it's going to blow up. But it would be very, very, very bad for the environment on a global scale, or at least for the ocean and all the creatures living within it for . . . let's say a thousand-mile radius. Then there's also the cloud of radioactive vapor and debris that would be released into the atmosphere. So, don't fuck around anymore, tell us what you two fuckers did with the second bomb."

Gloomy Knob stared at both of them. "Even if there were another bomb, what makes you think it is about to go off now?" he asked.

Jasper drummed his fingers on the edge of his laptop, then flipped through the edges of the schematic drawings that were piled in his briefcase. "Okay . . . here is what I have to think . . . if it didn't go off at the time, either the firing mechanism was destroyed or it wasn't. Okay? So, it's on or off. Someone could have snipped it off or it could have been destroyed on impact. It had a locator on it. That was destroyed, we know. The Koreans told us that much. We invaded, you probably remember that, right? Kicked their ass and everyone got fat on cheeseburgers and sticky rice. Okay so far? The generals helped us get things back in order to a certain extent. But low down on the list of surrender terms were the special outcomes for personnel. What was going to happen to the little fuckers. So . . . blah, blah, blah, turns out they don't really tell us about this missing warhead for a while. Until a guy who has all this info in some fucking silo in Hackaloogy, North Korea, happens to let it out that there is one timing device that is still transmitting, but it's intermittent. Damaged, but still ticking down, see what I'm saying. So I go to work. I do the estimates of the battery life, I get the records of the transmissions. First we have to make a deal with this Quan Fong fuck or whomever, but I have no idea if he is telling the truth. So, wise guy, my best estimate based on the size of the battery and how much juice it has put out . . . and being that it was designed to detonate before it ran out of juice—let me repeat . . . it is designed to use the last bit of power to send a charge through the circuits to blow the shit out of itself . . . and I know, I fucking know, no one likes it, but this part of the world, the part I myself am sitting in, is about to be blown to tiny little pieces of vaporized shit . . . soon-ish."

"We didn't find two warheads." Gloomy looked at both of the officials, his eyes wide.

"Lawyer," Ishmael said, still looking down.

"Itchy, what the hell are you saying?" Gloomy looked at his cousin. He tried to stand up but didn't seem to have the strength. "It's true, isn't it? We found the one, and that's the one that was on the boat. Jesus. Why would you want a lawyer at this point?"

Ishmael looked up at him slowly. "Cousin, shut up."

Gloomy looked around at Billie and Jasper in the little room.

"Tell us what you remember when you got on the boat, Christopher," Billie Shears said softly. "I'm serious. The clock is ticking."

"Would it help if I showed you the diagram for the bomb? Would you like to go see your daughter again?

Would you like to go to your parents' house, where your father is dying of cancer? Would you rather he be incinerated?" Jasper spoke down into the mouth of his coffee cup, without looking at Gloomy or Billie.

"No . . . but there was only one bomb. I don't know what else to say." He started coughing. At first it was a nervous cough and then it built until he was choking.

"Stop!" Billie Shears called out. "Get his cellmate."

The door opened and Lester Plays with His Face walked in, in a fine suit with his hair braided with red ribbon.

"Hello, boy," he said softly.

"What the hell?" Gloomy said. "You're supposed to be dead."

"I was never really real, partner," Lester said. "I'm a government agent. I was planted in your cell to gain information, and they faked my death to pull me out. Actually, I stayed around and became a friend of your family, of your father. I've been looking for that second warhead for some time now. Tell me what you remember now, Gloom."

Gloomy started to cry. Nothing was apparently real. His grandparents, Ellie and Slippery, were long dead, and Lester was alive. He never talked about the night that began the war. It was long over—only, this was apparently happening now.

"We will give you amnesty and parole so you can live back in Cold Storage, with privileges to travel by boat within the area if you help us now . . . but you have to do it now," Shears said. She held out some official-looking papers.

"Don't believe a word they say," Ishmael said.

"Why don't you want to help stop an explosion, Itchy?" Gloomy asked.

"Because I just don't care," Itchy said.

Gloomy thought about it and he looked at his cousin. His lungs burned. His head hurt. Tears ran down his cheeks.

"They were going to kill my mom," he said. "They buried her in that box. Somehow my sister got word of his plan, and she wanted to stop it."

"Whose plan?" Billie Shears leaned forward.

"The guy on the big boat, Wild Horses and his crew. They had the box all ready." Gloomy was pleading now, but to whom or why he was not sure. His lungs felt tight, as if he were about to drown. "I went up and checked on the warhead under the beach fringe. Some guys were moving it. I went back to try to get Mom out of the box. I thought my part of the deal was over. They beat the shit out of me. I ran to get Dad. I told him what was going on, but he didn't believe me. I went to the boat. Itchy was there, Wild Horses was there. I told him to let go of Mom. I told him I saw his men moving the warhead. Itchy asked me when I saw them, and when I said 'Just maybe a half an hour ago,' Itchy told me to get off the fucking boat."

"Stop," Billie Shears called out. "He told you to get off the boat?"

"Yes."

"Then you went down below, and you saw a little warhead, and all the shit went down with your sister and your cousin. You were on the boat until it caught fire, at which point you went ashore and were captured along with your cousin, correct?"

"Yes. I saw the warhead on the boat. I assumed it was the same one the men had been moving."

"But there wasn't enough time for them to get it on the boat . . . was there? You saw some men moving the warhead you assumed you found onshore. Then a little while later you saw a smaller warhead on the boat. After you got off the boat you never saw another warhead, correct?"

"I guess that is right. I thought the warhead I found was the one on the boat. But if you say it was a different one, if Itchy found another one I didn't know about, then that is possible."

"Okay . . . get him out. Now. We got what we need," Billie Shears said.

Hands fell upon him and belts were unbuckled and zippers undone. Water spilled from a rubberized helmet on his head and a lightweight backpack was lifted away from his shoulders. He was seeing Ms. Shears, the DA, in the exact same room. He was sitting near Lester Plays with His Face. Itchy was not to be seen. His cousin's chair was empty. Everything was less vivid, visually. But the air tasted cleaner. He opened his mouth wide and every inch of his tongue felt cool and clean, and then he realized he had had a strange medicinal taste in his mouth for a long time. It was very strange he hadn't been aware of feeling his feet at any time when he was sitting in the room, but now he was. They positively tingled.

"Okay. Now. A few explanations are in order." Billie Shears slapped her large file down on the table in front of Gloomy hard enough to make him sit up straight.

Chapter Nine

"Okay." Billie Shears gestured to the apparatus that Gloomy took off. It looked somewhat like a diving suit and had a helmet that contained a radio receiver and an intravenous drug attachment. "This is the Portable AV Medical Debriefer or the 'Porta Potty,' as some call it. We've been trying it out on you instead of the tank."

"With me?" Gloomy asked.

"Yes," Billie Shears said, staring straight at him.

Seconds ticked by.

"I haven't been in the tank before, have I?" Gloomy finally asked.

Lester started laughing. "Jesus, kid, you have barely been out of the tank, or out of some mixed states; they've been trying new stuff on you."

"Mixed states?" Gloomy tried again.

Billie Shears was agitated now. She smoothed down her linen skirt. "We don't have a lot of time. What we have to do now is get you and Mr. Wild Horses together and see if we can come up with the location of the mother."

"Mixed states? Ah . . . wasn't I supposed to volunteer for that? You know, sign something?" Gloomy looked around. "And not to be an asshole, but how much of what

I remember is real? And why didn't I get a happy ending? Isn't that supposed to be . . . you know . . . part of it?"

"Yeah . . . that," Shears said. "That was badly mishandled very early on, and I'm deeply sorry about that."

"What? My memory?"

"No, we don't have time for all that. Because of this suit, you were walking around and experiencing a lot of what was happening to you, but we were controlling everything."

"Norma? Rocket?"

"They did kidnap you. They thought they were doing it for the Iranians, for the money. They were going to double-cross them for their own Christian group, but whatever . . . that doesn't matter. Their Iranian contacts have scooped them up already. Ghost . . . we know he is working for the Iranians. We don't know what happened to him . . . or to them . . ."—Billie looked around—"Do we? No . . . ? They are missing as of now, but that's not important. Norma and Rocket were working with us by the time they got you to shore. You do have a wife and daughter . . . yadda yadda . . . back to that later. We've got to get you and Wild Horses together and see if he will tell us where the mother warhead is. The Iranian agents out at the prison don't want anyone finding the warhead at this point—or maybe they do. We don't know. It's possible by now they don't care if it goes off."

"Why don't you just do all this to Wild Horses if he is the one who knows where the bomb is? As I've been telling you, I don't know where it was. You must know that from all your spy computers. I mean, come on!"

Billie Shears leaned forward at the waist, holding her gold necklace back with the flat of her hand so it wouldn't bang against the table. "Mr. McCahon, we don't torture people *lightly* or just willy-nilly. We have good, sound reasons to suspect that you have vital information."

"But Wild Horses knows!" Gloomy said again.

"That fucking guy," Jasper finally snorted.

Billie Shears straightened her blouse again and even Gloomy could see it was a tic. "Mr. Wild Horses is a genius," she said.

"Fuck you . . ." Jasper spit out under his breath.

"And a complicated individual," she continued. "Let's just say he has many places to hide in his psyche."

"If I have to listen to one more word about Martin fucking Heidegger, I'm gonna puke," Jasper blurted out. "The only thing to figure out about that guy is if he is eighty percent full of horseshit or one hundred percent full of horseshit, the Nazi prick."

"Okay, enough philosophy for today," Billie Shears said firmly. "Believe me, we tried, Gloomy. But our debriefing of Mr. Wild Horses was fruitless."

"I bet he got a happy ending. Why no happy ending for me? I didn't volunteer for any of this." Gloomy lightly thumped his wrists on the table.

"That . . . they fried you early on. They horsed you. That's what they call it. They got too rough, too erotic with you early in the process. They didn't realize how sensitive your feelings for your wife were, that she was the only source of eroticism in your life. They horsed you, and it damaged your psyche for questioning. That's why it ruined your sex dreams."

"Now you want to humiliate me in front of the world?" Gloomy was looking at the cameras, which were still pointing at him.

"No, what I want is to let you know that your wife is a lucky woman and when you go to sue the federal government for the harm they did to you, I will happily testify for your lawyers." She slid a card across the table to him. "That has my real name and a good telephone number on it, and if you give it to any other shit bird I will have you killed . . . but, really, we've got to get moving."

Everyone stood up and started walking toward an open door that led to a helicopter.

"Am I awake now? Is this . . . is this real?" Gloomy asked Lester as they stopped into the outer office.

The well-dressed Lakota man leaned over and held on to Gloomy's elbow and spoke slowly and clearly, "Yes, the first thing you should know is this is not a dream. There is a bomb. It may or may not be about to explode. You told them something important."

"What in the heck did I tell them?"

"You told them that Mr. Wild Horses is the only one left who knows where that warhead is stashed. You found the baby sunk in the lake. But the mother had fallen with it and had sunk deeper into the muck. You told Ishmael, and he rounded up the baby, and Wild Horses found the mother probably when he was mucking around getting the baby out. You told them all this even though you didn't know there were two warheads in that lake. You told them that Wild Horses got ahold of a bigger bomb and was cutting Itchy out of the plan completely. Itchy thought the little bomb was the whole deal. The baby was already on the boat, but Wild Horses' guys were carrying the mother near the beach when you were coming to the boat. That's what you saw. Itchy figured that out and that's why Itchy wanted to destroy the boat. He wanted to undo the plan. He had been betrayed by the professor."

He helped Gloomy out of his vest, then handed him a

cup of coffee to help wake him up. "Can I ask you some-thing, Gloom?"

"I guess."

"Why didn't you ever talk about the incident with law enforcement?"

"I killed my sister." He looked around the darkened room with the computer monitors and the puddles of water at his feet. "It made me too sad."

The tall man smiled and shook his head. "Fair enough. Clive is not doing well, by the way. That part is true. I really am alive and I really am Lester. Your family calls me L.P., like the records."

"Nice to meet you," Gloomy said. "I'm glad you are not dead." They started walking toward the clattering machine.

"Me too. Like to stay that way."

"You friends with my folks really?"

"Yeah." Lester smiled at him.

"Just for work . . . to spy on them?"

"Naw, kid . . . well, a little, you know, but they good peo-ple, solid with the Spirit . . . You know that." Lester Plays with His Face rubbed Gloomy Knob's back and made sure he ducked his head to get into the helicopter.

SOON THE CHOPPER lifted up above them and above the hills of the sheltering islands. They could see the glow of the prison lights floating out on the calm water and up into the air surrounding the island, as if the structures themselves were melting into the rocks and evaporating away. There were two other helicopters clearing away from the landing pad as their chopper approached. Gloomy was not wearing a headset, but he could tell the pilot was arguing with someone. The pilot misjudged his landing and bounced hard onto the deck. Ropes were thrown and orders given. No one, not even the civilians or the officers, could stand and move until the ship was secure and the bell had sounded. Finally Gloomy was led away toward the compound, where he would be strip-searched once again.

Billie Shears turned him around. "I'm going to stay here on the island. I will be available. You can talk to me anytime. Just think about it, Gloomy. I don't have time to work on you anymore. I have to go all in with Wild Horses, you understand?"

"Yes," Gloomy said, and he turned and walked toward the chain-link tunnel topped with concertina wire. "Can I talk with my cousin? Maybe he will tell me something."

"Well . . . there are things about your cousin . . . Let's get checked in. Things are shitty in here right now. People are getting rambunctious about the prospect of a bomb going off," said Shears.

The search was not as rough as it could have been. The guards were polite and welcoming to Gloomy. An escape was a kind of validation for all the regulatory bullshit the guards had to put up with, so they felt a sort of exhilaration when they processed Gloomy back in. The first thing they did was hand him his old tags.

"We found these near the blast site. At first we thought you were dead, but that lasted only about twenty minutes or so. Then word came down from higher up in security that you were 'signed' out by security, whatever that means. So we stopped looking for you. You being dead was all part of some spook scene to find something, I guess." Norm, the really fat guard who was filling out some form on a clipboard, was speaking with the weary cynicism typical of an overworked DOC employee. He didn't really give a shit either way if Gloomy was alive or dead.

"Excuse me, sir. How's the fella who injured his arm and shoulder so badly in the explosion?" Gloomy asked.

"Lot of guys like that." He shook his head and looked mildly bemused at the notion. "There was a guy dressed like a guard who wasn't a guard got his shoulder mangled. He died. He was in on it."

Gloomy shook his head and kept silent.

"Now, Mr. McCahon," Norm said, looking at his clipboard, "Mr. McCahon, we've got you on a medical hold for at least the next thirty-six hours."

"Not punitive seg?"

Norm looked down at the clipboard again with the broad, exaggerated expression of a vaudeville straight man. "Why nooooo, Mr. McCahon. It appears they've got something else planned for you altogether."

When Norm laughed, Gloomy felt sick to his stomach.

He changed into the new suit and was hooked up again, but this time the cuffs were loosely done in front.

"Follow the yellow brick road," Norm said, and, smiling again, pointed toward the door. Gloomy walked up to it, and it slid soundlessly open. He walked into a segmented hallway. The walls were white with a green stripe and the floors were a light yellow. Gloomy had never been in this section of Stevens before. There were doors on each side and in front of him. Every twenty feet he would come to a dead end, and one of the doors would slide open. He went right and then left and two more rights. It was a mechanically operated maze that could lead prisoners to any part of the prison without being escorted. Sometimes he could hear radios buzzing or heavy footsteps on the catwalks above him. The guards in Heaven were following his progress.

Finally he came to a door that wouldn't open. Gloomy

waited. It may have been five minutes; it could have been a half hour. But he stood and waited without saying a word. The door behind him closed and he found himself standing in a cubicle without noticeable doors or windows. Finally the metal partition to his right slid open and he was on the edge of another cubicle.

It was a room with a large mirror on the right-hand wall and a wooden chair at the far end. Handcuffed to the chair was Norma, the barmaid who had smuggled him out of prison. Her nose appeared to be broken and blood was spattered down her shirt and pants. Her eyes were swollen shut and her breathing was shallow. At her feet was Rocket's dead body. Blood flowed out onto the floor toward Gloomy's feet and it puddled under the chair Norma was chained to.

The sight of this bloody woman certainly caught Gloomy's attention. Her face was battered. She was breathing unevenly and uttered slight, choking whines with each breath. But what alarmed Gloomy McCahon even more was that standing behind her now was not only Ali Wild Horses, but Lester Plays with His Face.

THROUGH THE CEILING, a deep rumble started building on the catwalks. People were running. Dozens of correctional officers' shoes were hitting the walkways like rattling metallic thunder.

"The local cops gave us over to someone with connections here. They are all working for the Iranians. I fucking swear. They brought us here. They beat us. They killed Rocket." Norma was crying. She felt as if her ribs might be separated.

Rocket had run into the woods when the police stopped their van back at housing. The cops caught her after

three steps and had smashed her face against the pavement. They wrestled Rocket to the ground in the woods
and threw them both on a transport boat out to Stevens.
They had been thrown into a segregation unit. All the
guards had been antsy and seemed distracted by some
disturbance in the prison. Everyone was thinking about
the prospect of a thermonuclear explosion. All the radios
seemed to be chattering at once, and people were running around above her. At one point a group of men she
assumed were convicts opened the door screaming and
started beating and kicking her. She had heard something
spraying and Rocket screaming, then choking until he
was quiet. She couldn't see through her swollen eyes, but
her head remained stuffed with noise. She had tried to
stretch her eyes open. She wanted to look up to where the
footsteps banged on metal but she couldn't. She sat there
trying to summon her "Dorothy feeling." She wanted nothing in the world so much as to rise up out of herself and
float like a sooty spark through the ceiling. *There is no place
like home. There is no place like home.*

"I didn't say a thing to them, Gloomy. I told them nothing. You have to believe me."

Lester stepped behind her. "Calm down, now. Nothing
bad is going to happen here."

"Something bad is already happening," Norma snuffled
through her tears.

Now Gloomy could hear men barking orders and keys
jingling on great rings, radios hissing and the clatter of
weapons slapping against utility belts.

"Why are you here?" Gloomy asked. His eyebrows were
arched and his voice had the pathetic, hopeless tone of a
lost little boy.

"Why the hell am I here? Why in the hell do you think

I'm here?" Norma screamed. She was weeping openly now. By the time her tears dripped off the tip of her chin, they stained her gray wool pants faintly red. "Iranians bought off some cops and some of these guards. I don't know . . . why . . . A man promised our group two hundred thousand dollars to break you out of jail," she wheezed, "half when we agreed, half when we succeeded."

"Those were Iranian agents. The same people who buried Gloomy's mother. They wanted him to take them to the bomb. We let you do that, hon." Lester was trying to calm her down.

"Come on!" Norma wept. "I really need to wipe my nose."

"What is going on now?" Gloomy yelled.

"It's complicated," Lester said, "but trust me. I'm here to help you," he added, a little falsely.

"We need protection, Lester." Gloomy reached out his hands toward his friend. Lester backed away. Norma kept swinging her head around.

Gloomy started flailing his arms around and scratching his head and his arms.

"*Am I in the tank again? Please tell me. Am I in the tank again?*"

"What the hell are you talking about? They're all trying to kill us!" Norma screamed at Gloomy.

"Hush . . ." Lester said. The partition behind him opened, and he stepped out of the room just before it slid closed again with a hydraulic shudder before Gloomy had time to even think about trying to get out. Muffled voices cried out. It was the slurred barking of doglike men. Hundreds of men calling out behind concrete. Gloomy heard the hissing of hydraulics, then the boom of a gas canister.

"They've killed Rocket!" Norma screamed, then she

jerked her head toward the sound of the closing door. "Who's that? Who's that? I heard someone."

"It's just a guy," Gloomy said absently. He leaned against the partition and slid down the wall to sit on the floor.

"Mr. McCahon," Norma said, "don't leave me here. Please don't . . ." Her voice was heavy with tears.

Gloomy looked at the plate mirror on the wall to his left.

"We won't be here that long," he said toward the mirror.

The rumble above them in Heaven grew. Hundreds of leather boots banged on the metal catwalk. Then they heard the crack of rifle shots.

"What's that? Christ almighty, what's that now?" Norma was screaming. The noises above the room burned into her skull.

"It's going off," Gloomy said with as much calm as he could muster. Then the riot became a slurry of darkness and noise.

Chapter Ten

Silver red flecks swirled up through his field of vision, and he tasted dead leaves and an autumn fire in his mouth. He felt as if he could push his tongue up through the roof of his mouth into the gray mud of his brain. Sparks began to jitter up his fingers with each breath. He couldn't move; he could hardly remember ever having moved. It was as if his body were a blob of wet clay being lifted slowly up out of a river. But also . . . he was pissed off. He was tired of being someone else's object to be shaped.

He was in Medical Ward 11. This was the holding clinic for the "meat pumps." There were three hundred beds in one open ward. All of them held men hooked to machines. There had been court cases that forbade the "mercy killings" of prisoners. There were too many men who wanted to be killed before they had suffered enough. As a result, a life sentence meant a life sentence and the higher courts had upheld the proposition that inmates were entitled to the best of Western pharmacological treatment and cheap nutritional liquid supplements to keep them alive in whatever condition for as long as possible. Some said it was a waste, but no one could find an acceptable way out of the dilemma. The courts hadn't given the doctors the authority to kill the aged inmates and no one wanted to give the inmates themselves the option to escape punishment by fleeing into the arms of death. So they ended up here: hundreds of old men serving out the last of their life sentences in a warehouse filled with cheap—if not so comfortable—life-support systems.

When Gloomy opened his eyes, he could see the rounded pinnacles of his feet under the covers. Beyond were row after row of metal beds beside monitor/respirator pedestals; bed turners to mitigate bedsores. Automated bedpans adapted from dairy machines, and catheters with the latest antibacterial agents. The good thing about limited human intervention was fewer chances of introduced infections. The room echoed with the soft churning and sighing of machines. The monitor lights blinked like fireflies. Gloomy was laid out flat in his bed. He was breathing on his own, though he had oxygen tubes up his nose and an IV needle in his arm. He could see no bags hanging above him, for the ward was plumbed directly to a secure pharmacy on the floor above. The ward was designed to be served from above and secured from below. Gloomy's head lay directly on the mattress, turned slightly to one side.

He lifted himself up and looked farther down the ward to where the exit sign was lit up like a distant cocktail lounge in the desert. Six beds down from him, he could see Norma, laid out on a bed, her arm hooked to a tube. Her eyes were closed, her face calm and wiped clean of blood.

It took him a moment to realize that he was now sitting up without any effort or pain, and he wondered how this could be, just as he wondered how he could be sitting up so straight without moving his feet at all. It seemed the most natural thing in the world to ask Karen about it.

"Am I dead, Karen?" he said to his wife out loud.

"No, honey, not yet. You're hurt pretty bad, though."
Karen sat next to him on the bed, and when he saw her,
the fire ants and burning leaves turned into a warm elixir
coating over the pain.

He couldn't guess her age. She was not the girl in the mountains with the gear and livestock spilling out on the road.
She was not the woman in labor delivering their daughter.
Still, she was beautiful: black hair across the shoulders of
her western shirt, her tight jeans and silver buckle clearly
visible at her narrow waist. Somehow he couldn't touch
her. Gloomy started crying because he wanted, with everything in his body, to reach out and put his hand against
her soft cheek but he couldn't.

"I'm sorry," he said finally.

She put her fingers through his hair and shook her
head slowly. Her face was kind and concerned and there
was the slightest hint of mocking in her expression, as if
she were scolding him for his childishness.

"I know you are, honey," she said in the softest voice. "I
know you are."

Gloomy looked around. Old men were walking slowly
up and down the rows of beds; the backs of their hospital robes were open and their shoulders stooped. Old
white men with thick muscles gone to sagging flesh, tattoos
faded and pulled out of shape by loose skin. Old black
men with white hair and pomegranate jowls. Indian men
with long gray ponytails making slight gestures with their
hands at their sides. They wandered up and down the rows
of beds, looking idly at the bodies breathing into the
machines. Gloomy could not hear their bare feet scuffing
the hard tile floor. There was just the ticking of machines,
like crickets.

Above him he saw birds, great black birds flying in the dark corners of the ceiling. As they flew, they trailed strings of light through the darkness, thin and filmy like spiderwebs on a clear, damp morning. Gloomy thought he could smell fire. Karen pushed her fingers through his hair. Gloomy turned and saw Billie Shears was also sitting on his bed, and it occurred to him that it was rude for the assistant district attorney to be there interrupting him during a visit from his wife.

"I brought her out to the prison. I'm sorry, Gloomy. I shouldn't have, but we don't have all that much time. They haven't got the riot clamped down. Someone has been tampering with the main security system. It's a mess out there."

"Why the heck did you bring her? Why am I drugged? Is this even real?"

"Yes . . . I'm sorry . . . really . . . but you've got to tell me more about what happened." Billie Shears's voice was loud and piercing; it almost hurt his ears. Gloomy turned away from her.

Karen bent over and kissed him. Her breath was warm, and as she put her lips against his, he felt a narcotic flare of morphine blush through his entire body. Her breath was sweet and it made him hungry; yet he could not reach up and touch her face. He pulled away from her . . . from this apparition.

The webs of light floated down from the ceiling and covered her hair, just inches from his face.

"You saw her. Isn't she a beautiful girl? Isn't she just the most beautiful thing?" The prosecutor's voice seeped into his head like deadly gas.

"I had to do what I did. It got so out of control so fast . . . I had to . . ." He closed his eyes.

Billie Shears nodded and her voice kept wheedling in. "I'm not here to judge you, Gloomy. I just want to know one last time, is there anything you can do to help us?"

"I can talk to my cousin."

"No. No, Gloomy you can't." Shears turned to her left and flicked on the light over the bed he was sitting next to.

Shadows filled the open mouth of Ishmael Muhammad. His long hair was braided down one side of his shoulder; his walnut skin appeared dusted with ash. His eyes were closed, and his nose was cankered with sores around where the tubes were inserted. On his chest he had a tattoo of the memorial for the Swiss Guard at Lucerne: the dead lion with the shield of the crusaders beneath its paws and the shaft of a broken spear coming out behind the beast's shoulder. It had become one of the symbols of the new indigenous movements around the world. The symbol of the brokenhearted Christian movement, it memorialized the place where Nietzsche had killed God. His cousin Ishmael lay there with his prison tattoo bleeding into his chest and his mouth a cavern in the light.

"He has been in a coma for eighteen months," Shears said. "We believe the Iranians got to him."

"Iranians?"

"When Wild Horses hid the bomb, the Iranian secret police sent people in and also started buying informants to try to find it. They had provided most of the parts to the North Koreans. They knew it was going to malfunction. They knew it was never going to reach its target, but they wanted the bombs. They wanted the nuclear devices. Ghost worked for them. We think he got to your cousin. He tortured him and finally gave him something that put him in this state."

"Did Itchy tell them anything?"

"For a time we thought he did. Not even Jasper knew about this. We thought there might be an imminent detonation, but it didn't come. We worked Ghost over pretty hard, but I have to tell you, Gloomy, these new enhanced interrogation techniques are not as good as they are cracked up to be."

"No kidding." The lights twinkled, the bellows of the breathing machines wheezed.

"Like anything else, in an expert's hands, they can be useful. But when you start digging and planting things in the mind"—Shears paused and looked at his hands—"things get messy real fast. Particularly when you're dealing with . . . non-normal personalities."

"Like who?" Gloomy looked up at the lawyer.

"Well," Shears sighed, "like just about everybody."

Gloomy laid his head back and slept.

SOMETIME LATER, HE woke up. Billie Shears was more in focus now. Gloomy felt the warmth of his wife's kiss being replaced by the thick flavor of blood in the back of his mouth.

Gloomy was in Heaven. The main control room. A riot was raging in the Ted Stevens Federal Penitentiary. There were chaotic winking lights on the main control panel, and the faint smell of an electrical fire filled the room. Billie Shears sat in a chair at the panel, looking nervous. She wore an elegant suit with a pair of work boots, which she bobbed up and down nervously as she waited for the violence to burst open like a cyst. Karen was crying. Ghost was standing behind her, holding a utility knife to her throat. Ali Wild Horses was slumped in a chair across from Shears.

It was clear Ghost wanted to kill Karen. He pulled her hair back, exposing the white curve of her throat, and looked deep into her eyes, as if to be sure that she would know exactly what was happening as he did it. He had a real knife now, a folding knife with a serrated edge that he had managed to take from a guard. The hand holding the knife shook slightly, and his lips noiselessly formed words: curse words mostly and names of people. Names, presumably, of people he loathed. He was lost to reason now, thinking not so much in complete thoughts but in sweeping bursts of memories: schoolyard taunts and long-ago slights. His words were fueled by something like a mixture of rage and simple irritation. He was an open fire hydrant of petty spite, and the tighter the grip of what was left of his pity, the harder the spray.

Ghost didn't really like this feeling of rage, for it brought him dangerously close to the edge of his control. He knew well enough that bad things would happen if he went any further. He wasn't excited by the fear pouring from the woman's eyes. He simply wanted her to know who he was. That it was *he* who was not to be disrespected. That it was *he* who was going to spill the life out of this nothing, this squiggle of tissue set in motion in her mother's womb so many years ago. The knife fluttered against Karen's throat as his hand shook.

Ali Wild Horses spoke in a soothing voice to Ghost:

"You should calm yourself. There is already enough chaos here. You need more control to get a good result . . . don't you think?"

Ghost spat on the concrete floor.

Ali Wild Horses had been transformed by his years of isolation and happy-ending torture. When Gloomy met him briefly back in the early days, he had angular features that seemed to focus his passions. But now Ali Wild Horses' face seemed both bloated and sunken in at the same time, like the collapsed tent of a dead animal. He looked at Gloomy and Billie Shears with a kind of sadness that Gloomy recognized from his years in prison as the self-mockery of the convicted.

"We are nothing now, isn't that true, Christopher?" He nodded at Gloomy and used the formal name, which Gloomy barely recognized anymore. The former college professor continued: "We have become cages. We have become drug-addled dream makers, story spinners for our captors." He nodded to the monitors on the wall and fiddled with a joystick to zoom in on Cousin Itchy.

"My poor brother is trapped in his body," Wild Horses said, as if he was going to cry. "He was so wrong . . . we did not kill God. God deserted us."

"Shut the fuck up," Ghost said.

"Just tell me where the fucking bomb is and then let me get the fuck out of here," Ghost said, as if he were a child on the edge of a temper tantrum.

"You, my brother, are an empty cage. Can't you see that? You are completely alone. No one will help you outside these walls. You carry your cage with you."

"A big fat bank account awaits me," Ghost hissed. The knife against Karen's throat began to blossom with bubbles of bright blood.

Gloomy sat, numb. "I don't believe any of this is happening," he said. He looked straight at Shears. "This is another one of your sessions. I'm telling you. I don't know where the bomb is. That is not Karen." He nodded at the woman who seemed to be shivering in Ghost's arms. "That is not Ghost or Professor Wild Horses."

Wild Horses smiled at him. "You should be a philosopher, my friend. The problem is and always has been 'subject-object duality.' You are the subject and they have scrambled you up like an egg. Indeed, you are the kind of citizen they now deserve."

"Let's get going, boys. I'm going to kill the bitch!" Ghost said.

"And you, my brother, are the other kind of citizen they deserve." Wild Horses was so sad, he could not even smile at his joke. He held his hand up. "I will take you anywhere you want. I will take you anywhere the authorities let me. Frankly, I doubt the warhead is still there. I suspect that one group or another has probably stewarded it off this island long ago. I was expecting it to detonate long, long ago, and I was disappointed when it didn't. Just more time to spend my life in a cage. But I will take you anywhere you want."

Gloomy looked at the monitor. There was a scene of prisoners ripping apart the mattresses in Ward 11. Men were bleeding from their heads and hands, beating each other with pieces of bed frames. Others were wrapping themselves in mattresses for protection. The incoherent screams of the men in Ward 11 came bleating out of the speakers over their heads, and the thudding of blows sounded like the clatter of a horse race on a muddy track. Gloomy closed his eyes.

Billie Shears stepped forward. "Listen, I'm sure we can work something out. But just to set the record straight, I mean, just in the interest of fairness . . . do you think you could ask that young man to step away from the young lady? He's making me nervous. We don't need any problems here, do we?"

Ali Wild Horses looked over at Ghost and scowled, and the convict returned his scowl with a petulant shrug. He held the blade on Karen's throat, and Gloomy could see her white skin jumping against the edge of the blade with each pulse.

"Anyway . . ." Billie Shears continued, affecting a matter-of-fact tone in her voice, "I think I can get us all out of here."

Ali let his eyes go down to the floor and then snapped his head back up to meet Shears's eyes. Then he looked up. They all watched different monitors of the prison. There were men piling against locked doors; men beating each other and some chewing on arms and fingers, trying to bite their way out of the crush of bodies. "It won't be easy. Especially with a sister being held that way." Here he looked at Ghost.

"Leave that to me . . . let's get to my money," Ghost said, and shoved the silent and trembling woman ahead of him.

Gloomy still felt the drugs coursing through his head. *None of this is happening*, he thought. He looked at his feet and saw a revolver. Billie Shears nodded toward it. It was a prison-issue wheel gun.

"Oh, heck no," Gloomy said. "Not even in your dreams am I going to grab a gun in Heaven. Jeepers. I don't know where the goddamn bomb is. Just take me out of the tank."

"*Gloomy, you are not in the tank!*" Shears yelled. "God damn it." The lawyer finally stood up and Gloomy could see that her hands were taped behind her back. Gloomy had apparently been too dopey for them to bother with binding him up.

Shears came over and chest-bumped him, then stepped on his foot. "You ever have foot pain in one of those sessions? Think!"

Gloomy didn't care that much about foot pain, but he was ticked off, so he bent down and picked up the gun. Ghost moved back against the wall and blood started to sprinkle like rain from his knife blade.

"Like this is going to do anything at all?" Gloomy shot Ghost in the head, and brain matter splashed back into his mouth, which woke him up quite a bit. The brain matter was thick and salty—clearly authentic. "Holy cow," he said softly.

Gloomy grabbed his wife and jumped over a chair, then slammed his shoulder against the door on the other side. Perhaps there were shots echoing at his back. He heard the crack of a gun, but then he heard a deeper boom of another weapon, and he hurtled down the catwalk away from central control. Still the drugs surged through his brain, but he held on to Karen, or what should have been Karen.

Gloomy didn't know where he was going. Men battered him with pieces of desks and fists rolled up in blankets. Up on the catwalk the voices of screaming men seemed to rain down from the sky. He didn't run. He kept plodding as if he were walking through fire. He heard footsteps pounding and felt his pulse searing through the wound in his chest. Blood was streaming down his side. Red lights twirled in clear glass bowls. Horns were blaring and men screamed underneath him. "Hey! Hey! I'm here. I'm here," one voice pleaded. "I'm done. I'm done. I'm on the floor. Now just make it stop, okay."

Gloomy walked the straightest, most direct route away from central control. Thirty yards. Then forty. The doors began to close behind them, so someone may have been back at the control panel. Doors started to slide open and then shut ahead of him, and he made three of them, just squeezing his torn shirt through the last after he shoved Karen ahead of him. They were locked in a tight cubicle with a hatch and only a narrow stairway down to Earth. Smoke was coming up from the trapdoor. This had been an entrance for an extraction team, and Gloomy dropped down through the opening. He sensed someone was creating a pathway for him now.

Three dead men lay in the room at the bottom: two uniformed officers, all their weapons and gear stripped off them. The third was a convict with a wound the size of a cantaloupe in the middle of his chest. The officers had pieces of a metal bed driven through their chests. Gloomy stepped over them and walked slowly toward the door just six feet in front of him. It was locked.

Gloomy heard a metallic hum and then a clicking. The stairs retracted back into the ceiling. The trapdoor to Heaven slid shut with an echoing thud and a snap of the metal bolt moving into its magnetized keeper.

Gloomy and Karen were in protective segregation. This was an examination room. It was empty now, the tables having been smashed. It was empty except for the dead men and himself. The men in the adjacent cells had not been sprung. Whoever the rioters were, they had come through the common rooms and the halls. The fish in protective seg were still locked down. These souls locked in their six-foot cells were the snitches and the compulsive touchers and pederasts: men whom everyone wanted to kill, men whose sanctuary was thirty-six square feet of concrete.

Gloomy heard them crying. On each side of him was the strange hiccupping sound of baritone voices sobbing uncontrollably. "Please. Please. Oh please, God." In the corner on the floor was a man's personal box broken open. Gloomy leaned over and picked it up. Like Gloomy's own box, there was a lone picture in it: a young black woman sitting on the hood of a car. Gloomy looked at it a long time. Then something odd happened. The box became his own box. This was his own cell. He felt the hollow of his throat fill with ice. He was frozen again, and when he looked at the picture he could see Karen holding his beautiful baby girl. Karen was holding Esme. He remembered, then as he was walking through the furor, his daughter was named Esme. Then the lights went out, and acrid gas started pumping through the ceiling.

Gloomy's eyes were in searing pain and he started choking. The gas was meant to force men to move from one space to another. To use it, there should be a door open. He flung himself around the walls. Nothing gave way to air. Everything he hit was hard. He was in the box, inside a box, inside a box, and somewhere in the center was the frozen bile of his fear.

The men called out through the gas. "Mother. Mother. Mother," someone said. Another called out, "Carol, baby, please make it stop. Please, God." They were beating their heads against the concrete floor, and Gloomy could tell their faces were pushed hard against the cracks under the metal doors.

The gas hissed into the room and sank toward the floor.

"Oh God, please. Stop. Stop. Stop. Stop. I'm dying here. Please," a voice somewhere pleaded.

There was no light anywhere. Only darkness as thick as the concrete itself. Gloomy could not tell whether his eyes were open or not. He felt his body going cold. There was not much feeling in his wound now, though he could discern his chest heaving up and down. His fingers were numb, and he couldn't feel his legs. He jutted his lips into the crack under the door, hoping to find some breathable air. When the door slid open he pulled back and billowing smoke poured through, and he knew now his eyes were open because the smoke sizzled against his eyeballs with the pain of finely ground glass.

"None of us are ready to be touched by God," a voice said.

All Gloomy cared about when the door opened was that he was able to breathe. He had no thoughts or doubts about that. He rolled out of the flooding cell and took in lungfuls of breathable air. None of the other cell doors opened. There was just a thin light from emergency floods high in the corner of protective segregation. It was just enough light for him to be able to see Karen.

She looked tired and worried, looking around the common room with some irritation. "What are you doing here, Gloomy?" she asked him. Her brow was furrowed.

Gloomy breathed hard, fighting to regain his breath. Men all around him continued screaming. Gas was leaking from under their doors. He could hear their fists beating a wild tattoo on the iron, palms hitting metal doors with faint wet slaps. "Oh, please," someone said. Gloomy was concerned about Karen. He grabbed at his arm. He wasn't hooked up to the IV of drugs. He shouldn't be experiencing the morphine rush of warm liquid through his body. She seemed real, not heavenly or hallucinatory. There was no halo or circle of light; there was no music. But still, when she held her hand out to him, his fear thawed, as if the frozen river that had been his life in prison had suddenly thawed and rattled loose with first a shudder, then a roar.

He took her hand and watched her walk with that wonderful sway she had. She turned her head, pushing her thick hair with her chin at first, and then smiling as she curled it out of the way with her bound hands. Blue eyes and dazzling smile, she walked toward the door and it opened with a cloud of gas.

"This is a beautiful life, Gloomy, no matter how it first appears."

When she smiled again and pulled him close, Gloomy remembered the sweetness of her skin, the smell of her on the night they were married and too tired to make love. His wife. Now he remembered every detail of her. Her courage. Her voice, the flavor of her lips when he had kissed her and the taste of their lives when they were happy. He was somehow warm with the touch of her skin.

The next door opened, and men ran past with body-armor shields, the red edges of their laser sights slicing through the darkness. Radios blared and disappeared, and the armed men ran by without noticing Gloomy and Karen. They stepped over the dead men and walked toward the next closed door.

"You've missed loving me, haven't you, Gloomy?" Karen said, and pulled him close as if she could sense his memory of their lovemaking.

"Yes," Gloomy said. He was walking slowly because his body hurt so much, but he was awash in memory now: he remembered the dress she wore to a particular dinner at the Elks Club when they ate shrimp cocktail, the smell of her wool jacket on the afternoon they came back from fishing in Necker Bay. He heard the sound of her voice humming as she worked over the flower boxes on the steps of their house. He even remembered particular sharp words and sullen moods. He remembered his moodiness and her frustration. He remembered her pleading with him not to follow his cousin. But none of the sadness could dampen the new feeling that coursed through him as he remembered their lives.

"I'll talk to you later," she said, and helped him up a narrow ramp where two convicts were piled near the door, both bleeding badly from slashes in their necks. The door opened to a long hallway. Convicts were lying on the floor with their hands laced behind their necks. Prison officials were roaming in and out of doorways, holding guns. There was a flash and deep concussion of a shotgun blast from behind the dark door of one of the cells. Blood was slick on the floor. They stepped over the men on the ground. One of them was shaking uncontrollably and wetting himself in a great yellow puddle. Another shotgun blasted in a cell behind them, echoing down the hall. No one talked to Gloomy and no one seemed to notice them.

Karen's hand felt soft, then he could smell lemon soap in her hair. He closed his eyes and thought of the cool mornings on hot days down in the dry eastern slope of the Cascades. He could make out cut hay and a hint of dust. Yet even as he inhaled, he could smell the gunpowder and gas. He could smell the blood and the shattered toilet bowls. In a strange way, this was reassuring; perhaps it meant he wasn't crazy.

She walked with him, holding his hand. They approached a large metal door that seemed to be the size of a movie theater screen. It must have been a service-vehicle entrance. As the door slid open, there was a clatter of a whirlwind: circles whirling in air, screaming turbines, and floodlights. The blinking eyes of the metal birds hovered in the dark clouds. All around him the straight threads of laser sights zigzagged through the room. Four helicopters hovered just over the fence line, each with the helmeted face of the pilot illuminated behind a windscreen. As Gloomy stepped beyond the last wall and into the open, all the laser sights swept around the area through smoke and gas and landed on his chest. It seemed as if a whole tapestry of light were fused on his heart. Gloomy held his hands up and slowly laced his fingers behind his neck. Then he got down on his knees, and when he looked up, Karen had disappeared into vapor, and he saw the dead Lester Plays with His Face standing over him, arms spread with a gun in one hand and a federal officer's shield in the other.

Chapter Eleven

"All right," Billie Shears said as she looked at the two men in the communications center back in Cold Storage. Off on the horizon the lights of the prison were a bubble rising up into the night. "I am authorized by the president of the United States to release both of you. That's both, if just one of you takes us to the missing warhead. Right now. This deal is available right now, and right now only. You have as long as it takes for me to explain it. If you both say yes, you can both go free if the bomb is found. If one of you says no, you both go back to the prison right now and don't go free no matter if the bomb is found or not. Right now, gentlemen."

She took a moment and retied her hair. She was met with silence. In the distance helicopters chuffed through the night with their lights blinking. Waves washed under the wharf. Ali Wild Horses was sitting quietly, looking down at his shoes. Blood dripped down his face from some fresh injury. He looked up at them, his eyes watering from the smoke; his shirt was ripped, and there was matted blood in his hair. Everyone looked at him for a long moment that clung in the air until at least a minute had passed.

"All right, let's go. Back to the boat." Shears looked at

one of the dozen guards behind them. "Cuff them up. Their old cells will be cleared in a matter of minutes and ready for both of them." Jasper was standing behind her, looking rumpled with his shirt untucked and his pants ripped out at both knees. His tie was loosened down to the middle of his unbuttoned shirt. His glasses were on crooked. He had no coffee cup in his hand and he did not look happy.

One of the officers put cuffs on Gloomy and Wild Horses, but in front, indicating there was more talking left to do. Neither of the guards jerked the prisoners to their feet.

"Yes," Gloomy said, "all right. Yes. I don't believe you, but I'll take a walk around. I have no idea where to find anything but . . . yes. Only, I want my cousin moved to a good hospital. I want him part of the deal, too. Otherwise, no." Gloomy looked at Shears. "You are responsible for fucking him up. If he was conscious he would be offered the same deal and you know it."

Wild Horses cleared his throat and spoke: "He should be moved to the head trauma unit in Bethesda, Maryland, where the US government and Harvard University are doing the most cutting-edge work on neurological repair: nanotechnology and embryonic cell regeneration. They do extensive neurotherapy. Best in the world. That should be his deal. As if he were a hero of your great war against the Koreans." Wild Horses looked at Shears, then at Gloomy. "Make that part of the deal."

"Yes. That's what I want. All that," Gloomy said without pausing.

"Okay . . ." Shears said, "I'll authorize it, but only when we find the bomb. Now, what about you?" She was looking at Wild Horses.

"I want the record to reflect the truth."

"You are a terrorist. You are a murderer."

"None of that is true. I wanted to keep the weapon out of the hands of the Iranians."

"You expect me to believe that?"

"I don't care what you believe. That is the truth. The Iranians infiltrated your prison population long ago."

"What did they want with the bomb?"

"I think they were interested to know if it would blow up. They designed it for the Koreans in the first place."

"What were *you* going to do with a bomb?"

"What does anyone in the twenty-first century do with an unexploded thermonuclear bomb? I was going to establish a free state. Maybe I was going to establish the free state of Palestine? Maybe I wanted to establish the free state of the Lakota people in the Black Hills? I didn't have time to think about it. They literally just fell into my lap. But I never detonated a bomb. I never killed anyone. I never planned a kidnapping. The Iranians and the boat crew did that. I want a full pardon. You say yes to that, and we will go. If the bomb is where I left it, I will take you to it right now."

"When did you find out about the second bomb?" Billie Shears asked.

"My brother Ishmael came to me with the first bomb. He said his cousin had found it. He took us to where he found it. Ishmael had dug it up and out of the muck. We moved it down into the woods. Later I went back to cover our tracks. I didn't want anyone following the drag marks. I was mucking around in the lake and on my last pass, my stick hit a metal object, and it was some strapping that led to the mother."

"What did you want with the mother?"

"As I said, what does anyone want with a bigger thermo-nuclear device that falls into your lap? All I knew is that it meant independence for a marginalized people: a place at the table. That's what it meant to the Pakistanis, the actual people of India and Israel, of North Korea."

"Why not give it to the Iranians?"

Wild Horses shook his head. "The Iranians would just sell it to some other repressive state like the North Kore-ans, and once it was clear their missiles didn't work the Americans would roll over them like a steamroller."

"You didn't have a missile, either." Billie Shears smiled knowingly.

"It was a big first step, though." He paused and looked kindly at her. "Ms. Shears, we can sit here and chat as long as you like, but are you going to give me that piece of paper?"

"Yes, I will do that." Billie pulled out a sheet of paper with a presidential seal. She wrote on the bottom of the page with a heavy silver pen, "With a full pardon of all charges." She had another letter for Gloomy and took several moments to write out the specifics of Ishmael's release. Then she handed the papers to both of them for signature.

Ali Wild Horses looked at Billie Shears and said, "I don't believe a word you say in this agreement, so let me ask you one more thing."

"You are pushing it, fella."

"Just this, why a deal for both of us?" Wild Horses stared at her without a smile.

"Saves time. We knew you weren't in it together but knew you wouldn't sell Gloomy out if he was going to rep-resent Ishmael. Clock's ticking," Shears said, and handed each of the bloody men a cheap ballpoint pen. They both signed the official papers.

"Let's go." Billie Shears motioned to the phalanx of men behind her, and they began to move out.

The rain had stopped and the wind was blowing hard up the inlet. The hemlock and spruce trees were waving their limbs around like frantic schoolchildren in the dark. Men surrounded the inmates in their tattered prison uniforms. The prisoners were uncuffed and unshackled. They walked almost like free men, their backs straight and their arms swinging. Ali Wild Horses asked for a flashlight, then asked if anyone had an aerial photograph of the area. Men dug in satchels and several appeared in front of him, then suddenly a powerful light was in the warrior's hand.

"Thank you," he said with genuine dignity. He stared at the photograph, then cast the beam of the light around. "That's north, yes?"

"Yes," Charlie said. "What are we looking for?"

"You are looking for me to take you there," the still young-looking man said, and off he walked with the clatter of all the white soldiers following him.

"I'm not going to be any help with this. Can I go see my dad?" Gloomy asked.

"I'll take him," Plays with His Face said, and Shears nodded.

The two former cellmates walked down the boardwalk toward Gloomy's old house.

Ali stormed over past the bunkhouse of the cold storage and into the woods by the road cut near the dump. Back in the 1990s, when the new road to the dump had been built, there was a shortage of shot rock in Cold Storage, and no one wanted to blow a new rock pit down, so they buried container vans along the side hill to support the new road. Container vans transported supplies via rail and truck and then ferried them from the Lower

48 to Alaska villages. They were like the fifty-five-gallon drums of the late twentieth century. They lay scattered all over bush Alaska because they were rarely sent back. So, along the hill beneath the road was a row of partially buried vans that had been used to support the surface of the narrow street to the dump. Each van was made of thick metal and only had one door for loading. One of these container vans had a door that looked accessible. This van, the one you could walk into, blocked the door of the next big metal container. Ali walked into the first container.

"We have checked all through this stuff," one of the officers said.

"It's not in here." Ali jerked the door and walked into the dank container and all the way to the end. At the far back wall, he asked for a crowbar and one appeared. He pried a panel off the back wall, which provided access to a panel to the next container van. "It wasn't supposed to be Fort Knox." He looked at Jasper, who was coming along in the shadows. "It was supposed to get vaporized. We worked on this for a while. I had some friends in here for a couple of days. I got things squared away, and when I heard SEAL teams charging up here, I just turned knobs and connected wires, then ran out. Left everything. I was storing it. I left it rigged in case I was captured."

"Why didn't you trade for this one?" Shears asked.

"I was informed it had been found by the Iranians. When it didn't detonate, I assumed that was the truth and they had it."

The last panel had some holes around the edges. When he pried it open, a wet, acidic smell of nitrogen and mold wafted toward them: rotten food, urine, unmistakable animal funk. "Gentlemen . . . this is where I left the North

Korean bomb." He gestured like a maître d' toward the entrance.

Technicians with lights and toolboxes walked past him. Shears and Wild Horses followed. Men with guns stood by protecting them, for some inexplicable reason.

"Jesus Christ," Jasper said.

Wild Horses walked toward the cylinder he had left behind in the makeshift crate so many years ago. Mouse shit and dead squirrels covered the ground. There were moldy humps on the floor that had once been loaves of bread, desiccated rotten fruit, and perfectly fine-looking cans of processed meat. Ali looked over Jasper's shoulder at the shrunken corpse of a bloated mouse. The fat mouse had bitten into the plastic and wires, where someone with greasy fingers had wrapped a connection, and the battery had fried it to perdition and shorted out the timer, causing it to connect only intermittently.

The timer was stopped at five hours and twenty-seven minutes and fifteen seconds. As they watched, a little spark flashed and the fat mouse jiggled when the timer advanced one second. As if out of pure spite, two more seconds ticked off, then the timer stayed still.

"Why, that little pig!" Ali Wild Horses said aloud.

NIX HAD LOST track of time. The box was collapsing down on top of her and the smell of her urine was sweet to her now. It was something other than intertidal sand.

She had begun to feel drops of water on her face, and gradually there was a steady trickle down the air hole. She heard waves close in, and her chest heaved as she sucked in air.

She hadn't even dared to consider that the sound she heard was digging. She assumed the chomping clatter above her was rocks rolling loose in the waves. She was approaching the calmness that overtakes the nearly dead, when she heard the voice so clear it almost seemed a familiar friend:

"There is nothing to worry about. There is no need to fear or struggle. Life is exactly as long as it is. All the rest is desire and imagination. Hush. You will not suffer. Hush. You will feel the light soon enough."

She closed her eyes and tried to imagine the face of Christ. His dripping-wet beard standing in the waves above her. His strong hands digging into the wet sand. What would she say to Jesus in those first moments? She had no idea, but her eyes were full of warm tears. She felt, she supposed, the way He must have felt before He left this earth. It was a wonderful feeling, as if she were lifting out of this box and into a bright rotunda.

Then she heard the metal ring of a shovel hitting stone and felt the pressure of something scraping on the top of the collapsed wooden box. Then the air pipe moved as someone wrenched it back and forth.

Here is Jesus, she thought. *Here He is, the Son of God, and I will rise up and He will hug me fiercely and we will be in that place where there will always be enough time . . . and enough room.*

The top of the box broke away. Water and mud gushed down on top of her dress. Her hands pushed up reflexively. Daylight spilled down on her chest. Air, water, and mud began filling up the hole. She raised her arms to Jesus. She raised her hand, wanting to be borne up into heaven. She was crying out in a language she didn't know. She was spitting sand and water from her mouth and uttering unformed words of praise and gratitude.

His hands pulled on her forearms. His large, strong

hands, the savior's hands, pulled her up out of her box and into the light of a beach on a small island. She was crying and shaking, and she wanted to hug the body of Jesus Christ, her savior. She wanted to tell Him how much she loved Him and how grateful she was that He had finally come. But when she did, she opened her eyes and stared in disbelief.

"We made it, Auntie," said the man with the gasoline on his clothes. "I'm sorry I made you wait."

She wiped her tears and the mud from her eyes and looked at the man who dug her up.

It was Ishmael Muhammad, and standing next to him was her husband, Clive McCahon. Ishmael had left the yacht before it blew up, found Clive, and found the air hole in the tideflat before the tide had reclaimed the beach.

THE NIGHT THEY found the dead mouse that had defused the bomb, Nix heard that someone had seen Gloomy get off a boat in town. She asked every prison worker she saw where he was, and she had gotten no answers. She was furious and desperately agitated with the prison authorities. They weren't telling her anything.

As she walked up the stairs to see Clive, she took her coat off and threw it in the corner. There was Gloomy standing by Clive's bed. He was thin, his clothes were torn. Someone, Lilly probably, had given him one of Clive's old sweaters. It had been seven years since she had seen the thin man with the battered face. The man who was her son, the man who had killed her daughter and had been a part of her being buried in the ground for those interminable hours.

Once it was clear that Gloomy had not actually died in

the explosion at the construction site, the DA had come to her. Nix told the district attorney that her house would, in all probability, be the last place in the world he would come. She had not written him, spoken with him, or visited him during the years of his confinement.

One enterprising young detective tried to plumb the depths of her psyche by saying, "You think of your son as dead then?" And Nix had snapped back at him, "No, detective. My daughter is dead. My son is locked away in a place I never want to go." The detective had changed his line of questioning and had suggested they were in possession of secret communications they would use to implicate Nix if she didn't cooperate with them in the recapture effort. Nix knew with a certainty that was deeper than the aching in her bones that this was not true. She had not communicated with the man who had been her son after her daughter had died, and she wanted him captured as much as anyone, so she let the police tap her phones and set up surveillance on her house.

In the last seven years Nix had done hundreds of hours of therapy. She was so familiar with the symptoms of post-traumatic stress disorder that she could recite them quickly and convincingly. She was restless and she had a hard time with trust, and she resented the presumption of her therapists that a diagnosis could explain a life or a family tragedy. Explain not only the night sweats but the acrid stink her body seemed to give off whenever she heard the crashing of the waves at night.

Nix had always loved to draw, and she loved making music. She loved to draw birds and seashells, and her music reflected the melody of curves. People in cities as far away as Hong Kong and Amsterdam felt that owning one of her drawings of a scallop shell could somehow make them closer to the moment of creation itself. In a world awash in suspect images, Nix's drawings had become talismans for wealthy urbanites, symbols of the rooted life they would never have, like a second home in the woods they rarely visited but would never sell.

Nix was the kind of beautiful woman whose confidence was banked deep down. She could not take a compliment. If anyone ever said something nice, she would flush red and turn her head away, but in the next beat of her heart she would gaze back with a look that had seared its way into many men's brains.

She had told the police that she knew nothing of the plot to blow up the yacht, but they were having none of her charms. The detectives asked her in thousands of ways, but she didn't know anything, couldn't remember a scrap of conversation or a misplaced notebook or map.

Even before the explosion she had sensed the world was off-kilter because of the narcissism of men. She knew the boys in town had been infected by it. Ideology and anger had overtaken love and caring even in this little town where caring for one another meant survival. In the weeks before the war, Gloomy's face had looked hard, more like the other men's. Nix remembered coming home to see him sitting at the kitchen table, staring down and saying nothing as he tapped his fingers lightly on the polished fir top. Even in this little wilderness town, Ishmael and Gloomy seemed to have a premonition that the president was going to take the country to war.

Nix walked into the room where her husband was dying and there he was. There was her boy. Karen stood next to him in the corner of the room. Gloomy looked up at her and then over to his mother. His right hand was holding his father's left. As he looked at his mother, tears were running down his cheeks. L.P. had his hand on his back, patting him softly. Lilly was wiping her nose. Clive had a smile on his pale and exhausted face.

"He woke up for a bit," was all Lilly said. "He recognized the boy."

Nix blustered out a sob with the words that came out of her mouth. "Well, that's a miracle. The boy looks a mess." She walked over and put her arms around him, weeping.

"Baby . . ." she sobbed. "I love you so much."

"Momma," Gloomy said through his tears. "I'm so sorry, Momma."

"Quiet, baby . . ."—and she rocked him in her arms—"You are here, that's all that matters now."

Chapter Twelve

Clive McCahon died the night they found the second North Korean warhead. His family stayed with him as his last breath poured from his open mouth and passed out the open window. Then they shut his mouth and eyes and held on to him as his body cooled. Then the sun rose for another day.

They waited to have the memorial service until all of the press left town. That took several weeks. Clive's brother, Miles, and Miles's wife, Bonnie, were called from their new home in Sitka. It took a couple of days to motor their boat up the coast. People used the time to get fish and to bake bread and pies. Pilots flew in fresh vegetables, wine, and beer. Victo and Karen even flew over gallons of borscht from Pelican via the mail plane. The Russian workers at the cold storage went in together and bought caviar and made paninis with sour cream. People from the bar built a large tent out in front of Mouse Miller's Love Nest, and on the day of the memorial it was sunny and there was a minus tide. People brought tables and put them out on the beach grass, and there were several fires along the beach. Children ran in and out of the bar, laughing and playing tag. There had been talk of cremating Clive right there on the beach in the fire, but the wood was notoriously wet, and getting the fire hot enough would require burning up almost all the pallets at the cold storage plant, which none of the fishermen were willing to do for something that would give their kids nightmares all winter long. So Clive was shipped to Anchorage and rendered to ash up there and flown back. Robert Rose in Sitka made a beautiful blue-green urn with herring etched on the side, and it sat back in a mahogany nook in its permanent home behind the beer spigots of the bar, where everyone could admire it.

Gloomy was there, passing plates of king salmon around, and Karen—the flesh-and-bone Karen—worked the grill. He still was not used to her not being a hallucination, so he kissed her every time he went back to get more fish.

Karen held a sweating cold beer bottle and turned slabs of salmon and black cod on the fire. Her heart was full, and when she saw her daughter chasing the boys around on the slippery boardwalk, she didn't bother to scold her and only laughed to herself. She was so happy that she could not imagine anything bad happening—not on the day of the funeral, not when her Christopher was back home.

Norma, who had cut her own deal with Billie Shears, ran the bar, while Nix prepared her remarks. Miles cooked steaks on a griddle inside, and Bonnie cut hard-boiled eggs for the potato salad. Ali Wild Horses sat outside near his tent. He had refused to sleep inside since he had been released from prison. Billie Shears had been as good as her word and had announced his full pardon to the world, and Wild Horses had been besieged with interview requests. He had presented himself as nonviolent and misunderstood.

He stated his intention to go back to the university setting to research Martin Heidegger's work, vowing to complete his understanding of the German philosopher's thoughts in *Being and Time*. He was also starting a new book about something he called new epoch studies. "Modernism really had its roots in the nineteenth century. You realize the famous Armory Show of modern art was in 1914? So what we feebly call postmodernism is a reaction to something almost a hundred and fifty years old. It is time to move on. My new book will be about nature, communalism, and the foundations of generosity." And indeed, Ali Wild Horses published a book by that title in five years' time to much acclaim.

Many people told stories about Clive. Before the children became overtired and before the adults became too drunk, Nix brought her old band out and she said a few words:

"Clive McCahon was a fool and a trickster. He was totally unself-conscious. He loved God and music and he saved my life." Then she paused. She struggled to read the paper where she had written many, many words, but tears had clouded her eyes.

Finally, the skinny drummer from her old band, who had flown in from Brooklyn, got up from behind his kit and handed her the bass fiddle, and he counted out the rhythm for Blind Donkey's original composition of "Love Is the Answer, but What Is the Question?" Then everyone, including the tired children and the drunken adults, grabbed one another and started to dance.

Then just as if on cue, a brown bear walked out of the woods between the bar and the bathhouse. The bear was as immense as anyone could ever remember seeing pass through town. His head seemed to be two feet from ear to ear, his hide a silky golden brown. Every step sent a shimmer of light through his hide. His front end swaggered, and his back end wobbled to keep up. He appeared to have the mass of a truck, with tiny pig eyes, and long black claws. The children instinctively clung to the nearest adult, and people reached to their belts for guns, even if there was not one there. The big bear was upwind of the party, and when he lightly stepped down the rocky slope to the beach, he turned to look and sniffed. His eyesight was poor, and the wind was against him, but he could sense the humanness of the noise and the fires. He could sense the food. There was danger but he was not afraid. He was within striking distance of the other omnivores, but anyone could see this creature was merely curious.

Gloomy and Karen's little girl, whose name was indeed Esme, came out from behind her mom and put her plate of fish down on the ground. "You can have mine," she said, but the big bear only paused, then circled wide and worked his way upwind, turned a few rocks over, and snuffled up two small crabs as the band started to play again, then disappeared up into the steep woods. As the big bear disappeared, lunging uphill through the underbrush, Gloomy felt happy, genuinely happy, for the first time in a long time, and he wondered if the big animal could hear its own heart beating in its ears as he had heard his own heart when he caught sight of the large animal on the beach. Gloomy wondered in fact, if the bear was ever confused by the irregular time clock of his own ursine heart beating, by what it was or what it meant.